Bed Of
Lies

Also by Shelly Ellis

Chesterton Scandal series

To Love & Betray
Lust & Loyalty
Best Kept Secrets
Bed of Lies

Gibbons Gold Digger series

Can't Stand the Heat
The Player & the Game
Another Woman's Man
The Best She Ever Had

Published by Dafina Books

Bed Of Lies

SHELLY ELLIS

Kensington Publishing Corp.
www.kensingtonbooks.com

DAFINA BOOKS are published by

Kensington Publishing Corp.
119 West 40th Street
New York, NY 10018

ISBN-13: 978-1-61773-405-2
ISBN-10: 1-61773-405-5
First Kensington Trade Paperback Printing: May 2016
First Kensington Mass Market Edition: February 2018

eISBN-13: 978-1-61773-404-5
eISBN-10: 1-61773-404-7
First Kensington Electronic Edition: May 2016

10 9 8 7 6 5 4 3 2 1

Printed in the United States of America

To Andrew and Chloe, my own little squad.

Acknowledgments

When you look at the odds of successfully getting a book published, let alone publishing several books in this kind of environment, where other talented authors lose contracts all the time—it can seem rather daunting to decide to become an author, to try to make a career out of it. And if you do decide to take the big leap and hope that you get a contract, agent, your contract renewed, etc., you need to find time to pursue your dreams. You need to find those hours to contemplate characters and craft perfect scenes. More importantly, you need a group of people who believe in you and are willing to support you with their time and effort. They basically become your own little support team.

So I'd like to say thanks to the biggest member of my support team (in duties, not girth), my husband, Andrew. You've been there through the highs and the lows and always believed that I can do it and that I had the talent to pull it off. It takes a strong, patient man to do what you do with our household and family while I sit alone in a room writing. I can never say enough how I appreciate everything you do.

I'd also like to say thanks to my backup team—my parents, Donna and Craig Stratton. You guys have been there since the beginning, since I was scribbling stories in notebooks and daydreaming of the day I would see one of my books on a shelf. You still provide encouragement and effort (in the form of babysitting your lovely, crazy granddaughter) to help me crank out each chapter. Thanks so much for your love and support.

I'd also like to thank my editor, Mercedes Fernandez. Thank GOD you love *telenovela*/soap opera drama like I do! (*Jane the Virgin* is beyond compare, is it not?) This will be our sixth book together and I appreciate you allowing me to embrace complex characters, dramatic storylines, and hot love scenes, and believing in my voice from the first book.

And a big thanks to my agent, Barbara Poelle. I had secretly always wondered why I needed an agent. I rationalized that I got a book contract without one. I was doing just fine. Of course, agent extraordinaire proved why I needed one. Thanks for being my advocate and pushing me to be an even better writer. Thanks for treating all your clients (from the authors waiting for their debut to *The New York Times* bestsellers) like they're all important to you. I see your skill and dedication and I appreciate and rave about it.

Thanks to my network of author buddies I talk to on the Web. Seriously, I will meet all of you one day in person! Your support and sisterhood help get me through the rough patches.

And thanks to the readers who have reached out to me to tell me how much you like my work. You complete the circle and make this all worth it.

Chapter 1

Terrence

"Yeah! That's what I'm talking about, baby!" Terrence Murdoch yelled over the heavy bass before tossing one-hundred-dollar bills into the air and letting them fall like confetti. The cute brunette in front of him showed her appreciation by doing a split on the stage, clad in only a smile and a bright yellow G-string that glowed under the blue-hued stage lights. Two other strippers danced beside her in clear platform stilettos, gyrating and swinging around each pole as Terrence and his friends hooted and yelled with delight in the VIP section of the club.

Terrence didn't know where to look first. It was a delectable sampling of full breasts, round thighs, and pert behinds. He just wanted to dive in and bask in all the womanly beauty.

He raised his beer bottle and toasted the sexy performance. "I've died and gone to heaven!" he cried. He then turned to his older brother, Evan, who had hung back from the stage and chose to stay at the table behind them. "Ain't they beautiful, man?"

When he saw what Evan was doing, his grin disappeared. He slammed his bottle back to the table in outrage. "Ev, what the . . . what the fuck? Are you kidding me?"

Instead of admiring the strippers, Evan had been peering down at his BlackBerry under the flashing strobe lights. At Terrence's cry of outrage, the company CEO glanced up from his phone screen.

"Huh?" Evan asked absently. "Oh yeah, it's great, Terry." He began to type on the phone keys again.

"Ev, put that damn phone down and look at this, man!"

"I'll be right with you. Just let me finish this e-mail," Evan said, still furiously typing. "Got to get this out tonight. They're in a different time zone."

Terrence reached over and yanked the Black-Berry out of Evan's hand, catching his brother by surprise.

"No, look at it now! How can you be doing business when you have this in front of your face?" he asked, jabbing toward the stage.

One of the women dropped to her knees before turning her ass toward the men huddled around her. She did a twerk that made the men holler for more. Another stripper hopped up on a pole and twirled around and around, letting her blond curls dangle inches above the ground.

"I mean . . . come on!" Terrence turned back to look at his brother with a grin that was so wide it could barely be contained on his face. "Look at this!"

Evan gazed at the two strippers, inclined his head, and nodded. "Nice," he said thoughtfully, like he was considering a new pair of shoes.

"Nice?" Terrence comically looked at the women onstage, whipped his head to glare at his brother, then stared at the women on the stage again. "What the hell do you mean, 'Nice'?" He jabbed his index finger at the strippers. "Those women are fuckin' perfect, Ev!"

Evan emphatically shook his head and smiled as he reached into his jacket pocket and whipped out another cell phone. He dragged his index finger across the screen, scrolling through a series of photos. "No, *this* is perfect."

He held the glass screen toward Terrence. Terrence squinted under the club lighting to see what his brother was showing him. It was a photo of Evan's fiancée, Leila. She was wearing a tank top and yoga pants and rolling her eyes as Evan took the picture, like she had wanted anything but to be photographed at that moment.

Terrence had to admit that his future sister-in-law was one gorgeous woman. And Evan had been pining after her for years—hell, *decades!* He had been secretly in love with her since he was nine years old. In Evan's mind, Leila Hawkins had probably reached almost mythical proportions in beauty, brains, and loveliness.

But still, how could a man ignore what was right in front of his face? It destroyed the whole purpose of Evan being here at the strip club if he sat toward the back of the room, fiddling on his BlackBerry.

Terrence had invited Evan out with his friends for a night of drinking and debauchery to give Evan a long-needed break. His older brother was a consummate workaholic, and now when he wasn't working, he was almost plastered to the side of his new fiancée. Terrence had wanted his big bro to have some fun. But Evan looked like he would be more entertained if he was sitting at his desk going over contracts and sales figures at Murdoch Conglomerated, where he was CEO. Or maybe he'd rather be sitting beside Leila, staring at tablecloth swatches for their wedding reception.

"Are you telling me you aren't just a *little* bit interested in looking at those titties?" Terrence pleaded. He once again pointed to the stage. "Not just a little?"

Evan burst into laughter. "I'm sorry, Terry, but from here they look like average breasts to me. But you know what? Go ahead and enjoy yourself. Don't let me ruin your fun." He yanked his Black-Berry out of Terrence's hand. "But if you don't mind, I'll take this back."

Terrence slowly shook his head in bemusement as he watched his brother sit down in one of the leather club chairs and start scanning through his e-mails again.

Operation: Get Evan Turnt Up was going downhill—*fast.*

Terrence glanced at the drink Evan was now sipping: a Shirley Temple. He could try to ply Evan with alcohol to make him loosen up, but he knew that wouldn't work. Evan didn't drink thanks to his alcoholic wife, Charisse. Her drunkenness had been part of the reason they were now getting a divorce—that and the fact that she had been cheating on Evan.

Nope, getting him drunk is out of the question, Terrence thought.

An idea suddenly popped into Terrence's head. A wicked smile crossed his full lips.

"Well, if they just look like average titties from here, I guess you're going to have to see them up close."

Evan frowned quizzically as he lowered his glass back to the marble tabletop and looked up from his e-mail. "I'm sorry . . . what?"

Terrence suddenly turned on his heel, marched toward the stage, and shoved a group of his friends aside so that he was front and center.

"Ladies!" he shouted as he whipped out a series of hundred-dollar bills, spread them into a fan and brandished them in the air. "My brother would like a lap dance. *Now!* A grand to the first woman who does it."

The three strippers paused mid-routine. One almost fell off her pole. Another scrambled off her knees. The three women ran off the stage and came barreling toward Evan, whose mouth was agape. One looked like she nearly twisted her ankle trying to make her way down the short staircase.

"No!" Evan said, holding up his hands in protest and furiously shaking his head. "Really, ladies, I'm fine. I don't . . . I don't want a lap dance!"

Terrence cackled as he watched the strippers shove and elbow-check each other to get to Evan first. The blonde turned out to be the victor and promptly fell onto Evan's lap and started gyrating for all her worth.

"Terry!" Evan yelled, trying his best to rise out of his chair without touching the half-naked women who were huddled around and over him. "Terry!"

"Enjoy it, Ev!" Terrence grabbed his beer and held it up before tossing the hundreds in his hand into the air and taking a swig. "You deserve it!"

"Hey, you forgot this," Terrence said as he handed Evan his suit jacket.

The two men walked out of the strip club almost two hours later into the chilly February night. A few of Terrence's friends trailed behind them, laughing and joking with one another.

"I didn't forget it," Evan mumbled as he tossed the suit jacket over his forearm. "It was *stolen* from me."

Terrence chuckled.

One of the strippers had ripped off Evan's suit jacket as soon as they had descended on him like a herd of locusts. His necktie had been removed, too, when one of the other strippers used it to bind his hands behind his back when he kept struggling. Another had smothered his verbal protests by shaking her double-Ds in his face.

"Come on! Admit it!" Terrence prodded, looping an arm around Evan's neck in brotherly affection. "You had fun, didn't you?"

"It was . . . interesting," Evan said just as one of the guys behind them leaned over and vomited on the walkway not too far from the club's red carpet.

"Oh, hell no!" the burly bouncer boomed, hopping off of his stool in front of the door. "Y'all better get his ass outta here!" he ordered, making one of the guy's companions nod and grab his sick friend around the shoulders. Another helped guide him toward a car that was parked at the end of the block.

Evan and Terrence shook their heads in disgust as they watched the trio walk off.

"Is your friend gonna make it?" Evan asked.

Terrence waved his hand dismissively. "He'll be fine. One of them will get his sorry ass back home tonight. I don't know what his wife will think when she sees him like that, though, but"—Terrence shrugged—"that's his problem."

Evan narrowed his eyes at Terrence. "You had plenty to drink yourself. Are you going to be okay driving back to your place?"

"*Me?*" Terrence pointed at his chest and laughed. He had a slight buzz, but that was about it. He could remember being in far worse states than he was now. "Man, please! I am far from drunk. Trust me. I'll be fine."

"You sure about that?" Evan asked again, just as a black Lincoln Town Car pulled up to the curb. Evan's driver climbed out, quickly walked to the rear door, and held it open for him. Evan paused before climbing onto the leather seat. "I could give you a ride, you know."

Terrence waved him away again as he started to walk in the opposite direction in search of his Porsche. "I'll be fine, Miss Daisy. Just give Lee a kiss for me. All right?"

"Oh, I most certainly will," Evan said with a wink

before climbing into the sedan. The driver shut the door behind him.

Terrence turned and walked down the block back to his car. He raised the collar of his wool coat to block out the chill and rubbed his hands together to warm them. He bet Evan would give Leila a kiss as soon as he got home. Thanks to the erotic performance the men had witnessed tonight, he bet Evan would give her a lot more than that.

After a few minutes, Terrence spotted his silver Porsche two-seater and he breathed a sigh of relief.

"There's my baby," he whispered, almost with reverence.

The strip club hadn't had valet parking and he had been loath to leave her parallel-parked along the curb in this neighborhood, but he had had no other choice.

Terrence inspected his car with a careful eye and whispered a prayer of thanks when he saw no dents or scratches. The paint on his Porsche still glistened and the rims still sparkled from the wash, waxing, and buffing the car had gotten earlier that day.

If the love of Evan's life was Leila Hawkins, then the love of Terrence's life was certainly his 2015 Porsche 911 S Coupe. A close second was maybe the De'Longhi ESAM6700 Gran Dama Avant Touch-Screen Super-Automatic Espresso Machine on the granite kitchen countertop back at his condo in Chesterton, Virginia. If he could be buried with that thing, he would.

Terrence didn't have a love of the female variety and he had no desire to fall in love with anyone.

Oh, he was no monk; he dated often. He had his fair share of girlfriends and one-night stands. But so far, no woman had made him want to "put a ring on it," so to speak. Terrence had seen the ravages married life could have on a person by witnessing his parents' horrendous marriage for decades and the trials Evan had gone through for the five and half years he was married to his soon-to-be ex, Charisse.

Though Evan often encouraged him to finally settle down, Terrence couldn't work up enough optimism about love and relationships to try his hand at anything permanent with a woman. He'd rather live in the moment and collect honeys like they were Pokémon trading cards.

He opened the door of his Porsche and climbed inside. As he drove, he listened to the voice messages on his iPhone. Unlike Evan, he had turned off his cell while inside the club, not wanting to be disturbed.

"Hey, Terry," a female voice cooed over the phone's speaker as Terrence merged onto a roadway, "it's Asia. I've texted you three times today, baby! Where are you? I was hoping we could meet up this weekend. Give me a call back when you get this. I miss your fine ass. Byeeeeee!"

Asia was a waitress at a Cuban restaurant downtown. She had full lips, big thighs, and a beautiful smile, but lately, she had become kind of clingy. Terrence wondered if he should call her back or cut her loose.

"*Bonsoir, mon ami!*" Terrence heard next, instantly making him smile. "*Ça va?*"

He knew that throaty purr from anywhere. It

was Georgette, a blond Victoria's Secret model based out of Montreal whom he had met back during his modeling days. He loved Georgette because of her good taste in food and wine, her French accent, and because she understood the true definition of "no strings attached" sex. They had been hooking up off and on for the past six years.

"I will be in the city for a few weeks," Georgette continued. "Let me know if you wish to meet, huh? I packed the lace teddy you like and the . . . you know . . . the stuff that you lick . . . *qu'est-ce que c'est?* Ah, who cares! I show you, Terry! *Je te veux!* Can't wait to see you, *mon ami. Au revoir!*" He heard kissing sounds and then the line clicked.

Oh hell, yeah, he thought.

He would call her back as soon as he got home. He would check her schedule and make reservations at their favorite spot. After dinner, he'd take her back to his place and they would try out "the stuff that you lick."

"Terry!" a voice suddenly screeched from his iPhone, snatching him out of his sexual reverie and making him wince. "Terry, you know who this is. Don't play like you don't! I saw you with that chick yesterday. Yeah, she was all up on you. Is she your new girl now? How dare you dump me like I was yesterday's trash, you son of a—"

Terrence reached over the armrest and immediately pressed a button on the phone's glass screen to delete the message.

Oh, Monique, he thought with exasperation.

Now, that was a girl who *definitely* did not understand the definition of "no strings attached" sex.

Monique Washington had given off alarm bells the moment he had met her—she had been high-maintenance, constantly had checked her reflection in mirrors, and had wanted to talk endlessly about trips to Europe and trust funds. But he had pushed his misgivings about her aside. So what if she was a little shallow? He wasn't a deep man himself. And besides, she was good in bed and when he had told her that he wasn't ready for a real relationship, she had seemed okay with his revelation. But he should have trusted his first instincts. She had turned out to be a real nutcase. She went past clingy and straight to *Fatal Attraction*, showing up at his condo at all times of the day, threatening other women that he was dating. When he had tried to shake off Monique, she started blowing up his phone, leaving pissed-off and threatening messages.

He wouldn't make that mistake again. If he sensed that a woman wasn't up to staying at a distance, then he wouldn't bother to start anything with her. For now, he would just have to block Monique's number.

"On to the next one," Terrence murmured as he pulled to a stop at a stop sign.

"Hey! Heeeeeeey!"

Terrence frowned and turned to find two women smiling and waving at him on the sidewalk. Despite the temps being in the low thirties, both women were wearing short skirts and flimsy shawls. One had flowing dark hair. The other looked like she was wearing an auburn wig. They both seemed to be heading home from a hard night of partying.

"Hey, cutie!" the dark-haired one yelled, motioning wildly for him to lower his car window.

Terrence obliged.

"Evening, ladies," he said in his smoothest Billy Dee Williams voice.

They ran toward his Porsche—or more like stumbled—holding on to each other for balance. "Is that your car, baby?" the auburn-haired one slurred, leaning on her friend.

Terrence inclined his head. "I'm driving it, aren't I?"

"Where you headed?" the other asked eagerly, sticking out her chest.

"Home," he answered.

The dark-haired one licked her red lips and smiled. "Well, it looks like we're headed there, too."

"Home with me?" He raised his brows.

The two women nodded in unison. "Yeah! Let us in!" the auburn-wigged one shouted before groping for the passenger door handle and missing it by several inches. Shc fell back onto the sidewalk instead and landed on her rear, making her wig shift askew. Her friend burst into laughter.

Terrence shook his head. "I'm afraid not, ladies. But get home safely, okay?"

Terrence waved at the comedic duo and floored the accelerator, unaware of the Mitsubishi Galant that was simultaneously plowing through the four-way stop in the opposite direction. It hadn't paused or stopped.

"Hey! Watch out!" one of the girls shouted.

Terrence turned in just enough time to see the

bright headlights of the Mitsubishi coming toward him, but not in enough time to brake before the two cars collided.

Tires squealed. Metal crunched. Glass shattered in all directions. That's when the two women began to scream.

Chapter 2

Evan

"Goodnight, Mr. Murdoch," the driver said as Evan climbed out of the Lincoln Town Car while it idled in the circular driveway in front of his home.

"'Night, Bill," Evan called back. He paused to tiredly rub his neck. "Oh, and tell your wife I'm sorry for keeping you out so late. All right?"

The driver waved away Evan's apology and grinned over his shoulder. "Don't worry about it, sir. If you keep giving me those bonuses you've been giving me, she won't care if I don't *ever* come home!"

Evan laughed and shut the passenger door. He watched the car pull off and then slowly climbed the stone steps leading to Murdoch Mansion. Though the floodlights were on, illuminating the exterior of the expansive estate, only one light inside the mansion burned bright. Evan smiled when he looked up and realized that light was in his own bedroom. Though it was almost three o'clock in the morning, Leila had waited up for him.

Unlike Charisse, he thought grudgingly as he inserted his key into one of the French doors and stepped inside the silent three-story foyer. Charisse either would have been passed out drunk on her bed or too preoccupied sharing that bed with someone else.

While he had been pulling long hours at Murdoch Conglomerated after taking the position of CEO, trying to maintain the legacy that his father had left to him, Evan's wife, Charisse, had been occupying her time carrying on a hot-and-heavy affair with his backstabbing half-brother, Dante. But Evan wasn't too upset when he finally had proof that she had been cheating on him. He had suspected it all along. His marriage to Charisse had been in name only for years, even if Evan had been unable to admit that truth to himself until he caught his wife screwing Dante in their marble shower. The blow of betrayal had been softened because he had been already firmly in love with someone else: Leila.

Evan quickly climbed the staircase to the west wing, hearing his footsteps on each riser. His steps echoed off the walls and high ceilings. He couldn't get to the second floor fast enough, so impatient to slide into bed next to his fiancée.

Leila had been his childhood friend and lifelong crush. For years, he had hidden his feelings for her, only to watch her marry another man, whom he still despised. It had taken more than twenty years, Leila getting married and divorced, and Evan getting married and separated, before the two finally ended up together.

They no longer had to hide their feelings. Leila was no longer another man's wife and he would soon no longer be another woman's husband. No more clandestine nights at his office, where they made love on the leather couch with the door locked. No more ultimatums from Leila about ending their relationship or revealing to his wife and everyone else in the world their own affair.

"We're better than this, Evan," she had told him back then and it had humbled him to admit that she was right.

They were engaged and out in the open. She lived in his mansion and so did her daughter and mother. Evan was ready to start the next chapter in his life and he was beyond happy that he was starting that chapter with Leila at his side.

A minute later, he pushed open the door to his bedroom. The crystal pendant lamp on Leila's night table was on, but unfortunately, Leila was fast asleep. She was propped up on several pillows in her silk nightgown. The hardback novel she had been reading had fallen from her hands and was fanned open on the bed beside her as she snored.

Evan inclined his head and smiled. *Well, at least she* tried *to wait up for me,* he thought before softly shutting the bedroom door behind him. He tiptoed across the room so as to not wake her, though it wasn't necessary. The plush carpet drowned out any sound his footsteps could make. As he walked quietly, he took off his coat, tossed it onto a footstool, and began to unbutton his dress shirt and remove his cufflinks. He finished undressing and prepared for bed in the bathroom after shutting the door behind him. Minutes later, he returned to the bedroom in his boxer-briefs to find Leila still slumbering.

She had sunk lower on the pillows and was now partially splayed onto the bed. She was on her side facing him. Her peach silk nightgown was bunched around her hips, showing a great deal of thigh, both of her calves, and all of her delicate, red-painted toenails. The top lace panel of the nightgown had fallen open on one side, revealing one lone honey-hued breast and a dark nipple that was already hardening and puckering with goosebumps in the cool bedroom air.

Evan's smile widened as he leaned against the bathroom doorframe. *This* was what he had been trying to explain to his little brother as they had watched the cosmetically enhanced, topless strippers pump, grind, and hump on stage. It wasn't that he hadn't found the women or their performances seductive, but he found it exceedingly more erotic to stumble on a subtle scene like this: a beautiful, sexy, *natural* woman whom he loved, fast asleep, unwittingly showing all her assets to him and turning him on in the process. Watching her lying there, Evan hardened.

He walked around the bed, extinguished the light, and placed her book on the night table. The bedroom fell mostly into darkness except for the glow of the full moon filtering through the gossamer curtains on the other side of the room. Leila didn't stir as he turned off the light or even when he walked around their king-sized bed to the side where he usually slept. She shifted slightly only when the bed dipped as he climbed in naked beside her after tugging off his boxer-briefs. She mumbled something unintelligible, then started snoring again.

Evan let his eyes trail over her in the dim lighting. His gaze not only lingered on her breasts and long legs, but also rested on her slightly parted lips and the dark lashes that swept her cheeks. He pushed a lock of hair off of her brow, then let his fingers lightly trail down her neck and along her collarbone before descending even lower. He ran a finger along her breast, then her nipple, before cupping the full breast in his hand.

Leila still didn't rouse, but her breathing instantly changed. Her snores halted and became sharp, quick breaths. She shifted and moaned softly in her sleep as he trailed his thumb over the nipple again and again, flicking his finger across the dark bud. When he leaned forward and lowered his mouth to her breast, she breathed in sharply. Her eyes fluttered open.

"Ev," she murmured sleepily as he eased her onto her back, "what are you—"

"*Sssshhhh,*" he urged, holding a finger to her lips. He grinned. "Just lie back and relax."

He then returned to suckling her breast and her strangled moans became even louder. As Evan tugged the straps of her nightgown off her shoulders, he raised the hem of the nightgown even higher. He was delighted to discover she wasn't wearing underwear beneath it.

Good, he thought. There would be less fabric in between him and what he wanted: her.

His mouth didn't leave those delectable nipples

even as he eased his hand between her legs, coaxing her to spread them wider. He massaged her clit with a practiced touch and felt her grow wet beneath his fingertips. Her moans shifted to yells and back again. Just when he sensed her getting close to the edge, he pulled his hand and mouth away and she whimpered in protest.

"What the . . ." She pushed herself up to her elbows so that she could glare down at him.

Leila was barely wearing her nightgown. It was now nothing more than a silken, crumpled belt around her waist. At that moment, she was naked, resplendent, and absolutely indignant. "What the hell, Ev? Why'd you stop?" she grumbled.

She looked so angry that he had to laugh.

"I didn't stop, baby," he said as he climbed between her legs. "I'm only getting started."

He reached down and started massaging her again, bringing her back to the brink of ecstasy that he had dragged her to before. But this time he quickly replaced his hands with his mouth, licking and kissing the juncture between her legs until she was bucking underneath him, until she was balling the sheets in her fists and screaming his name. His dick ached to be inside her, but he held back, wanting to give her pleasure first. When the orgasm hit her, he sat back on his elbows and watched her stomach rise and fall. He watched her thighs tighten, then go slack.

When the last wave washed over her and she fought to regain her breath, he slowly climbed back on top of her.

"I love you, Evan," she whispered to him in the

dark, wrapping her arms and legs around him, drawing him close.

"I love you, too," he assured her just before he entered her and she cried out his name again.

Evan drove hard and deep, loving the way she felt around him, loving her welcoming warmth. Leila clawed at his back and dug her nails into his shoulder blades. She widened her legs even further to let more of him inside her and he readily plunged into her over and over again. She bucked her hips to meet each stroke.

As they made love, Evan rode the rollercoaster of sensations, felt the thrill of each plunge, and knew what awaited him at the end: pure bliss.

He closed his eyes and let out a long, tortured groan when the release finally came. His hold around her tightened to the point that he worried he might be crushing her and then he suddenly went slack. He collapsed his full weight on top of her and panted against her ear. When he finally regained his strength, he peered down at her. She was beaming.

"So this is what you're like when you come back from a strip club?" Leila asked with laughter in her voice. She licked her lips seductively. "Remind me to send you there more often."

Evan pushed that bothersome lock of hair out of her eyes once more and kissed her chin, cheeks, and lips. "We could save the money and *you* could just strip for me every night?"

"For free?" she asked with mock outrage, cocking an eyebrow.

He chuckled. "No, for a nominal fee."

She inclined her head and pretended to consider his offer. "Eh, you're cute. I guess I could give you a discount."

"I'd appreciate that." He pulled out of her and turned onto his side, dragging Leila with him. Evan wrapped an arm around her shoulders as they lay naked beside each other in bed. Sex with Leila was always amazing, but the quiet moments they spent in bed alone together afterward were definitely a close second.

"Did you guys have fun tonight?" she asked, trailing her fingers along his arm and shoulder.

"It was okay." He shrugged. "I think Terry had a better time than I did, though."

She chuckled. "Of course Terry did. Strip clubs are right up his alley."

"I felt bad while I was there."

"Why?" she cried, looking taken aback. "I told you I didn't mind! I meant it."

"I know, but it's not like I have a lot of nights at home. I mean, I'm always at the office. Tonight could have been time we spent alone together."

"You have nothing to feel bad about, Ev. You can have some nights out with your brother and your friends. I don't mind!" She shook her head. "Besides, tonight I had to help Izzy with her science project. I was up to my ears in Styrofoam and glue, trying to re-create the solar system."

Izzy was Leila's daughter.

"I could have helped, though."

"You didn't have to help. We had it covered!" She waved her hand. "We've got just a few more finishing touches and we'll be done. She's going to present it to her second-grade class on Thursday. She's excited."

"If you have a few more things you have to do, I can help. I did science fair projects back in the day, remember?"

"I told you . . . We have it covered, Ev."

"No, seriously, Lee, what can I do? I want to help."

Leila's smile faltered. For the first time, she looked uncomfortable. "Actually, I think Izzy would . . . would prefer if just . . . you know . . . she and I work on it . . . alone."

He tightened his jaw. "You mean she doesn't want my help."

"Ev," Leila began, "she's still adjusting to all this, to us being together. I told you, bonding with her isn't going to happen overnight."

"I know that, Lee," he said tightly, releasing his arm from around Leila's shoulders.

He was a businessman. He understood things took time and that building relationships with people could sometimes be a slow process, but his relationship with Izzy was painfully stilted, almost prickly. She wouldn't even let him call her Izzy.

"My name is Isabel," the precocious seven-year-old had softly but firmly corrected him once when he used her nickname.

He had tried to be kind to Izzy, to shower her with attention, to joke with her, to pull her into conversations. Hell, he had even tried to ply her with gifts, but so far, nothing had worked.

"You're just trying too hard, Ev," Leila had insisted. "Let it happen naturally."

Maybe Leila was right. Maybe eventually Izzy would warm to him. But for now Izzy was adamant that she had one dad and one dad *only*, and his name was Bradley Hawkins, not Evan Murdoch.

"She will eventually bond with you," Leila now argued as they lay in bed together. "Please just give it—"

"*Time?* I know. But all the time in the world isn't going to help if Brad keeps making her hostile toward me."

Leila bit her bottom lip and fell silent. She knew he was right.

Though Brad, who lived back in California, was also engaged and planned to get married in the upcoming months, he didn't seem as willing to let his ex-wife move on with her new life. He argued with Leila by phone and had threatened to file for sole custody and "take back what's rightfully mine." The only thing that kept Leila from worrying about losing Izzy was that Brad had been found guilty of fraud and embezzlement for an elaborate pyramid scheme and now faced jail time. With a criminal record, the likelihood of him getting custody of his daughter was very remote. But that didn't stop Brad from pouring poison into Izzy's ear, saying things about her mother and her mother's "bigshot, millionaire sugar daddy." So far, Brad hadn't managed to turn Izzy against Leila, but it seemed he was having much more success in turning her against Evan.

"I'm sorry, but I have no control over what Brad says or does," Leila now whispered, gazing at Evan in the darkened bedroom.

"Which is why you need to try even harder to sway Isabel in my direction," he argued.

"Ev, that's not how kids work."

Leila sounded tired and it wasn't just because it was three o'clock in the morning. He knew she was tired of having these arguments, and frankly, so was he. But he also knew that even though Leila loved him, she would end their engagement if Izzy gave her an ultimatum or told her she didn't want her to get married. He had seen before how much investment Leila had in making sure that her daughter was happy. On the rankings of importance in Leila's life, Isabel Hawkins came first. That left Evan with a lot at stake in this.

"Then how the hell do kids work, Lee, because I don't know what else to—"

He was stopped short by the ringing of the telephone. Both Evan and Leila paused, surprised to get a phone call at this late hour. When the phone rang a second time, Evan's stomach instinctively tightened. Whenever he received late-night calls like this, it was always because something had gone wrong. And something *had* gone wrong—he could sense it.

He slowly picked up the cordless phone on his night table. "Hello?" he asked with a frown.

"Hello, this is the Metropolitan D.C. Police Department," a woman's voice answered. "Am I speaking to Evan Murdoch?"

"Y-yes. This is he."

"Are you the next of kin for Terrence Murdoch?"

"Yes," Evan nearly shouted, sitting bolt upright at the mention of his brother's name. Leila jumped at his side, startled. "I'm his brother. What's . . . What's wrong?"

"Sir, your brother has been in an accident."

Chapter 3
Paulette

Paulette lowered the phone back into its cradle, her hand trembling as she did. Her eyes were filled with unshed tears as she sniffed. She quickly shoved back the duvet and sheets in her four-poster bed and rose to her feet. She walked across the bedroom floor to her bathroom, prepared to hurriedly wash her face and brush her teeth. She didn't have time to do much more. Time was one thing Paulette could not afford to waste. Evan had said that he and Leila were on their way to D.C., to the Medstar Washington Medical Center to see their brother, Terrence. If Paulette left in the next fifteen minutes, she would arrive soon after them and they all could hold vigil in the hospital waiting room together.

Paulette flicked on the bathroom lights, blinking furiously and squinting at the sudden brightness. She turned on the water to its coldest setting in one of the double sinks, cupping her hands underneath the faucet and splashing her face over and over again.

The last Evan had heard, Terrence was in critical condition and on a respirator in the intensive care unit. As Evan had relayed the news to Paulette over the phone, he sounded dazed. When Paulette frantically started asking him to tell her more about their brother—the severity of his injuries or his chances of survival—Evan had only mumbled his replies.

"I don't know . . . That's all they told me . . . I wish I knew more," he had blurted out to her steady stream of questions, frustrating her even more. Finally, Leila jumped on the phone, probably after wrenching the receiver out of Evan's hand.

"We won't know anything until we get there, Paulette!" Leila had barked, her tone sounding more anxious than harsh. "We're heading out now. Just meet us there, okay?"

He's still alive, Paulette reminded herself as she stepped out of the bathroom a few minutes later, shaking with each tentative step like she was walking on a tightrope. *At least Terry is still alive.*

And if his last hour was drawing near, she would see her brother for the last time if it killed her.

Paulette walked toward her armoire to quickly grab some clothes to dress and head to the hospital. She tugged her cotton nightgown over her head and glanced at her reflection in the gilded-edged, free-standing mirror near her walk-in closet. She stopped in her tracks and stared, stunned as she gazed at herself.

Her body seemed to have changed overnight. Her breasts now spilled over the tops of her balconette bra and the straps cut into her shoulders from holding the burden of the additional weight. Her waist had grown by several inches. Even when she sucked up all the air in her lungs to make her stomach flat, she still had a slight potbelly—like she had had one too many burritos and was bloated with gas. She wasn't sure if it was her imagination, but even her hips and thighs were starting to look a little wider. She was almost three and a half months' pregnant, and yet her body was already showing all the telltale signs of the impending baby.

Now frantic for quite a different reason, Paulette rushed the remaining distance across her bedroom and yanked open one of her armoire drawers. She searched for one of the many fashionable billowing, long wool sweaters she often wore nowadays. Paired with a set of leggings, it cloaked her changing body perfectly. But she wouldn't be able to hide the pregnancy much longer—not at this rate. Either her body would betray her and reveal her secret, or the changing weather would. It would be April in only a couple of months. The weather in Northern Virginia would get warmer soon. Wool sweaters and thick leggings would start to look strange if she continued to wear them.

You didn't really think you could keep up this charade forever, did you? a little voice in her head mocked as she threw one of the sweaters over her head and shoved her arms through the sleeves. *Come on, Paulette. You're not sixteen anymore. No one's* that *naïve!*

No, she wasn't sixteen anymore. When she was sixteen and pregnant, she had had an abortion. The guilt over that was the reason she had chosen not to have one this time around, even though she wasn't sure whether the father of her baby was her husband, Antonio, or her ex-boyfriend, Marques, who had blackmailed her into giving him thousands of dollars and having an affair with him. She had decided to risk the damage this baby could have on her marriage because she couldn't talk herself into walking into that women's clinic and putting her feet in those stirrups again.

But the risks were great. When Paulette finally had to reveal to Antonio her pregnancy, she was terrified at what the aftermath would be. Would he divorce her? Would he kick her out of the house? Would he *kill* her?

Her hands stilled after she tugged on her leggings and she reached for one of the brown leather riding boots at the foot of her bed.

Will he kill me?

Marques's murder was still unsolved. There were no eyewitnesses and Marques's seedy drug ties had left police detectives with a long list of possible suspects. But Paulette had her own suspicions, though she hadn't shared them with the boys in blue.

Marques had been killed in his apartment in the wee hours of the morning and according to neighbors, there had been loud voices before sounds of a struggle. Marques was found beaten and strangled by police soon after.

Antonio had stormed out of their house the night before the murder after Paulette, crippled by guilt, had finally told him about her affair. Her husband hadn't been reachable for hours and hadn't returned home until the next morning. He also had never told Paulette where he had been all that time while her calls to his cell went to voice mail and her texts went unanswered.

She didn't want to believe Antonio was capable of such a horrendous act. Before the rancor that had entered their marriage, her husband had been a funny and loving gentleman. No matter how furious he had been at her, he wasn't capable of cold-blooded murder. He wasn't capable of beating a man to death and strangling him with his bare hands, was he?

Paulette took a deep breath, sat on the edge of her bed, and tugged on her boots. Though questions about her husband still clouded her thoughts, she momentarily pushed them aside to finish dressing.

I can only deal with one crisis at a time, she told herself.

Minutes later, Paulette stepped out of her bedroom and walked down the hall to the stairs with keys in hand and her purse thrown over her shoulder. As she passed the guest room, the door creaked open. Antonio stood in the doorway in striped pajama bottoms, catching her by surprise.

"Oh, Tony, you scared me!" she exclaimed, throwing her hand over her chest, feeling her pulse quicken beneath her palm. She stared at her husband, who practically loomed over her in the shadow of the doorway. "I-I didn't know you were . . . were awake."

Since she had told him about the affair several months ago, he had moved his things and now permanently slept in the guest room. Because of his busy work schedule, sometimes they could go days without seeing each other. Paulette suspected that not seeing her occasionally suited Antonio just fine, which broke her heart. The man whom she loved no longer wanted to be around her.

"Where are you going?" he asked, narrowing his eyes with suspicion and pushing his door open wider. He glanced over his shoulder at the alarm clock across the room on his night table, then turned back and glared at her. "Where the hell are you heading out to at three a.m.?"

I'm not cheating on you, Tony, she wanted to tell him, but instead she cleared her throat and said, "Evan called. Terry's in the ICU at Medstar. I'm heading into D.C. to see him. We all are."

Antonio's face suddenly changed. He abruptly shifted from anger and mistrust to unmasked concern. "What's wrong with Terry? What happened?"

"He had a car accident," she whispered, lowering her eyes. "It's bad . . . *really* bad. Evan said he doesn't know if . . ." Her voice choked a little. She cleared her throat again. "Look, I have to go. I told them I would—"

"I'll go with you," he said suddenly, turning around and yanking down his pajama pants. She watched in shock as he walked naked across the guest room and turned on the overhead light. He began to open drawers, pulling out underwear, a pair of jeans, and a T-shirt.

"Tony, you don't . . . you don't have to come with me. I can—"

"No matter what's going on between us, Paulette, Terry is still my brother-in-law," he said loudly and firmly. "I think of him like a brother. I want to know what's going on with him, too. I'm going."

At that, she fell quiet.

They pulled out of the garage in Antonio's Mercedes soon after. As Antonio made the forty-five-minute drive into the city, the couple sat in such a strained, uncomfortable silence it made Paulette fidget in the passenger seat. Unable to take the silence any longer, Paulette reached forward and pressed a button on the dashboard to turn on the satellite radio. She slumped back into the seat and listened to the drone of sports radio banter.

So many questions for Antonio filtered through her mind that she wanted to ask.

Do you still love me?

Why do you stay?

Will we ever be able to go back to the way things were?

Do you hate me for bringing that man into our lives?

What will you do when I tell you I'm having a baby?

What will you do if I tell you I don't know whether the baby is yours?

But all her questions went unanswered. She stayed silent and her husband continued to diligently stare out the windshield, acting as if she wasn't there.

When Antonio pulled into a spot in the multi-story parking garage, Paulette almost leaped out of the car. She couldn't get out of that stifled compartment fast enough.

"Do you know where we need to go?" Antonio asked as he shut the driver's side door and walked around the car toward her.

She quickly nodded. "Ev said he was on the sixth floor."

She turned away and marched across the garage

to the stairwell, not looking back to see whether Antonio followed her. When she and Antonio stepped out of the steel-walled hospital elevator ten minutes later, they were greeted by the sight of the ICU waiting room. Several leather brown chairs were lined along the walls and in the center of the room in an L shape. A flat-screen television sat on the far wall facing the elevator and a CNN anchor sat behind a glass desk on the screen. A half-stocked vending machine sat along the adjacent wall.

Paulette quickly spotted Evan and Leila. Save for an elderly woman who looked like she was nodding off in her chair, Evan and his fiancée were the only other people in the quiet waiting room. Evan was leaning forward with his elbows on his knees and his head bowed as he stared bleakly at the linoleum tile beneath his feet. Leila sat at his side, her face grim and her eyes red and glistening with tears. She was rubbing Evan's back and whispering something to him.

Seeing them both like this, Paulette's mind instantly leapt to the worst-case scenario.

Oh God, she thought, starting to tremble all over again. *Terry's dead! He's dead, isn't he?*

"Ev?" she called out weakly.

At the sound of her voice, Evan immediately raised his head. He staggered to his feet and slowly walked toward her with his arms outstretched. He looked absolutely decimated.

Paulette raced across the room, closing the distance between them. She leapt into her brother's embrace. She didn't care whether he felt her hard, round stomach. She just wanted her brother to hold her.

"I'm too late, Ev!" she sobbed into her brother's ear, tightening her arms around him. She clung to him like he was a life preserver in a vast ocean. "I'm too late, aren't I? Terry's dead! Oh my God! Oh my God! Terry's—"

"Calm down, Sweet Pea," Evan whispered, patting her gently on the back and using her childhood nickname. "Terry's still alive. The doctor said he's stable."

At those words, she sobbed even harder—this time with relief.

Maybe it was the hormones from the pregnancy or the constant stress she had been under because of the affair, her broken marriage, and keeping her pregnancy a secret, but Paulette sobbed and sobbed and Evan let her do it. He let her cry on his shoulder as long as she wanted. Meanwhile, Leila and Antonio stood mutely to the side, allowing the siblings to have their moment.

When Paulette's sobs finally tapered off, her brother slowly pulled away and gazed down at her. "Do you want to see him?" he asked.

"Of course." She sniffed, wiping her eyes on the sleeve of her sweater. "Take me to him."

Evan reached down and took Paulette's hand. They both walked to the waiting room's entrance. When they reached the doorway, Evan paused and turned to look back at Leila.

"Go ahead," Leila said, answering his silent question. She dabbed at her watery eyes with Kleenex. "We'll wait for you guys here." She smiled up at Antonio before falling back into one of the chairs along the wall. She patted the seat of the chair beside her. "Park it here, big guy. Keep me company."

Antonio gave her a half smile before dropping into the seat.

As Paulette walked out of the waiting room, she heard Leila say, "Tell me what you've been up to, Tony. I haven't seen you in a while."

Antonio then began to speak. His voice was calm and without the spite that Paulette often detected nowadays whenever he spoke to her.

Paulette was grateful to her future sister-in-law for offering a distraction and keeping Antonio preoccupied. She liked Leila. In the twenty-plus years Paulette had known her, they had only argued once and that was due to deceit and machinations on her brother Dante's part. He had lied and insinuated that Leila had divulged secrets about Paulette that Leila had promised to keep forever. But now the two women were friends again. They met regularly for lunch. They laughed and gossiped together over the phone, but Paulette still hadn't told Leila her current secret—that she was pregnant. Paulette was hesitant to trust *anyone* besides her obstetrician with a secret this big again.

Evan's hold around Paulette's hand tightened as they walked past the nurses' station and down the quiet corridor to Terry's hospital room. They passed several glass-enclosed rooms with patients of all ages, many hooked up to a myriad of IVs, respirators, and so much tubing that they looked like extras in science-fiction movies. Several nurses in blue scrubs shuffled in and out of the rooms.

"I'm gonna warn you that he's in bad shape," Evan said softly, glancing down at her. "It was a very serious accident, Sweet Pea."

Usually she hated it when her brothers used the nickname that their mother had bestowed upon her when she was one year old. But today she found it comforting.

"I know," she whispered as they walked.

"The doc said they're going to transfer him out of ICU soon because he's doing better, but Terry still doesn't look good. There are bruises and . . . and swelling. He has some broken bones."

Evan was trying to prepare her for something awful. She could sense it. But nothing was more awful than her brother dying.

"As long as he's alive, Ev, I don't care," she said as Evan drew to a stop at one of the doors.

He nodded, let go of her hand, and wrapped an arm around her shoulders as she took a timid step into the room. The curtain around the hospital bed was partially drawn, so the only thing she could see was a lump at the end of the bed. Probably Terry's feet.

When they stepped around the curtain, she breathed in audibly. She clamped a hand over her mouth to keep from shouting out. Evan's grip around her shoulders tightened as she started to weep again.

Terrence Murdoch, former model and unrepentant playboy, lay at a slight angle in the hospital bed, propped up by several pillows. His face was covered with a mix of purple and red bruises and so much swelling that Paulette could barely recognize him. His head was now so lumpy and misshapen that he looked less like someone who had once graced Italian and Parisian runways, and more like the Elephant Man. Bandages were wrapped around his head and a large white patch surrounded by cotton covered his left eye. Plastic tubing was in his mouth. His bloated lips hung slack, like he had fallen asleep while watching television or sitting on his living room couch. A cast was around his left arm. The other arm sat lifeless at his side.

Paulette slowly shook her head as she cried.

What had happened to her brother, and would he ever be whole again?

Chapter 4
C. J.

C. J. furiously flipped through her reporter's notebook in search of a blank page before resting it on the steering wheel of her Honda Civic. She ripped off the lid to her ballpoint pen with her teeth and held her cell phone in the crook of her shoulder.

"Hello, Mr. Mayhew! Thank you for calling me back," she said, trying her best to keep the giddiness out of her voice but not succeeding.

She had been just about to climb out of her car and head into the offices of the *Chesterton Times*, where she had worked for the past two and half years, when she saw Philip Mayhew's number on her phone screen. He was a source she had been hounding for weeks, trying to get an interview with him. The owner of several local restaurants—one of which was located in Chesterton—had been accused of improperly paying his employees or not paying them at all. Mayhew had threatened those same employees with deportation if they complained to the authorities. One of the waitresses at his restaurant had come to C. J. last month with the accusations, looking terrified and taking frequent, hesitant glances over her shoulder the whole time she spoke with C. J. at a small coffee shop outside of town.

"Thank you for coming to me with this," C. J. had told her, trying her best to calm the woman's worries. "You're very brave."

"No, you are the one who is brave. I read your . . . your stories," the woman had said quietly in her heavy accent, gazing timidly at C. J. "I see how you stand up for poor people."

Of course, the woman was referring to the stories that C. J. had written about the corruption at Murdoch Bank and how the bank had conspired to foreclose and push out homeowners from one of the oldest neighborhoods in Chesterton to make way for a tacky new shopping center.

C. J. had worked hard on those stories for more than a year, seeing them as not only a way to bring attention to the plight of hardworking people who deserved better, but also to stick it to the late George Murdoch, whose shadiness was legendary. She despised men like him, who used their money and power to lord it over others, who reminded her much of her own domineering, manipulative father.

But despite C. J.'s best efforts, the stories hadn't accomplished much besides winning a few investigative journalism awards from the Virginia Society of Professional Journalists. The homes had been foreclosed on and the four blocks of houses were scheduled to be bulldozed by the end of the next year to make way for the new mall. Murdoch Bank was still in existence and the last she had checked, the share price of its parent company, Murdoch Conglomerated, was the highest it had ever been. The company had expanded even further under the leadership of George's eldest son, Evan Murdoch.

C. J. was an optimist, but she wasn't deluded; she knew you couldn't always win. Sometimes the little guy got the short end of the stick no matter how hard you tried. But that didn't mean she would stop trying. It didn't mean she couldn't make sure scum like Philip Mayhew was held accountable for what he did.

"Yeah, I called you back," Mayhew now answered bitingly. His voice was so brittle that she could have mentally snapped it in half. "I heard you were going to write some bullshit story about me in your little newspaper. I wanted to tell you I was going to sue your ass for defamation if you printed that goddamn story."

"Libel," she corrected, leaning back in the driver's seat and taking her pen top out of her mouth, unfazed by his threat.

"Huh?" he barked.

"I said you'd have to sue me for libel, Mr. Mayhew, because I'm a reporter. You couldn't sue me for defamation. But know that the requirements for proving libel in the United States are tough. You'd have to prove intent to destroy your character and—"

"What are you . . . a fuckin' law expert?" he snapped.

"You'd also have to prove that I *lied*," she continued, undaunted, self-righteous indignation spurring her on, "and we both know that I am most definitely *not* lying. You haven't been paying your staff the same amount that you've been reporting to the government, Mr. Mayhew. That is not only unethical, but also a federal crime."

"Look, lady, I don't have to—"

"I have pay stubs and money orders proving this. I also have statements from several of your employees."

"Oh yeah? Well, whoever talked to you is fucking fired! I'll make sure they'll be on the next boat to Honduras!"

C. J. rolled her eyes. According to her sources, this was a threat Mayhew made often.

"I wouldn't advise that, sir. If you fire them, I'll just print a story saying how they were penalized for telling the truth. You'll look like the biggest bully in the county and it would make operating several businesses in this area very challenging."

At those words, Mayhew finally fell silent.

"Look, I believe in balanced reporting. I'm offering you the courtesy of responding to these allegations. I'd like a quote from you, Mr. Mayhew. Here's your chance to defend yourself."

"You want a quote from me, bitch?" he yelled over the phone, making her pull it away from her ear. "You *really* want a quote? How about this? Fuck you and suck my dick!"

He then hung up.

C. J. sighed and dropped her cell phone back into her satchel. She shrugged. In her early days as a cub reporter, such words would have left her devastated and badly shaken. But after five years of working everything from the crime beat to city council, she had developed a thick skin.

"'When reached, Mayhew had no comment,'" she muttered as she scribbled it on her notepad. She then threw open her car door.

Less than a minute later, C. J. strode into the *Chesterton Times* newsroom on the second floor of a two-story walk-up on Main Street. It was an unassuming office with wall paneling and old carpet that was so stained that its checkered-pattern was no longer identifiable. A lone window kept the room's inhabitants from feeling like they were stuck in a musky basement. All of the five reporters' desks were in a bull-pen arrangement. C. J. beelined straight for her desk, where her laptop already sat open, waiting for her to file her next story.

"The African queen has arrived, everybody!" Sports reporter Eddie exclaimed, throwing up his arms. "All hail the queen!"

C. J. bestowed him with a withering glare and gave him the finger as she passed. He and a few of the other reporters burst into laughter.

She knew she had a reputation in the newsroom for being snobbish and unapproachable. Maybe it was a product of her reserved upbringing, or maybe it was because she was the only female *and* black person on staff, but she had never bonded with the other reporters, though she had been at the newspaper for two years. Whenever they went out for drinks after hours, she declined their invitation to join them. Whenever they grabbed a quick bite to eat or took a doughnut break at Mimi's Café up the street, C. J. begged off and said she had already eaten or had to get to her next assignment and didn't have time for lunch. After a while, the other reporters stopped inviting her. Now they were content just to ridicule her and make flippant remarks—hence the nickname "African queen."

"Still saving the world and protecting it from evildoers?" Eddie asked sarcastically, leaning back in his rollaway chair. He sucked through the straw of his Big Gulp, emitting a loud, annoying sound that made C. J.'s skin crawl.

"Don't you have some Little League game to report on?" she replied, dropping her satchel onto her desk. "Or isn't there a mascot somewhere you can interview?"

Eddie laughed again, though this time there was no levity in his voice. "Well, not all of us want to pretend that we're working at the friggin' *New York Times*, sweetheart. And last time I checked, this ain't the *Wall Street Journal*! You're at a Podunk, small-town paper just like the rest of us, even if you like to pretend that you aren't. So you can just climb off that high horse of yours!"

"Oh, believe me, I know where I am," she muttered before lowering herself into her chair.

When C. J. had graduated from Spellman, she had had dreams of working at *The New York Times* or maybe being a foreign correspondent for the Associated Press or Reuters. Her family name and connections certainly would have helped her get one of those positions. But she hadn't used the Aston family name. She didn't want to be beholden to her parents for yet another thing in her life. She didn't want her father to have something else to hold over her head. Besides, he never would have helped her anyway, not with how she had "betrayed" him. So instead she applied for jobs at smaller newspapers, abbreviating her name on her résumé from the more identifiable "Courtney Jocelyn Aston" that gave away her identity, to the less conspicuous "C. J. Aston." She took her first reporter job across the country at a local paper in Southern California and never looked back. Not only did she not owe her success as a reporter to her family, she hadn't spoken to any of them in years.

"Cut it out, Eddie," their managing editor, Jake, ordered. He stepped out of his office and into the newsroom. "At least let her boot up her laptop first before you start ribbing her."

C. J. turned to find Jake standing over her shoulder. The squat man had his glasses perched on his bald head and one of his hands in the pocket of his gray slacks.

Jake dressed and looked like an insurance salesman or a high school principal, but there was nothing mundane about him. If C. J. was tenacious about covering the news, Jake was just as tenacious in running his newsroom.

"I've got a story for you, C. J." He tossed a sheet of paper onto her desk and she slowly picked it up. "There's a rumor going around that Terrence Murdoch got drunk and plowed into some poor old lady's car in D.C. He's at Medstar Medical Center recovering. I need you to talk to Metro Police and get a statement from ol' Terry."

C. J. frowned as she stared down at the paper where Jake had scribbled a few basic details.

In the process of covering Murdoch Bank, C. J.

had learned a lot about the Murdoch family, or the "Marvelous Murdochs," as they were called around Chesterton. She certainly had heard a lot about hazel-eyed, pretty boy Terrence Murdoch, who made most women in Chesterton swoon.

C. J. had caught a glimpse of him a few times while he was sitting behind the wheel of his silver Porsche, or as she liked to call it, his "big dick on wheels." She had even run into him once. Well, actually he had run into *her*, almost hitting her with a door he was holding open for a model-looking type in a short skirt whom he was squiring around town.

"How serious was the accident?" she asked, staring at the sheet of paper.

"Don't know," Jake answered before turning around and heading back toward his office. "Guess you'd better get to the hospital and find out."

C. J. pretended not to be one of the small throng of reporters waiting in front of the hospital's automatic doors with cameras and notepads at the ready, hoping to get an interview with Terrence Murdoch or his family. With the same ease, she strode to the nurses' station, already working out the lie in her head that she'd have to tell in order to get past the desk, down the hall, and into Terrence's hospital room. She wasn't family, neither was she Terrence's friend. This would be quite a challenge, but for now at least, she was up to it.

She had made a few calls and gotten a few more details about the accident from Metro Police. Terrence had been in the car accident at around

2:15 a.m. at a four-way intersection in Northwest D.C. No one knew for sure who was at fault. The other driver—a sixty-five-year-old woman who had been on the way to pick up her granddaughter—said she couldn't remember whether she saw Terrence waiting at the stop sign prior to driving through the intersection. But two eyewitnesses said that Terrence had definitely come to a full stop, then drove on before the other driver plowed into him. Of course, these eyewitnesses had been drunk so their credibility was in question. Terrence also had done plenty of drinking earlier that night while he partied at a local strip club. Now both drivers were waylaid in the hospital with injuries.

According to one cop, "We're still going over accident reconstruction, but off the record, I think that rich boy is at fault."

If that was the case, Terrence might get sued or worse, face criminal charges for what had happened that morning. C. J. had already updated Jake on her findings. He was holding the slot open on the front page for this baby.

"Hello," C. J. said as she stopped in front of the nurses' station, trying her best to look distraught, "can you please tell me where Terrence Murdoch's room is?"

The nurse, who had shoulders wider than a linebacker's, leaned back and squinted up at C. J. "Are you related to Mr. Murdoch? Only relatives are allowed to visit patients in this wing."

"I'm his . . . his fiancée," C. J. whispered before lowering her head demurely.

She also broke the nurse's gaze because she

couldn't continue to lie and look at her at the same time. She might have developed a thick skin after years of reporting, but she was still a horrible liar.

"I'm not a blood relative, but I might as well be one, right?" C. J. said with a nervous laugh. "I heard about the accident and I just want to see him. To . . . to make sure he's okay."

The nurse hesitated, then slowly nodded. "Well, I guess you can see him." She held up two fingers, showing C. J. the "peace" sign. "But only two people are allowed in the room at a time. His brother and sister are already in there. When they leave, you can—"

"*They're already there?*" C. J.'s head snapped up. Her eyes widened with alarm.

Her reaction made the nurse narrow her eyes further at C. J. "Yes," she said slowly, "they're in the room with him now. When they leave, you can see him."

"Oh, uh. Okay. I . . . I have no problem waiting."

She didn't want to run into Evan Murdoch. If she did, her whole plan, along with her cover, would be blown. He had seen her before when she tried to interview him a few times for her stories on Murdoch Bank. She had tracked him down a year ago while he was having a business lunch in town and he had not been happy to be interrupted by her.

"The next time you ambush me like this, my lawyer will be contacting your paper and I'll have a restraining order filed against you. Understood?" Evan had said tersely, before storming off.

Evan did not like her, and if he found her standing here in the hospital, he'd like her even less.

"I'll just go grab something to eat . . . you know . . . in the cafeteria . . . downstairs," C. J. said hastily to the nurse. "I'll be back in a sec."

"But here they come right now," the nurse called out just as C. J. turned away from the desk.

"What the hell are you doing here?" a baritone voice boomed, making C. J. wince.

Damn, she thought. *I was so close!*

She loudly swallowed and turned to find Evan Murdoch glaring at her.

The last time she had seen him, he had looked the part of a company CEO in a pin-striped business suit, sensible blue tie, and crisp white shirt. The other reporters thought C. J. was stuck up, but Evan Murdoch had her beat. He gave off an air of superiority that only came with growing up rich and knowing that you would always be rich.

But he didn't look like that today. He was wearing a baggy sweatshirt and wrinkled jeans. He was even sporting a five o'clock shadow. Bags were under his eyes. If she had seen him in a crowd, she might not have recognized him.

"What are you doing here?" he repeated tightly.

A woman stood at his side, looking confused. C. J. instantly recognized her as Paulette Williams, Evan and Terrence's little sister.

"I . . . I was . . . I was here to . . . uh . . ." C. J. struggled to make up a lie. To say that she was also visiting a patient in the recovery ward, but she wasn't fast enough.

"You were here to see my brother, weren't you?"

Evan said, taking a step toward her and making her take a step back. "Are you writing a goddamn story about this?"

Lie, C. J.! Tell him anything! a voice yelled frantically in her head, but she was tongue-tied. She could be bold when she knew she was doing the right thing, but that resolve always faltered when she felt like she was doing something wrong.

The guilt trips her father had exerted on her for more than two decades had worked wonders.

"I . . . I wanted to hear Mr. Murdoch's side of the story," she said. She forced herself to stop trembling, pushed back her shoulders, and met Evan's gaze. "I wanted to give him a chance to defend himself. I believe in balanced—"

"He could have *died!*" Evan shouted, taking another step toward her. This time his sister grabbed his arm, tugging him back. "He could have fucking died, you heartless bitch!"

At the sound of his shouts, a few people stepped out of the nearby waiting room. One was a pretty woman in a turtleneck and yoga pants. She quickly stepped forward and rested a hand on Evan's shoulder.

"Ev, what's wrong?"

"Sir," the nurse said quietly, "this is a hospital. You're going to have to keep the noise down."

"She's here to write a goddamn story about my brother!" Evan said to anyone who would listen, jabbing an index finger at C. J. "He's hooked up to a fucking respirator and she wants to get a quote from him! Are you kidding me?"

C. J. quickly shook her head. "I-I didn't know."

No one had told her the extent of Terrence's injuries. She had tried to get that information, but the police hadn't even known.

Now as she gazed at his family and she could see how much they were grieving, she knew she had made a mistake coming here.

"Look, I'm . . . I'm sorry." Her knuckles went white as she tightened her death grip around the straps of her satchel. "I—"

"*You're sorry?*" Evan repeated, still glaring at her. He tried to tug his arm out of his sister's grasp, but she only held on tighter. "You're fucking sorry?"

"Evan, calm down," the other woman beside him said. In contrast, his sister continued to stand mutely at his side, looking befuddled and overwhelmed.

"Sir, you're going to have to leave if you continue to yell like this," the nurse ordered.

"I'm not leaving! He's my brother! Make this fucking parasite leave! She shouldn't be here, anyway. You just let reporters walk into patients' rooms? What kind of goddamn hospital is this? Where the hell is security?"

"I'm sorry, sir, but this young woman told me she was his fiancée," the nurse argued. "I wouldn't have—"

"Well, she fucking lied!"

C. J. stood frozen, like a deer caught in headlights. She wanted to escape, but she felt paralyzed. The woman at Evan's side suddenly wrapped an arm around C. J.'s shoulder and steered her back toward the elevator, catching C. J. by surprise.

"Let's go," the woman whispered into C. J.'s ear,

walking swiftly down the corridor and dragging C. J. along with her. "You need to get out of here before he kills you."

The woman was being hyperbolic, right? C. J. gave a wary glance over her shoulder at Evan Murdoch, who was still railing.

"Ev's not normally like this," the woman said, stopping in front of the elevator doors. She pressed the Down button, not giving C. J. a chance to tell her where she wanted to go. "Terry's accident really scared him. He's more than just a little distraught."

"I'm sorry," C. J. whispered again.

"It's okay," the woman replied as the elevator doors opened. "You just came at a *very* bad time."

C. J. stepped onto the metal elevator and turned to the woman. "Thank you, Miss—"

"Hawkins," the woman said. "Leila Hawkins. But everyone calls me Lee."

Leila Hawkins. She recognized her now. Evan's mistress, according to the town gossip.

The elevator doors shut and C. J. collapsed against the metal walls.

Chapter 5

Dante

Dante whistled a peppy tune as he strode and practically skipped off the elevator and down the corridor. He was excited and could barely contain the enthusiasm that surged through him at that moment. He felt like today was Christmas and the Fourth of July rolled into one. Dante hadn't been this happy in weeks, maybe even *months* and it was all because his half-brother, Terrence, had decided to crash his Porsche into some poor old lady at a D.C. intersection.

Just thinking about it made Dante beam.

"Umm, excuse me," the nurse called out as Dante passed the hexagon-shaped desk. "Excuse me, sir!"

He didn't pause or even acknowledge her. Instead, he glanced at the doorways of each hospital room, in search of Mavis Upton—the woman who had been in the accident with Terrence.

Dante had used his legal connections as a lawyer to finagle her name from the local cops and now he was on a mission to not only meet Mavis but also to make her his client. They were going to sue the pants off of Terrence Murdoch.

To say that Dante disliked his wealthy siblings was putting it lightly; he utterly *despised* them. While they had been born and raised in the lap of luxury, he had grown up poor in the inner city. While they carried the Murdoch name, his father had succeeded for decades in keeping Dante a secret. In fact, Dante hadn't known that George Murdoch was his father until he was a grown man. The week after his mother made the deathbed revelation, he had gone straight to George's office at Murdoch Conglomerated to introduce himself.

"Why are you here?" George had asked Dante coldly within seconds of him stepping through the office door.

Dante had just laid eyes on his father, gazing in awe at the man he strongly resembled. George had had the same skin tone as himself, had been balding, and had shrewd hazel eyes that seemed to bore into Dante's very soul. He had admired George already based on what he had heard and read about him over the years. Seeing George in person, looking so dignified and commanding in the penthouse office of the company he had built from the ground up, only made Dante admire him even more. But his father's chilly tone had been like a splash of frigid water.

His mother had warned him that George had been embarrassed about his liaison with her—a poor waitress he'd had a one-night stand with in the early days of his marriage. Because of that, Dante hadn't expected a bear hug or even a tear-filled apology for ignoring him for thirty-six years, but he had at least expected his father to offer him a seat in one of the two leather wingback chairs that had been facing the immense mahogany office desk. He hadn't expected the first words out of his mouth to be "Why are you here?"

"Do you want money?" George had asked, eying Dante. "Is that what this is about?"

"Money would be nice," Dante had said. He had forced a laugh to let his father know he had been joking, but he had stopped laughing and cleared his throat when his father remained silent and continued to glare at him. "But no, the real reason I came here was to meet you, to . . . to see the man who made me."

"Well, you've met me. You've seen me." George had raised his hands in a "*Now what?*" motion.

"I was . . . also hoping that I could . . . uh, get to know you," Dante had said, feeling his usual overwhelming confidence starting to falter. "I'd like to meet your fam—"

"That's out of the question." George had shaken his head, risen from his chair, and adjusted his tie. He had walked around his desk. "Look . . . Dante, is it?"

Damn, Dante had thought, feeling a stab to his chest. *He doesn't even know my name.*

"I see no reason to change the arrangement that I had with your mother before she died. She agreed not to make your presence known if I agreed to help her financially. I'll offer you the same deal." George had walked the short distance across his office to stand in front of Dante. The two men had been the same height and had the same build. They were almost replicas of each other. "I'm assuming you'll want an amount more substantial than your mother's. I sent her a stipend of five thousand dollars a month. How about I increase it by another five thousand for you?"

"You think . . . you think you can just buy me off?" Dante had asked tightly, feeling an acidic burning in his throat.

And besides, if he got money from George, it wouldn't be a measly ten-thousand-dollar check once a month. He wanted what was rightfully owed to him as the *true* eldest son of George Murdoch. He wanted his father to treat him like he mattered.

"I don't think I can buy you off, I *know* I can." George rested a hand on his shoulder, making Dante sad to realize his father only touched him when he was attempting to bribe him. "Come on, you seem like a reasonable man. I'm willing to negotiate a monthly stipend. And hey, if you continue to keep my secret, I'll even add you to my will. Just name your price."

Dante had angrily shoved his father's hand off his shoulder. For a second, he was too furious to speak. "To hell with you," he had muttered before storming out of his father's office.

Dante knew he had a chip on his shoulder the size of Gibraltar, but he felt that chip was warranted. He had been ignored and rejected by his own father. He had tried to take his rightful place as the head of the Murdoch family, but his siblings had thwarted him at every turn, uniting against him and shutting him out entirely.

But that's okay, Dante thought as he peered into another hospital room, finding an old man sitting in his hospital bed with a plastic tray at his waist. The old man turned and gazed at Dante quizzically while chewing on mushy string beans.

I'll fix their asses, Dante thought as he continued his search.

Dante saw Terrence's latest mishap as an opportunity. Dante still might not be the head of Murdoch Conglomerated, or even officially part of the Murdoch family, but this would offer him a chance to exact long-overdue revenge on the so-called Marvelous Murdochs, the M&Ms. He was almost salivating at the chance.

"Hey, don't try to blame me for this shit!" he heard a woman shout. Dante slowed as he drew closer to the room where the voice came from. "Nobody told you to run into that damn car!"

"But Tasha said you left her alone in the apartment again. She was scared, Renee," another woman replied. Her voice sounded older and fatigued. "You can't just leave a child alone like that and go running around in the streets all night! I told you that before. She's only six years old!"

Dante stepped into the doorway and saw an older woman with graying hair propped up by a stack of pillows. A bandage was on her right cheek. Her left eye was bruised and swollen like someone had punched her. A younger woman in a pair of skintight jeans and black knee-high boots with towering high heels paced back and forth in front of the older woman's hospital bed. She was dressed like she had just walked out of a nightclub.

"Whatever, Ma!" Skintight Jeans shouted, dropping a hand to her hip and pushing out her chest over her low-cut, sequined top. "Like I said, don't try to pin this on me. Because I ain't—"

"Excuse me, ladies," Dante said, striding into the room. He glanced between the two women. "I hope you don't mind if I interrupt, but—"

"Who the hell are you?" the younger woman snapped. Her burgundy lips curled with a sneer.

"It would behoove you not to speak so loudly about the accident," he continued, "especially here in the hospital. We wouldn't want everyone to hear. And from what I understand, Terrence Murdoch is also on this floor."

He likely would get moved to a private room in one of the nicer parts of the hospital, but for now, he and Mavis were both in the recovery ward.

"You definitely wouldn't want *him* to hear all of this," Dante said.

The younger woman fell silent while the older woman's eyes pooled with tears.

"I-I can't remember what happened, but I know I was in such a . . . such a rush to get to Tasha," the woman murmured, her voice shaking with emotion. "I didn't mean to go through that stop sign! I wasn't trying to—"

"Ssshhh," Dante whispered, stopping her mid-sentence. He walked toward the bed and raised a finger to his lips. He then removed his wool coat and tossed it over the plastic handrail. "Your name is Mavis, *right?*"

She hesitated, then nodded.

"Well, Mavis, my name is Dante Turner. I'm a lawyer with the law offices of Nutter, McElroy, and Ailey, and I'm going to offer you some free legal advice: Don't confess to something you didn't do."

She frowned and fisted the bed sheets in her hands. "But I-I don't know for sure if I didn't do it. I mean, I-I think I—"

"Mavis"—he placed his hand on top of hers and gave it a squeeze—"you're a caring woman. I can tell. You have the best of intentions. But, believe me, you don't want to accept responsibility for what happened today. Do you know the other driver in the accident?"

Her frown deepened and she slowly shook her head.

"What the hell difference does that make?" the younger woman barked. "Who the hell cares?"

"Renee, don't be so rude," Mavis admonished, though Renee waved away her chastising. "He's only trying to help."

"Yeah, I bet he is," Renee snapped, tossing her long ebony weave over her shoulder.

"She's right, I am trying to help. And you *should* care who the other driver is," Dante said, shifting his gaze to Renee. "His name is Terrence Murdoch of Murdoch Conglomerated, a multi-million-dollar company that specializes in food products and restaurant franchises. Terrence comes from money—*lots* of money. And if he and his family decided to unleash their lawyers on you for the accident, your mother would end up in the poor-house. They'd find a way to destroy her."

"Oh Lord," Mavis whispered. She looked visibly shaken. She started trembling again. "I'm sorry. I'm so sorry! Please tell him I didn't mean to—"

"Mavis, I told you to stop apologizing," Dante repeated. "You weren't the cause of that accident. As far as I'm concerned, *he* was the one who went through the intersection and hit *you*, and that's what you should say in court."

"*Court?*" Renee raised an eyebrow and crossed her arms over her bountiful chest. "Who said anything about going to court?"

"Well, your mother would have to go to court if she intends to sue Mr. Murdoch," Dante said.

Mavis looked confused. "You . . . you think I should sue him? But I don't know for sure if he was the one who caused the crash. I wouldn't feel right blaming him for something he might not have done."

Dante returned his gaze to Mavis. The old woman was going to be a challenging client, he could tell. She was obviously crippled by guilt for what had happened and would not be willing to lie—at least for now. He glanced at her daughter, Renee, who was listening to him keenly. She was hanging on to his every word. He might have an ally in Renee. That woman looked more carnivorous than a gray wolf. She would have no problem lying and probably could aid him in pressuring Mavis to say what needed to be said when the time came. But for now, Dante would have to choose his words carefully.

"You're not really blaming him. This is more of a preemptive measure, Mavis," Dante explained.

"If you sue Terrence first, he's less likely to try litigation with you."

"That makes sense," Renee said, vigorously nodding. "You fire the gun first, Mama . . . the warning shot to scare him off."

"You'd file a lawsuit for your injuries," Dante said, "for your pain and mental anguish. You'd argue that it's only right that Mr. Murdoch pay a sizeable settlement to make you whole again."

"But I wouldn't . . . I wouldn't really be expecting that money, though, right?" Mavis asked. Her gray brows furrowed with distress. "I'm not really suing him for real. I'm . . . I'm just doing it so that he won't sue me . . . *first?*"

Dante nodded and indulged her with a warm smile meant to convey empathy, though he felt absolutely none.

She lowered her gaze, then finally nodded. "Well, I-I guess it's all right, then. But only if I'm not really going to get the money in the end."

"Of course not," Dante lied.

"So I guess you're offering to be her lawyer, then," Renee said, pointing her long silver nail at him that looked like the talon of a vulture. "Is that what all this talking's about?"

"I'd be happy to assist Ms. Upton." He quickly turned to the older woman. "On a pro bono basis, of course."

"*Pro bono?* That means you don't get paid up front, right?" Renee asked.

"Exactly," he said, giving her a wink.

Renee's smile widened. She stuck out her chest even further, almost pushing her breasts entirely over the top of her shirt.

Oh, he definitely had an ally in Renee, and judging from the heated gaze she was now giving him, he might have a lot more.

"It all sounds good to me, Mama," Renee urged. "I say hire him."

Mavis pursed her lips, forming them into a thin line that almost looked like a grimace. Finally, she nodded. "Okay. You're . . . you're hired."

Chapter 6

Terrence

Terrence sat alone in the dark in his spacious living room, gazing through one eye at his television, where ESPN played on the flat screen. One leg—the one he had shattered during the accident—was perched on the suede ottoman in front of him. A beer, already warming to room temperature, was in one hand. He absently scratched at his beard with the edge of his remote, careful not to touch his eye patch and the sensitive tissue underneath it.

When a commercial came on the screen, he raised the remote to flip to another channel and gazed at an action movie where the leather-clad hero ran across jungle terrain on two legs.

Two healthy legs, Terrence noted bitterly.

The hero also had two working eyes, rather than one that had been mutilated and blinded during a car crash.

Terrence had always been vain about his eyes. "They're like drops of liquid caramel," one of his girlfriends had told him back in college, before bestowing his eyelids with a sultry kiss. But they didn't look like "drops of liquid caramel" anymore. Now the damaged eye beneath his black patch made him shudder with disgust whenever he looked at it. It was red and inflamed tissue, mangled meat that would never serve its purpose again.

The eye and the leg weren't the only things that had changed since the accident. He looked like a completely different person now. Gone was the immaculately dressed, handsome man he once had been, and in his place was a slovenly couch potato.

Terrence hadn't shaved in weeks and now vaguely resembled a crotchety backwoodsman. All he needed was the flannel shirt and ax. He hadn't changed his clothes in days, either; he had been sporting the same stained, wrinkled T-shirt, striped pajama bottoms, and gray terry-cloth bathrobe since Tuesday. He didn't see any reason to change clothes unless it was for the mailman's benefit. That was the only person he had seen in more than a week.

Evan and Paulette had tried to visit, but he had told them he was busy. A few of the women he dated had called in the nearly two months since the accident and asked if they could stop by and play nurse.

"I can wear my French maid costume," Georgette had cooed over the phone.

But he had refused. He didn't want any of them

to see him like this. After a while, the women stopped calling—even Georgette.

That's just fine with me, he thought before taking a swig from his bottle. He wanted to be alone. That was the reason Terrence hadn't left his condo in days, even though the doctor had encouraged him to walk around and get some fresh air.

"Your leg and arm are healing nicely, but you've still got to work those muscles, Terry," Dr. Sidda had lectured in his lyrical Hindi accent as he'd lowered his stethoscope from his ears and draped it around his neck two weeks ago. He had stared at Terrence over the plastic rims of glasses that sat on the tip of his aquiline nose. "That is the only way you will regain full use of your limbs. It is how your strength will return, my friend. Have you been doing those exercises the physical therapist showed you?"

Physical therapist, Terrence had thought with annoyance. *You mean the asshole who kept barking at me, "One more! Two more! You can do it! You can do it!"*

Meanwhile sweat had poured from Terrence's brow as he held on to the handlebars in the hospital gym and tried to walk with his busted leg. He had felt like he could collapse at any moment.

Encouragement didn't mean much when your body was this broken, this weakened.

"What's the point? You said yourself that I'd probably always walk with a limp," Terrence had muttered sullenly to Dr. Sidda as he sat on the examination table. "It doesn't matter how much I hop around with that damn cane, Doc. Nothing is going to change that."

The doctor had studied him carefully for several seconds before lowering himself onto a rollaway chair at a sleek black desk on the other side of the examination room.

"You still have to try, Terry," Dr. Sidda had said softly before grabbing a notepad on his desk along with a pen. "And I know someone who might help you. I'm writing you another referral."

"Please, Doc, don't send me to another damn physical therapist," Terrence had grumbled. "I hated that shit! That's why I stopped going in the first place."

Dr. Sidda had scribbled something on the notepad before ripping off a sheet. He had extended the sheet toward Terrence. "It's not a physical therapist."

Terrence had squinted down at the sheet of paper as he took it out of Dr. Sidda's hand. "Then what's it for?"

"Psychotherapy."

When Terrence heard the word, he flinched. "You . . . you want me to see a *shrink?*"

Dr. Sidda took a deep breath, set down the notepad, and linked his hands in front of him. "Dr. Sweeney comes highly recommended. She specializes in patients like yourself who may be—"

"I don't need a shrink. I'm not crazy!"

"Terry, I don't think you're crazy. But I *do* think you may be dealing with mild depression as a result of your accident."

"I'm not depressed," Terrence had argued with tightened lips. His heart had started to thud wildly in his chest. He had balled his fists at his sides. "I'm just pissed off! I'm blind in one eye and I can barely walk! I'm getting fucking sued! If anyone else was going through what I've been going through, they'd be fucking suicidal. But you don't see me climbing up on a chair putting a rope around my neck!"

"And this depression may be your biggest obstacle to making a full recovery," Dr. Sidda had said, ignoring Terrence's tirade. "The only help I can offer is of a physical nature, but perhaps you need something more than that . . . something deeper." Dr. Sidda had held up his hand. "Please, just consider it."

I don't need any goddamn therapist, Terrence now thought angrily as he reclined on his sofa and a Mediterranean-style house exploded on his television screen. Fireballs silhouetted the action-movie hero, who ran in slow motion.

In all the years that Terrence had lived in the Murdoch household, witnessing his parents' dysfunctional marriage and dealing with his father, who had all the warmth of an arctic iceberg, Terrence hadn't gone to therapy. He had survived and thrived without sitting on any shrink's couch complaining about his problems and his doubts about whether his father had really loved him or any of his other siblings. Terrence Murdoch wasn't a whiner; he handled his shit privately and moved along to the next thing. Terrence saw no reason to see a therapist now. He wasn't depressed; he just wanted to be left alone. Was that so hard for everyone to understand? Besides, black people didn't do therapy.

Suddenly, Terrence heard his doorbell ring. He

lowered the remote and beer bottle to a nearby end table and glared at his front door.

"Who the hell is that?" he mumbled aloud before shrugging and deciding to ignore it. He returned his attention to the movie. The doorbell rang again and Terrence started to grumble.

He grabbed the stainless-steel cane that was propped up on the edge of the ottoman and slowly pushed himself to his feet. It was a slow process, crossing the distance of twenty feet between the living room sofa and his front door. He could have made the trek in less than sixty seconds in the old days. That wasn't the case anymore. While he limped toward the front door, his left arm shook with the burden of carrying the weight of his body. The doorbell kept ringing. Hearing that singsong chime over and over again was infuriating.

"I'm coming, goddamnit!" he yelled, breathing heavily.

Finally he reached the front door and practically fell against the wooden slab. He peered through the peephole into the condominium's hallway. When he saw who waited on the other side, he cursed again.

It was his brother, Evan, wearing a long-sleeved polo shirt and khakis, looking concerned as he glanced down at his watch.

I told him I didn't want to see anyone today, Terrence thought angrily.

Momentarily forgetting his fatigue, he quickly undid the deadbolt and bottom lock. He snatched the door open and glared at his older brother.

Evan's handsome face instantly brightened. "Hey, you're alive! Paulette, Lee, and I were starting to wonder. You didn't return my phone calls."

"I didn't know that not answering phone calls constituted being dead. Maybe I just didn't want to talk to you."

Evan nodded, ignoring his brush-off and peered around him at the condo's interior. "Well, I'm here anyway. Can I come inside?"

Terrence groused again before throwing the door open all the way, then he turned around to begin the slow trek back to his sofa.

"Jesus!" Evan exclaimed, shutting the front door behind him. "It smells horrible in here! Like a men's locker room. It looks horrible, too. When's the last time you had this place cleaned?"

Terrence didn't answer, but instead kept walking, finally reaching the edge of the Afghan rug.

"I thought you had a housekeeper," Evan continued, frowning down at the stack of unopened mail, dirty dishes and glasses, and discarded beer bottles that were piled on the glass coffee table. He glanced around him. "You know, I could recommend one for you if she isn't—"

"I don't need a goddamn maid," Terrence said as he collapsed onto the sofa and sighed with gratefulness at being back in its warm, reassuring embrace. "I got rid of the one I had. I don't need a new one."

Evan leaned over and turned on one of the end table lamps, flooding the room with light and making Terrence squint his good eye. Evan's frown deepened. "Why'd you get rid of your housekeeper?"

"Because I don't need one, all right? Besides," Terrence said, returning his attention to the television screen, "I need to save all the money I can, so

I can hand it over to my lawyer and the woman who's suing me."

Evan sighed as he fell back into one of the armchairs facing the sofa. "Your lawyer told me you haven't been returning his phone calls."

"You talked to my lawyer?" Terrence asked tightly, eying his brother.

"He can't do his job if you don't work with him."

"So what? He went crying to you? What are you, my fucking mother?"

"No, I'm your brother—and I care about you. We *all* care about you."

Terrence didn't respond. Instead, he raised one of the half-empty beer bottles to his lips.

"Should you be drinking that and taking your painkillers?" Evan asked, now frowning. "I thought you weren't supposed to mix that stuff."

"Don't worry. I'm off of Vicodin now, *Mom.*" He raised his brows again. "Is that why you're really here? Were you worried that I'd overdosed?"

"I just hate seeing you this way, Terry."

"Jesus! *What* way?" Terrence shouted, slapping a hand on the sofa armrest. "What are you—"

"When's the last time you've taken a shower?" Evan asked, inclining his head.

"What does that have to do with anything?"

"When's the last time you brushed your teeth or shaved?" Evan pointed at Terrence's scraggly beard. "Hell, you could have a family of forest animals living in that thing for all you know!"

"I'm going for a new look," Terrence mumbled sarcastically, taking another drink.

"You don't leave the house except to go to the

doctor or physical therapy and you're not even doing physical therapy anymore! You don't talk to anybody. You just sit in the dark like a mold or a fungus. And when you finally do talk to someone, you fly off the handle! Paulette said you yelled at her yesterday and now you're being pissy with me. I mean . . . I just . . ." Evan paused and took a deep breath. "Look, I'm sorry for what happened to you."

"I don't want your fuckin' apology," Terrence said icily, "or your pity."

"I'm sorry you got banged up and you lost your eye," Evan continued, undaunted. "But, Terry, honestly, I'm just happy that you're breathing and you're still here with us. We didn't know if you were gonna make it. I'm happy that you're alive!"

"At least *you* are," Terrence muttered before taking a drink.

Evan closed his eyes. "I hate seeing you this messed up. I hate seeing you this depressed. I know it's hard, but—"

"I'm not . . . fucking . . . *depressed!*" Terrence yelled, pulling back his arm and throwing his bottle at an adjacent wall. Glass exploded everywhere, making Evan jump from his seat, catching both men by surprise.

"Then what the hell would you call that?" Evan asked seconds later, pointing at the oozing stain that was now on the living room wall and pooling on the Brazilian hardwood floor.

"Frustration," Terrence said through clenched teeth. "I'm frustrated at being stuck in this fucked-up body! I'm angry that even if I wanted to leave the house, I don't want to deal with the looks of pity I see in people's eyes whenever I go into town. You think I don't know what they're thinking, Ev? *Oh, poor Terry Murdoch! He was such a big, handsome guy who had the world at his fingertips. Well, he doesn't have it anymore, does he? He's just a one-eyed cripple. That poor, poor boy! That* loser*!"* He furiously shook his head. "I don't need that shit. I don't want people feeling sorry for me! You included, Ev."

"So what? Are you just going to stay hiding in here forever? You're just going to wait until you gain two hundred pounds from all that shit you eat now and die of a heart attack? Or is your plan to drink enough beer and tequila that you die of cirrhosis of the liver first?"

"I haven't decided yet," Terrence said, as he reached for another half-empty bottle. "When I do, I'll let you know."

Terrence watched as his brother loudly swallowed, like he was fighting back a myriad of emotions. Instead of seeing pity in Evan's eyes, he saw a desolate sadness that almost made him regret what he had just said—almost.

"Fine," Evan murmured as he walked back across the living room toward the front door. "Whenever the time comes, I'll have someone come and pick up your body before it starts to stink and we get complaints from the neighbors." He reached for the doorknob, then paused. "But just remember this, Terry. Whenever I was at my lowest point, whenever I felt like I'd be better off dead, you were always the one to give me a pep talk and set me straight. You were the one who gave me perspective about being with Leila and told me that none of what other people thought about us mattered. You're the one who told me to pull it together and go after what I wanted or just stay fucking miserable. Now you're at your lowest point and you won't even listen to your own advice. You'd rather listen to the voices of people who feel sorry for you, but those people mean *nothing* to you! You're listening to them instead of the people who really care!" He shook his head again in bemusement. "That doesn't make you a loser, Terry. It makes you stupid and a fucking hypocrite!"

He then opened the door and slammed it closed behind him. The sound of the television filled the empty room.

Terrence lowered his head at his brother's words.

Yes, his body was broken. There was no getting around that truth. But did he finally have to admit that his spirit was broken too? Did he need help to heal it?

"You need something," a little voice in his head said. "Because what you're doing ain't working, bruh! What you're doing will have you dead in a year!"

After a few minutes, Terrence reached for his cane again and slowly hoisted himself to his feet. He limped toward the coffee table, where his mail sat along with the discarded referral that Dr. Sidda had written. He made his way to the granite kitchen island, where his cordless phone was perched. He settled himself onto one of the barstools and slowly dialed the number Dr. Sidda had written.

"Uh, h-hello," he said to the woman who answered. "I'd . . . I'd like to make an appointment with Dr. Meredith Sweeney." He listened to the voice on the other end of the line, then nodded. "Yeah, whatever slot you've got, I'll take it. The sooner the better."

Chapter 7

Evan

Evan closed his eyes as his head fell back against the leather headrest.

"Where to next, Mr. Murdoch?" his driver asked.

"Let's just head home, Bill. I'm exhausted," he muttered. And he was.

Evan had had plans to go to his office in Arlington even though it was the weekend. He had wanted to get some badly needed work done, but that no longer held any appeal for him. Besides, he wouldn't be able to concentrate. His thoughts would keep coming back to his brother, Terrence.

Evan felt like he was watching his brother drowning, but instead of Terrence reaching for the life preserver that was thrown to him or even fighting the current on his own, Terrence seemed to be waiting patiently for the raging river to drag him under. It was painful and heartbreaking to watch.

I wish I could reach him, Evan thought as the car

made a left turn onto the roadway that would take him back to Murdoch Mansion. *I wish he would listen.*

But Terrence had always been cocky and stubborn. Neither one of those traits did him any favors in his current predicament.

The sorrow Evan felt for Terrence was only equaled to the rage he now had for their half-brother, Dante. While talking to Terrence's lawyer about the lawsuit the other woman in the car crash had filed, the lawyer had mentioned in passing the name of her attorney.

"Dante Turner," the lawyer had said. "He's with Nutter, McElroy, and Ailey."

The instant Evan had heard his half-brother's name, his jaw tightened. "Yeah, I've heard of him."

"I asked around about him to see if he's a reasonable guy," the lawyer had continued, unaware of Evan's growing anger. "Maybe he'd be willing to lower the four million in punitive damages that she's asking for. I asked if he might force it to go to trial, which isn't ideal since the police still haven't been able to determine who was at fault in the accident." The lawyer had paused. "I want to warn you that none of what I've heard from my colleagues about Mr. Turner was good, Mr. Murdoch. They said he's one mean son of a bitch—*and* he's money-hungry."

Of course, Evan knew all of this already. Dante had gone out of his way to ruin the lives of his siblings—from having an affair with Evan's wife to trying to blackmail and bully Paulette into selling him all her shares in Murdoch Conglomerated. And he had done it out of sibling rivalry and to exact some revenge on their deceased father, which was so delusional it wasn't even funny. Now it looked like Dante had turned his laser sights on Terrence and of course, it had to be the moment when Terrence was most vulnerable and the least likely to defend himself.

Evan gritted his teeth again as he glared out the Town Car's tinted window at the passing cars and scenery. His fists tightened at his sides.

He wanted to wring Dante's neck. He wanted to punch his half-brother in the face over and over again. He had let Dante off the hook too easily in the past. It was time he dealt with him once and for all.

"So, what are you going to do?" the voice in his head mocked. "Put a hit out on him? What are you? Michael Corleone?"

No, Evan wasn't going to order a Mafia hit, though frankly, with the right amount of money, anything was possible. He would find a way to take care of Dante. He just needed time.

Evan's cell phone began to ring. He opened his eyes and sighed before glancing down at the phone screen. When he saw the name on his caller ID, he frowned. He slowly raised the phone to his ear.

"Charisse?" he said, not succeeding in keeping the shock out of his voice.

"Hi, Ev, how . . . how have you been?" she answered timidly.

Evan hadn't heard from his wife, Charisse, in months—not since she had entered rehab to avoid jail time for a drunk-driving incident. From what he had heard, she had already fallen off the wagon.

She had just finished another thirty-day program and was living with her mother again in her childhood home.

"Why did you call me, Charisse?"

There was no need to be civil. They hadn't been civil for most of the years that they were married; he didn't see any reason to start now.

Evan heard her anxiously clear her throat on the other end. "I just . . . I just wanted to talk to you. I *need* to talk to you, Ev."

"About what?"

"About us. About our marriage. I need to—"

"We don't have a marriage. Let's be honest. We haven't had a real marriage in years. And if you'd finally sign and send back the documents my lawyer sent to you, we would be well on our way to being legally separated, divorced, and out of each other's lives permanently."

"I'll . . . I'll send you the papers if you agree to talk to me."

"We *are* talking," he said tightly.

"I mean really talk. We can't do this over the phone. I need to see you in person . . . please," she whispered, sounding desperate.

Evan's frown deepened. What was this about? Why was she reaching out to him now? He wondered if she was stalling. Maybe she wanted to negotiate more alimony or more of their marital assets.

Fat chance of that, he thought. She had forfeited all her rights to negotiation when he caught her having sex with Dante, and he had the cell phone pictures to prove it.

"Ev, are . . . are you still there?"

"Yes, I'm here," he muttered, though he didn't know why. He should have hung up on her already.

"So, will you meet me? Will you do it?"

He sat quietly for several seconds and then finally exhaled and nodded. "Fine, Charisse, if you'll sign the goddamn papers, I'll agree to meet you. We can do it next week."

"Okay, that works," she mumbled, not sounding the least bit victorious even though he had given in to her. "I'll see you next week, then."

Evan hung up without saying good-bye. The instant he did, he felt his fatigue grow. He glanced out the window and saw his mansion coming into view—its soaring portico and neat green hedges. He breathed a sigh of relief. He was finally home.

"Is Ms. Hawkins around?" he asked his housekeeper as soon as he stepped through the doorway.

The petite woman nodded. "I believe she's upstairs in your room, Mr. Murdoch. Do you want me to tell her you're looking for her?"

"No, I'll find her myself. Thanks." He headed toward the staircase leading to the west wing. The housekeeper nodded again before shutting the front door behind him.

A faint smile came to Evan's lips. Leila was in their bedroom.

Good, he thought.

With the day he was having, Evan was badly in need of some sexual healing. He could envision Leila in her walk-in closet, peeling off the jeans and blouse she had worn that day to her doctor's appointment. He could take her right there on one of the cedar shelves where she organized her sweaters and pashmina shawls. Or maybe she had decided to take a quick shower. He could step in naked with her, lather her from top to bottom with soapy water, and have her in the shower stall, right against the glass tile.

As he climbed the stairs, taking them two at a time, he fantasized about the numerous ways he could make love to his fiancée: missionary, up against the bedroom wall, or doggie style on their Egyptian cotton sheets. Just thinking about Leila moaning beneath him made his pulse race. It made him hard as granite.

He rushed down the corridor to their bedroom. When he threw open the door, he started to tug the hem of his shirt out of his pants. "All right," he called out, "I hope you're ready for what I'm about to—"

Evan's words faded when he saw his fiancée smiling and lying on her stomach across their California king– sized bed. She wasn't alone.

"Ready for what?" Leila asked, pushing herself up to her elbows. She raised her brows expectantly.

Izzy, who was sitting on the bed facing her mother, turned to stare at Evan as she bit into an Oreo cookie.

A board game sat between Izzy and Leila. It looked like a Monopoly set, though the pieces and board itself were covered with some girlie iconography Evan vaguely recognized. Disney princesses, it looked like. Two opened Coke cans sat on Leila's end table. The flat-screen television seemed to be blaring the lyrics from the Disney movie *Frozen*.

Evan had rushed upstairs to make love to his fiancée, but that obviously was out of the question right now. He felt his hard-on deflate like a balloon.

He nervously cleared his throat. "Nothing! Ready for nothing," he lied before forcing a smile and stepping farther into the room. "How are you, Isabel? What are you and your mom up to?"

She wrinkled her nose at him. "We're playing a game," she said between cookie munches, sounding mildly annoyed that he would ask such a stupid question. She then turned back around to face the board.

"I promised Izzy that I would play Monopoly with her," Leila explained.

"And I'm winning!" Isabel said proudly, brandishing a multicolored stack of fake bills.

Leila chuckled, leaned forward, and kissed Izzy's forehead. "Yes, you are definitely winning. You are kicking Mommy's butt up and down this board!" Leila's smile faded and she became somber as she gazed over Isabel's head at Evan. "So, how'd the talk with Terry go? Did he hear you out?"

Evan had told Leila that he was on a mission today to get his brother out of the funk he had been wallowing in for months. Now he had to tell her that he hadn't succeeded in his mission. He walked toward the bed and shook his head. "Terry's too stuck in his self-pity to listen to me."

"Your turn, Mommy," Isabel said, breaking into their conversation.

"But you have to keep trying, Ev," Leila insisted. "We both know the only person who could ever reach Terry would be you."

Evan tiredly closed his eyes. "But he has to want to get better, Lee. I can't force him to do it."

"Mommy, your turn," Isabel repeated before pointing down at the Monopoly board.

"I *heard* you, Izzy," Leila said tightly before bestowing a stern gaze on her daughter. "Evan and I are talking right now. All right? We're going to play again in a sec." She then returned her attention to Evan. "So, is he going back to physical therapy? I know it was painful for him, but it got him walking. Is he—"

"He won't even leave the house." Evan opened his eyes and slumped back against one of his dressers. "He didn't look or smell like he had washed in days. But he's not on painkillers anymore. At least, there's that. We don't have to worry about him swallowing a handful of those."

"Jesus," Leila whispered breathlessly, pushing herself upright. She looked horrified. "Do you really think he's that bad off?"

Evan shrugged. "I don't know, Lee. I just . . . I just don't know."

Her shoulders slumped. "Why is this happening? Just when things start to settle down, something pops up to send the whole family into—"

"Your turn! Your turn! *Your turn!*" Isabel started to shout, slamming her fists on her thighs.

"Izzy, stop it!" Leila ordered. "Stop yelling like that. You're acting like a baby and you're being rude. Stop it now!"

"No, *he's* being rude!" Isabel shouted, jumping

to her feet and glaring at Evan. "We were playing a game and he stopped us!"

"Izzy," Leila began with tightened lips, "you had better apologize right now to Evan, or I will cancel your party in a few months, because birthday parties are for good girls. I will—"

"No!" Isabel screeched. She then flipped over the board game with a swipe of her hand, sending little princess figurines and cards flying across the plush carpet and the silk duvet. Leila jumped back in surprise. Evan went rigid. "No! I won't apologize!" Isabel screamed. "And you can't make me!"

Evan couldn't take it anymore. He had walked around on eggshells with this kid for months, trying his best to be patient and supportive of her, but he had officially hit his limit. She wasn't a sad little girl who was trying her best to adjust; she was a manipulative little tyrant, and he was tired of her bullshit.

"Izzy, don't you ever, *ever* talk to your mother that way again. Do you understand me?" he said in a booming voice and with an icy coldness that he had learned well from his father.

It was the same voice that had made Evan tremble in his sneakers when George Murdoch had used it with him when he was a little boy. Evan watched now as Isabel started to shake in front of him on her skinny legs, as she gnawed her chapped bottom lip.

"Now you go over there and pick up every single piece you knocked off that board," he ordered. "Do you hear me? Do it now."

Leila rose from the bed. "Ev, she doesn't—"

He held up his hand to silence Leila. "Every . . .

single . . . piece," he repeated, enunciating each word with a deliberateness that let Leila and Isabel know he meant what he said.

The room fell silent. Isabel's shaking only increased, but she took a hesitant step toward him then slowly bent down to the carpet. She grabbed one of the plastic pieces and set it on the bed. For the next five minutes, she gathered the missing pieces and cards, crying softly as she did so. When she was done, she kept her head bowed and wiped her nose with the back of her hand.

"Now, the next time you decide to talk to your mother like that, I want you to think very carefully before you do it," he continued, ignoring the beseeching look Leila was giving him. "Because you got off easy this time, but it won't happen again. I won't allow that kind of behavior in my home, Isabel. Not under my roof."

She mumbled a reply that he couldn't hear.

"What did you say?" he asked, taking a step toward her.

Isabel stopped trembling. She raised her head and met him with a defiant gaze. "I said, 'Then I don't wanna live here!' " she shouted between sniffs as tears spilled onto her cheeks. Isabel then turned and ran toward the bedroom doorway, stumbling slightly near the entrance before fleeing into the hall.

Leila glared up at him. "You didn't have to talk to her like that."

He stared at Leila in amazement. "Talk to her like what?"

"Like she was some underling at your fucking company! You can use that tone in the boardroom, but you can't talk like that to a seven-year-old."

"Oh, come on, Lee! I wasn't talking to her like she was an underling. I was talking to her like she was a disobedient kid, which she was! And, I might add, I was also defending you!"

"Defending me to my own daughter? You shouldn't have said anything, let alone punish her! She's *my* child, Evan." She pointed at her chest. "*I'll* handle her. Not you! Besides, I had it covered!"

"Oh, you did?" He barked out a laugh. "Is that what you would call it? Her screaming and throwing shit around the room . . . is that what you call having it 'covered'?"

Leila didn't answer him. Instead she marched to the bedroom door. "I'm going to find Izzy," she mumbled, not looking back at him as she said it.

Evan watched Leila disappear into the hall. He tiredly fell back onto the bed, bouncing slightly on the bedsprings.

"To hell with it," he muttered minutes later after furiously rising to his feet.

Terrence wants to slowly kill himself, so be it, Evan thought as he stripped off his clothes, tossing them carelessly to the bedroom floor.

Charisse wants to drag her feet on the divorce, I couldn't care less, he thought as he walked into his expansive closet and grabbed a pair of swim trunks.

Leila wants to let her daughter rule her life and decide the fate of our relationship, then there is absolutely nothing I can do about that, he thought as he headed to the east wing to take out his frustrations in the indoor pool.

He'd had it with the people around him. As far

as he was concerned, everyone—from Terrence to Charisse to Leila—could do whatever the hell they wanted with their lives and their life dramas. He was staying out of it.

An hour and a half later, Evan was finishing yet another lap in the pool when he saw Leila's distorted image above the water's surface. She was gazing down at him with her hands on her hips. She was still gazing at him when he climbed out of the pool a minute later and sat on the tiled edge, his body sapped of all energy.

"I thought I'd find you in here," she said, handing him the towel he'd left sitting on one of the stone benches lining the pool.

"I needed to clear my head," Evan mumbled, taking the towel and wiping the droplets of water from his face and body. He didn't meet her eyes.

She sat on the stone bench as he toweled off. "Look, Ev, I'm . . . I'm sorry."

He paused and lowered his towel.

"I know you were only trying to help. I shouldn't have told you to butt out. You're going to be Izzy's stepfather and I can't keep treating you like some interloper. I . . . I apologize for doing that."

Evan rose from the pool's edge and sat on the bench beside her, feeling the cold air on his bare back and shoulders and the cold bench on his bottom. He sighed and rested his elbows on his knees as he peered at the water in the pool, watching how the overhead lights gleamed off of its blue surface.

"Look, Lee, maybe you were right. Maybe I'm just trying too hard. I'm a square peg trying to bang myself into a round hole. Maybe I'm just not one of those guys meant to be a dad."

She suddenly sat upright and stared at him. She shook her head. "That's not true, Ev. Don't say that! Of course you'd make a good dad!"

"But we have to consider the possibility that I won't. It's not like I have a good example to follow. You know how my dad was—withdrawn, demanding, and manipulative. Maybe I would better serve Izzy and you if I don't try to take on a fatherly role with her. She says that she has only one dad, so let her have just one. I'll just be her mom's husband. The guy she goes to when she needs money or a letter of recommendation."

Leila winced and squirmed uncomfortably beside him. "That's not funny."

"I'm not trying to be funny! I'm being honest. Maybe, with time, my relationship with Isabel will change, but for now, I'll back off. I'll stay in my lane, so to speak. Besides, parenting isn't my strong point."

"It *has* to be your strong point, Ev."

"No, it doesn't." He reached out, held her hand, and squeezed it reassuringly. "Look, I'm not throwing in the towel completely. I'll still keep trying with Isabel. I'm just saying that being a father isn't something I had planned to—"

"I'm pregnant," Leila blurted out, making him pause again.

"What?"

She pulled her hand out of his grasp, closed her eyes, and gradually exhaled. "I said, I'm pregnant. We're going to have a baby." She opened her eyes again and gave him a timid smile. "That's why I went to the doctor today. I wanted to make sure the at-home pregnancy tests I took were right before I told you for sure."

He stared at her, now struck speechless.

"I know it isn't what we planned. I was on the pill, though frankly, I've never been very good at taking it. That's how I ended up with Izzy. And you're still married to someone else. This probably isn't the ideal time to have a baby, but"—she lowered her hand to her stomach and rubbed it gently—"life happens, right?"

Life happens. That was the understatement of the year! Had all the air left the room? Evan suddenly felt light-headed.

"So, I hope parenting can become 'your thing.' I hope you can envision yourself as a real father because you're . . . you're going to be one whether you're ready or not."

"I'm going to be a father," he repeated dazedly.

"Yes, you are going to be a father, Evan Murdoch." Her smile faded. She tilted her head and eyed him apprehensively. "Please tell me you're okay with all of this. You're not going to faint on me, are you? Or run out of here screaming?"

He slowly shook his head, still too stunned to speak. He was going to be a father!

Evan had given up on the idea years ago, after Charisse had had miscarriage after miscarriage and their marriage took a tumble off a steep cliff. He had told himself that he wasn't the type of guy who would make a great father anyway, with his screwed-up childhood and the lifestyle he had. He worked long hours and sometimes traveled at a moment's notice. Not having a child was for the best.

The lies we tell ourselves, he now thought, beyond amazed.

But life happens when you least expect it and now the chance to be a father had come again. Evan didn't know whether he was ready, but he didn't care. Short of Leila, he hadn't wanted anything so badly in his life than to be this baby's father.

"Evan," Leila whispered, "please say something. You're starting to scare me."

"I'm going to be a father!" he yelled, making her jump in surprise. His voice echoed off the tiled walls and high ceilings. He was pretty sure the entire mansion had heard him yelling. He then wrapped his arms around Leila, making her laugh. He drew her close and kissed her senseless.

Chapter 8

Paulette

"All right, you can sit up now," the doctor said. "Do you need some help?"

Paulette nodded and held out her hand. "I'd appreciate it, Dr. Rodriguez. Thanks."

Whenever Paulette got on her back nowadays, it took a lot of shimmying and rocking back and forth to get upright on her own. If she stayed down for too long, she started to feel faint, thanks to the baby resting on a major artery.

The joys of pregnancy, Paulette thought with exasperation.

"One, two, three," Dr. Rodriguez said after taking her hand in a firm grasp. She hoisted Paulette from the examination table with a soft grunt. Paulette sighed with relief as she sat upright and gazed around the examination room. Several magazines on parenting and newborns sat on the ledge near the window facing the hospital parking lot. A chart on the wall showed a dilated vagina during the stages of labor. Several plastic fetuses sat on a shelf near the door.

"Well, Mrs. Williams," the doctor said before glancing at her chart, where she scribbled a few numbers. "Your labs look pretty good. You're starting to experience some swelling in the legs and ankles, which is normal at this stage in the pregnancy. Just keep an eye on it." She glanced at the chart again. "Yep, everything looks fine, but . . ."

Paulette frowned when she heard the "but."

"The baby is measuring small for twenty-two weeks," Dr. Rodriguez said, pursing her full lips and narrowing her brown eyes at something on her chart. "Smaller than I would like."

Paulette's hands instinctively flew to her stomach, where her son now squirmed, perhaps sensing his mother's anxiety. Paulette had considered herself lucky that she was still so small. It made covering up the pregnancy a little easier than she had hoped, being this far along. To cloak her changing body, she had switched from billowing wool winter sweaters to loose-fitting halter dresses and sheaths accompanied by shawls now that the weather was warmer. Besides Dr. Rodriguez and herself, no one else seemed to know she was pregnant. But now it turned out Paulette's small size meant she wasn't quite as lucky as she'd thought.

The doctor sat down in her rollaway chair. "You're not gaining much weight, either. Are you eating well, Mrs. Williams? You aren't skipping meals, are you? Some women get so concerned about pregnancy weight gain that they can be a bit too restrictive with their diets."

"I've been trying to eat, but I haven't . . . well, I haven't had much of an appetite."

Dr. Rodriguez inclined her head. "Why's that?"

"I've been a little stressed out, I guess," Paulette said softly, releasing a nervous laugh as she rubbed her stomach again.

"Stressed out about what?"

Keeping my pregnancy a secret, my marriage falling apart, and my husband possibly killing my lover, Paulette thought. *You know . . . the usual.*

"Just . . . stuff," she said, in no mood to unburden herself to her OB/GYN. "Lots and lots of stuff."

Dr. Rodriguez nodded, making her springy curls bob.

"Well, whatever that stuff is, please learn to let it go or take care of it. We don't want it to affect your health or the health of your baby." She placed her chart on the desk next to her and gazed at Paulette. "For now, I'm going to order an ultrasound with a specialist to confirm that everything is okay with the little one. After that, we can decide what steps to take."

"What do you mean, 'steps to take'? What . . . what steps, Dr. Rodriguez?"

"Well, if the specialist thinks you're experiencing intrauterine growth restriction and that's the reason the baby is measuring so small, we might consider bed rest or a stay at the hospital, where we can do intravenous feeding. We'll just have to see."

Paulette blinked. "W-what?"

She didn't know how she could possibly explain

a stay at the hospital or bed rest to Antonio or any-one else without revealing her pregnancy. She rubbed her stomach more furiously now and the baby squirmed even more. Her lies and secrets were getting more and more complicated and now she ran the risk of losing not only her marriage, but also her infant son.

The doctor rose to her feet and smiled. She reached out and grabbed Paulette's hand. "Hey, I didn't tell you this to make you stress out all over again. The bed rest and intravenous feeding are just possibilities at this point. Let's see what the specialist says and then make a decision. All right?"

Paulette gradually nodded.

"I'll see you at your next appointment and keep your chin up. If anything comes up, we'll take care of it."

"Thank you, Dr. Rodriguez," Paulette whispered as the doctor stepped out of the exam room, closing the door behind her.

Paulette pulled into her driveway a half hour later, just as her mother-in-law opened the front door and shut it closed behind her. At the sight of her, Paulette rolled her eyes. The older woman had had a key to Paulette and Antonio's home since they had moved into the four-bedroom colonial. Paulette had asked Antonio to take back the key to give them more privacy, and he did for a while. But since the affair, Antonio seemed to disregard all of Paulette's wishes and requests. It looked like Reina Washington had full access to their home again and she was taking full advantage of it.

"Well, well! Look who's here," the large woman exclaimed sarcastically before throwing her rattan tote bag over her shoulder. Reina was decked out from head to toe in a plum-colored top, capri pants, a wide-brimmed hat, and ill-fitting ballet flats that squeezed her fat feet so tightly that they looked like two brown, plump sausages on an open spit. In her current getup, Reina vaguely resembled Barney the Dinosaur.

"I left some brisket and biscuits in the fridge. Tell Tony he can heat it up for dinner."

Paulette opened her Mercedes car door and stepped onto the asphalt. *"Why don't you tell him yourself?"* Paulette wanted to say, since Reina spoke to her son daily, but Paulette prudently kept silent. She didn't want to argue with Reina. She just wanted her to leave.

"I wondered if you were out grocery shopping since there doesn't seem to be any food in that house but"—Reina glanced at Paulette's empty hands—"that don't seem to be the case."

"Hello, Reina, it's always a pleasure to see you," Paulette said flatly, slowly climbing to her feet and shutting the car door behind her.

"Uh-hunh," Reina grunted before looking her up and down. "So, do you plan to buy groceries someday, or is the only home-cooked meals my Tony gets gonna be the ones that I bring to him?"

"When I have the time, I'll go shopping. I've been a little bit busy lately," she said as she stepped around the older woman and headed to her front door. "Trust me. He isn't starving."

"I guess young women these days don't consider it their responsibility to take care of their husbands and their homes," Reina said loudly over her shoulder, "but in *my* day, you weren't much of a woman if you couldn't do that."

Paulette stopped midway of inserting her key into the front door. Her jaw tightened.

"I told Tony you weren't gonna be much of a wife. 'Sure, she can sit around and look pretty, but that's just about all she'll do.' Yep, that's *exactly* what I told him." Reina dropped a hand to her ample hip and narrowed her eyes at her daughter-in-law. "And I was right. You don't take care of my boy. He seems less happy now than he was before he married you. If you ask me, he'd be better off cutting you loose."

Paulette clenched her keys in her hand. It took all her breeding, all the years of her mother, Angela, encouraging her to "behave like a lady at all times," to resist the urge to hurl her keys at Reina's big, fat head. Instead she turned and painted on a syrupy smile. "It was nice having you over, Reina. I guess you'll be leaving now. Drive safely, okay?" she said in a false, chirpy voice.

She then opened the front door and slammed it shut behind her, not giving Reina a chance to say anything else—insulting or otherwise.

Paulette locked the door, tiredly set her purse on the polished foyer table, and walked into the spacious kitchen, unwinding her shawl from around her shoulders. She exhaled and opened the stainless-steel fridge in search of lunch, following her doctor's orders to finally eat something.

"What does Mommy want to eat, bean?" she asked her son as she rubbed her belly and scanned the metal shelves. "There has to be something in here!"

It turned out that Reina had greatly exaggerated. Though the fridge wasn't stocked with lots of food, it wasn't exactly empty, either. Paulette managed to find a loaf of multigrain bread, lettuce, several slices of deli ham, slightly hardened Swiss cheese, and a jar of mayo that had just enough left for her to make a decent sandwich. Five minutes later, she walked into her living room and fell back onto the couch with a sandwich in one hand and a glass of apple juice in the other. Just as she set both on the coffee table and raised the remote to turn on the flat-screen television over her fireplace, the doorbell rang. She sighed heavily and slowly hoisted herself to her feet. It rang again.

"I'm coming!" she shouted.

She glanced longingly at her sandwich before grabbing her shawl, draping it around her shoulders, and making her way to the front door. She drew back the curtain near the door and gazed at the front steps, surprised to find a man in a drab, navy blue suit standing there. She unlocked the door and stared at him uneasily.

"Yes?"

He was short with a sweaty bald head and ruddy cheeks that made it look like he had just finished running a mile, but he really had only been standing still for the past two minutes. His suit looked even worse up close. It was wrinkled and made of a cheap polyester blend that Paulette would never wear. His laced-up black shoes also looked cheap, though they were at least polished.

"Mrs. Paulette Williams?" the man asked gruffly. His blue eyes scrutinized her with laser-like intensity, making her unease multiply tenfold.

"Y-yes. May I help you?"

He reached into his suit jacket pocket and pulled out a wallet. He flipped it open and showed his ID. "Ma'am, I'm Detective Joe Nola with the Mannock County Sheriff's Office. I've tried to reach you by phone, but had no luck. Have you not received my messages?"

Paulette swallowed audibly. Yes, she had gotten Detective Nola's voicemail messages. He had called three times in the past two weeks. Every time she heard them on her cell phone, she promptly deleted them. She knew why the detective was calling her and she had no interest in talking to him.

"Well, regardless," he said, closing his wallet and tucking it back into one of his suit jacket's inner pockets, "we're still investigating the death of Mr. Marques Whitney. We're following up on all leads. Do you mind if I come inside and ask you a few questions, ma'am?"

No! Go away, her mind silently screamed.

"Uh, Marques Whitney? Umm, I I don't know how I could help you, Detective. I just . . . I just knew him from the gym," she lied.

The detective squinted at her and she immediately looked away.

"Well, we have information to the contrary, Mrs. Williams."

Her eyes snapped back to his face, zeroing in on those cold blue eyes. She frowned. "Ex-excuse me?"

"I'd really like to speak with you and ask you a few questions, if that's all right."

"Tell him that you want to talk to a lawyer first!" a voice yelled frantically in her head. "Tell him that unless you're being charged with something, you don't want to be part of his stupid investigation. Hell, just tell him that you're busy!"

But she didn't make up an excuse or tell him to go away. Instead, she slowly nodded and opened the front door even farther before motioning him to come inside.

"All right, but please . . . can we make it quick? I was just about to eat lunch."

"This won't take much of your time, Mrs. Williams," he said, before stepping inside her home. "I can assure you of that."

Maybe the detective knows something I don't, she thought as she watched him shrewdly scan the room around him, like signs of some crime were painted on the walls or hanging from the windows like silk drapery. She had been wondering for months whether Antonio had murdered Marques. It had eaten her up inside and made her doubt the man she loved the most. Maybe the detective could shed some light on the mystery that had been plaguing her. Maybe he could finally calm her fears.

"Would you like some water or tea?" she asked, shutting the door behind him. "I could—"

"No, that won't be necessary." He stalked toward her suede sofa and plopped down. He pulled out a notepad and began to flip the pages.

"Please, have a seat," she murmured sarcastically before walking into her living room and sitting in one of the armchairs facing the sofa.

"So you say you knew Mr. Whitney from your gym?" he asked, taking out a pen and scribbling on his notepad.

"Yes, he was . . . he was one of the trainers there."

"Was he your trainer?"

"Uh, no." She reached for the glass of juice that sat on the coffee table. "Just a trainer at the gym. I ran into him a few times, I guess."

"Uh-huh." He flipped a page in his notepad as she sipped her drink. "Is there any reason he would be calling you then? We saw your cell phone number appear several times in his phone records, especially on the night of the murder."

Paulette almost choked on her apple juice. She painfully swallowed the bit that clogged her throat. "Uh . . . he called me?"

"Yes, he called you *several* times. Three times that day, to be exact." The detective dropped his notepad and stared at her. His wrinkled face drew tight. "Do you want to revise what you told me earlier? Is there anything else to your relationship with Mr. Whitney besides him being a trainer at your gym?"

"Stop the conversation now," the voice in her head cautioned again. "Tell him to leave. Pick up the phone and call your brother Evan. Tell him everything and ask him to recommend a lawyer for you."

But she couldn't do that. Evan knew about Marques, but he didn't know about Marques's murder or that she suspected Antonio might be involved. She didn't want to drag her brother into this mess.

I'll be honest with the detective, she thought, tired of lying, tired of the mountain of secrets. *I've got nothing to hide from him! I didn't do anything wrong! I'll just tell him the truth.*

She lowered her glass back to the table and loudly cleared her throat. "Okay . . . he . . . he was more than a trainer. Marques was an . . . an ex-boyfriend of mine. We knew each other when we were teenagers. We met up again at the gym and got . . . reacquainted."

"Reacquainted?"

She nodded.

"So you rekindled the friendship, then?"

Paulette forced a smile. "I guess you could say that. Yes."

"Had you been to his apartment?"

"His apartment? Umm, let me think." She pretended to look up at the ceiling and contemplate that one.

Paulette had been at Marques's dingy apartment more times than she cared to remember and each time she left in tears, tormented by what she and Marques had done in his bedroom. But the detective didn't need to know that little detail.

"Uh, yeah," she said. "I had been there a few times."

"Were you there on November twenty-fourth? The night of the murder?"

"No!" She emphatically shook her head. "No, he called me and we talked briefly, but that's about it. I was home the entire night."

The detective nodded, scribbling in his notepad

again. "Well, that answers all my questions. I've taken up enough of your time, Mrs. Williams. I should be on my way."

She inwardly breathed a sigh of relief as she watched him rise from the sofa. She immediately followed suit. "Let me walk you to the door, Detective."

See, that wasn't so bad, she told herself as she watched him stride across the living room's hardwood floor and back into the tiled foyer. *I was worried for no reason!*

The detective reached for the brass door handle, then paused. He suddenly turned to gaze at her again, tilting his bald head. "Mrs. Williams, why didn't you tell me the truth when I first asked you about your relationship with Mr. Whitney?"

"Well"—she gazed down at her hands and began to twist her wedding ring around and around on her finger—"I'm a married woman, Detective Nola. I didn't tell my husband that I'd become friends with Marques again. It would have been too . . . awkward. He's my ex. Remember?" She looked up at the detective. "I'm sorry I wasn't more upfront about it, but you . . . you understand, right?"

He squinted again, not looking the least bit understanding. "Do you know when your husband will arrive home today, Mrs. Williams?"

She blinked. "M-my h-husband?" A wave of heat shot over her body. She started to shake a little. "Why do you want to know that?"

"I'd like to talk to him. You said you were home the night of November twenty-fourth, but I need someone to verify your whereabouts. He would be the best man to do that, am I right?"

Her pulse started to race. Someone to verify her

whereabouts? *Oh God*, she thought, now panicked. She had been home the entire night—but Antonio hadn't. He had been gone for hours, including during the time frame when Marques had been murdered.

"I don't know when he'll be home, to be honest. He works long hours lately. He's . . . he's trying to get promoted at his engineering firm," she said weakly.

"If that's the case, I'll leave this with you," the detective said, handing her a business card. "Tell him to give me a call ASAP."

"Yes. Of course!" she cried with a grin. She took the card from him. "I'll let Tony know as soon as he gets home."

Though the truth was, she'd rip the card into a million little pieces, dump them in the trash can, and hoped never to see the detective again.

Paulette watched as the detective opened her front door. "You enjoy the rest of your day, Mrs. Williams."

"You, too," she piped before shutting the door behind him. Paulette drew back the curtain and watched the detective as he walked back to an unmarked Ford Taurus. She watched him until he climbed inside his car and pulled out of her driveway.

When the Taurus disappeared, she lowered her hand to her stomach and walked across the living room. She gazed at her sandwich, then turned away, no longer hungry.

Chapter 9

Dante

"Oh God! Oh God! Oh *Goooood!*" she said in a guttural growl.

Dante smirked. *God has nothing to do with this, honey,* he thought as he gazed down at the woman in front of him who was naked, sweaty, and on all fours. Her back muscles trembled, making the tramp stamp of butterfly wings at the base of her back look as if it was about to take off in flight. Her long black locks (it was a weave—he had seen the tracks) whipped from side to side as she thrashed like she was reenacting a scene from *The Exorcist.* But if this chick was quivering and speaking in tongues, it was all Dante's doing; it had jack shit to do with any celestial or demonic being.

He pounded into her again and again, ordering her to scream his name, feeling himself draw closer to climax. The headboard thumped against the wall at a rhythmic pace. The framed photos of her mother and daughter clacked against the plaster like a chorus of clapping hands.

"Yes! Yes! Yes!" she shouted, balling the bed sheets into her fists. She then bit down hard on the cotton pillow beside her head, gnawing it like some rabid dog.

After a few more pumps, Dante came with a euphoric rush. He pulled out of her, then fell back against the bed, releasing a contented sigh.

She slowly pushed herself upward. "Why'd you stop?" she shouted, shoving her weave out of her face. "I was almost there, dammit!"

"Yeah, well, I'm done and I'm tired," he said between huffs of breaths.

She grabbed the pillow she had been biting and thumped him over the head with it. "You selfish son of a bitch," she spat, making him chuckle.

"Don't worry. I'll break you off later."

She crawled across the bed and landed on his chest, knocking the air out of him. She sucked her teeth. "Yeah, right."

He chuckled again before slapping her ass and closing his eyes.

Dante's relationship with the Uptons was working out splendidly. Not only did he stand to make a couple mil from his cut of the lawsuit Mavis Upton was filing against his brother Terrence, he also was having a wild, freaky time with Mavis's daughter, Renee. He and Renee now met up at least twice a week to have sex—some of the best sex that he had had in quite a while, he had to admit. Renee definitely was no shrinking violet in the bedroom. That woman could get downright kinky when she wanted to.

"So, did you think about that thing I told you about last week?" Renee asked while trailing her long nails over his muscled torso. She then gave a saucy lick to the corner of his mouth.

Dante cracked open one eye to stare up at her. "What thing?"

She slapped his chest playfully and smiled. "You know . . . that Groupon deal to Barbados!"

Dante closed his eye again, pretending like he hadn't heard her.

"Well?" she persisted a few seconds later, shoving his chest harder this time. "Wouldn't it be a bomb-ass trip for us to go on? I've never been there before, and my girl Kemayaunda said it's hella nice! We should go, baby!"

Dante wasn't sure whether he wanted to take travel advice from a woman named Kemayaunda, but he kept that thought to himself. He turned on his side, opened his eyes, and bestowed Renee with an indulgent smile.

"Look, why don't we talk about it after your mom's lawsuit is done?" he answered diplomatically.

"But that could take forever, *babeeee!* The Groupon deal is only good until the end of May!"

She was whining. Dante hated it when women whined. Those manipulative bitches really knew how to play on a man's sympathies. Luckily, he wasn't very sympathetic.

"I get that, honey." He rubbed her shoulder soothingly. "But your mom doesn't know what's going between us. I don't think it's a good idea that she does until the case is over."

"But why we keeping it a secret, anyway?" She

narrowed her eyes and eased away from him. "You ashamed or something?"

Dante was momentarily tempted to give her an honest answer: The reason he wanted to wait until after the case was done was because he planned to dump her as soon as the judge ruled in their favor, or, if he was lucky, as soon as Terrence made an offer to settle out of court. Yes, the sex with Renee was good, but there was no way in hell he would pursue something permanent with this chick. She was so low-class it was almost pathetic. She talked about dinner at the Olive Garden like it was fine dining. He had to constantly fight the urge to correct her grammar. And she dressed like a Las Vegas hooker. He could only imagine taking her out to one of the cocktail parties his law firm regularly held. They would laugh him out of the room!

Besides, he had turned down women who were a lot more deserving of his time and attention than Renee. Hell, he had broken off things with Evan's wife, Charisse! She was the personification of class, old money, and power with the pedigree she had, even if she was also a sloppy drunk. Unfortunately, Charisse, like Renee, had tried to make their "relationship" into a lot more than what it was. Eventually, he had to let Charisse know she was sadly mistaken. Eventually, he would do the same with Renee—but not tonight.

"Of course, I'm not ashamed of you, honey." He raised his head and kissed her. "It just would make things too complicated if your mother knew we were together. We don't want her to get cold feet, now, do we? There's millions of dollars at stake here."

Renee rolled her eyes. "She's already getting cold feet! She asks me all the time when you plan to tell that boy she ain't really suing him. I told her I don't know. I think she's starting to think about tellin' him herself."

Dante perked up at that news. He raised himself to his elbows to gaze at her. "Your mother wouldn't really do that, would she?"

"I don't know." Renee shrugged. "Maybe."

Dante's brows lowered. He frowned. That old bitch wouldn't ruin his plans, would she?

"Look, the next time your mother talks to you about this, tell her—"

Their conversation was cut off by the sound of a door opening, then slamming shut.

"Mommy!" a little voice called out.

"Renee, you home?" Dante heard Mavis say. "We're back from the store. I got Tasha most of those school supplies she needed. I couldn't get all of it. That stuff is awfully expensive."

"Shit," Dante said before shoving Renee off of him and leaping to his feet.

Renee scrambled off the bed, too. She dropped to the floor in search of the shirt and jeans she had discarded earlier.

"I thought you said they wouldn't be back for hours," he snarled in an angry whisper as he pulled on his boxer-briefs then reached for his shirt, which was crumpled near her nightstand.

"That's what she told me!" Renee whispered back with widened eyes.

"*Renee?* Renee, you in here?" Mavis called again.

All the while, the duo frantically dressed, tossing

each other their clothes wherever they found them.

"Renee," Mavis asked as she pushed open the bedroom door, "are you asleep? You feeling o—" She paused when she realized Dante was in the bedroom with her daughter. She raised her brows in surprise. "Mr. Turner, what . . . what are you doing here?"

Dante pasted on a smile and buttoned the last jacket button on his single-breasted suit, covering his pants zipper, which he hadn't had the chance to close before Mavis had stepped into the bedroom.

"I was just stopping by to pay my favorite client a visit," he said, stepping forward and giving her a hug. "So, how are you doing, Mavis?"

"F-f-fine," she said uneasily as she shifted her gaze between him and Renee. "I just . . . I just wasn't expecting to see you here today. You came to Renee's place to see me?"

"I thought I might find you here. Renee was nice enough to give me a tour of her apartment while I waited. Weren't you, Renee? And what a *lovely* place it is," he lied, gazing at the bedroom's popcorn-covered, water-stained ceiling, the dirty shag carpet, and the particleboard furniture. "So minimalist." He turned and ran his hand appreciatively over Renee's dresser. "Where did you say you got this beautiful piece of furniture, Renee?"

Renee's mouth twisted and she scratched her head. "Uh . . . Rent-A-Center, I think."

"Interesting." Dante wrapped an arm around Mavis's shoulders and eased her out of the bedroom into the living room. "Look, Mavis, I came here to talk to you today because I wanted to update you on your lawsuit."

Mavis's granddaughter, Tasha, looked up when they entered the room. She sat in the adjacent kitchenette at a small table with a coloring book open in front of her and half of a peanut butter and jelly sandwich poised near her mouth. She glanced at Dante with mild interest, then returned her attention to her coloring book. She bit into her sandwich.

Dante surmised that she was probably used to finding random men coming out of her mother's bedroom.

"Well, I'm . . . I'm glad to hear you wanna talk about that, Mr. Turner," Mavis said, gazing up at him and shifting her purse on her arm. "I was just meaning to ask you about that. See, I thought you told me that we were just going to file a case but not really do anything with it. We just wanted to scare him off. Shouldn't we tell—"

"Yes, that is exactly what I wanted to discuss." He walked toward the plaid sofa dotted with mystery stains and sat down before motioning Mavis to take the seat beside him. "We can't withdraw the lawsuit quite yet."

She frowned and sat down. "B-but why not?"

Renee flopped in the loveseat facing them and reached for a pack of cigarettes and a lighter on the coffee table.

"Well, he still could file a civil suit against you, Mavis."

"But wouldn't he have done it by now?" Mavis asked. "It don't seem like that boy is really interested in—"

"And besides," Dante continued, talking over her, "we have to hold out for arbitration. We have to wait for his lawyer to approach us with an offer."

Mavis's frown deepened. "An . . . an offer? An offer for what?"

"An offer to pay you back the income you lost while you were in the hospital. An offer that will help you buy another, *nicer* car since the one you had was totaled. You're only asking for what's due to you."

She slowly shook her head. "But I thought . . . I thought I wasn't really asking him for money."

"And you aren't!" Dante assured. His smile widened. "You're not asking for money, Mavis . . . not *real* money, anyway. This would be a drop in the bucket compared to how much Terrence Murdoch has in his bank accounts."

"But I still don't know if I caused that accident! I wouldn't feel right asking him for—"

"But think about how useful that money could be for you, Mavis. How you could help make your life better . . . how it could help your family." He glanced at Renee, who was reclining on the sofa, smoking and looking bored. He raised his brows, beseeching her silently to stop sitting there like a slug and offer him some help.

She immediately sat upright and tugged her cigarette out of her mouth. "Yeah, Mama, just think about how you could help me and . . . and *Tasha* with that money. You said yourself you couldn't afford all her school supplies. Wouldn't have to worry about that no more!"

Mavis glanced over her shoulder at her granddaughter. She watched as Tasha grabbed a red crayon and continued to draw.

"Tasha *does* need a new book bag," Mavis mumbled. "There's a hole in the one she has now. And new shoes . . . those tennis shoes she wears are getting too small and—"

"See!" Dante said. "With the money you're awarded, you could get Tasha a new book bag, shoes, and anything else she needs."

Mavis seemed to contemplate Dante's words. Finally, she said, "But we won't ask him for *a lot* of money, though, right?"

"We wouldn't think of it!" Dante widened his eyes in mock innocence. "We'll only ask for what you're rightfully due. Only what will help your family."

She looked down at her wrinkled hands, which were now in her lap. "All right. All right, but please don't ask for too much."

Dante grinned. "Of course not!"

Chapter 10

C. J.

C. J. strode into the newsroom, yanking the strap of her satchel over her head as she made her way to her desk.

"Oh, look, everybody, Her Royal Highness is here!" Eddie the sports reporter yelled, glancing up from his laptop. He took a sip from his Big Gulp and grinned.

"No time for your crap today, Eddie. I'm busy," she mumbled before waving her hand dismissively at him as she passed.

She had just come back from the state police barracks and now had to quickly file a story on a local bank robbery for the paper's crime reporter. In exchange, said reporter had covered a chamber of commerce meeting chaired by Evan Murdoch that had been assigned to her.

"Why can't you do it?" Mason, the crime re-porter, had whined as she walked out of the newsroom hours ago. "I don't want to go to that meeting. You've got to wear a tie to those things!"

"I have my reasons. Don't worry about it," she had halfheartedly explained. "I'll pay you back with a doughnut and a cup of coffee later."

The truth was, since that incident at the Medical Center a couple of months ago, C. J. had avoided the Murdochs like the plague. Evan Murdoch's accusations and anger at her that day still stung. She had been called names by subjects before—many of those names of the four- and five-letter variety—but she had never been called a "parasite" before. She had never been accused of taking advantage of someone else's pain. It had been way too much to bear and it left her shaken for quite a few weeks afterward.

I'm not a parasite, she would tell herself when she lay alone in her bedroom at night. *I'm a human being. I care!*

In fact, C. J. wondered every now and then how Terrence Murdoch was faring. The last she had heard, he had become a bit of a hermit since the accident, as well as a raging alcoholic. She hoped the rumors about Terrence, like many of the other rumors in Chesterton, weren't true.

C. J. tapped on her mouse pad and stared at the digital clock on the right side of her laptop screen. She only had about an hour or so to write this story. After that, she had to head to the mayor's office for a scheduled interview about the new Chesterton business incubator. She refused to be distracted by nonsense, specifically in the form of bullshit from Eddie.

She pulled out her rollaway chair, sat down, and

frantically flipped in her notepad to the quotes from Sergeant Mitchell.

"You're back," Jake, the managing editor, said as he stepped into the newsroom, holding a stack of envelopes, magazines, and folders. "And you're just in time for the office mail."

"*Ooooh*, how exciting!" Eddie exclaimed before twirling around in his chair.

"Isn't it?" Jake said dryly. He tossed a stack of magazines onto Eddie's desk. "Here you go, smart-ass." He then walked toward C. J. and glanced down at a solitary envelope he held in his hand. "Hey, this looks official. You know many people in high places, C. J.?"

He handed it to her and she frowned. It was thick and made out of a parchment that you usually only found in papier and crafting stores. She recognized the gold seal on the back of the envelope instantly. It was the same seal she had stared at for most of her life but hadn't seen up close in the past few years. Beneath the seal in scrolling blue script were the words *Aston Ministries, Inc.* with the headquarters address beneath it.

"Anything important?" Jake asked.

C. J. quickly slapped her hand over the seal and stared up at Jake. She forced a smile. "Uh, no! No. It's . . . uh . . . just . . . just junk, probably. Thanks for bringing it to me."

He stared at her quizzically, then shrugged before walking off to deliver mail to another reporter.

After Jake moved on to the next desk, C. J. gazed at the envelope again. Her hands were shaking as she ripped open the seal with her thumb and stared at the handwritten note that was folded inside of it.

> *You've been a bad, bad girl, Court. You and I have a lot of catching up to do. Meet me at my office at 10 a.m. Wednesday.*
>
> *I'm guessing the people at your little newspaper don't know who you really are, hence your new name. Unless you want them to know, you won't think about standing me up.*
>
> *—V.*
>
> *P.S. If you didn't want to be found, you shouldn't have moved back to the East Coast. You know how Dad is. Not a smart move on your part.*

"Shit," C. J. muttered as she closed her eyes and balled the note in her fist. She ripped the envelope into several pieces before tossing both into her metal waste bin.

"What's the matter with you?" Eddie asked. "Didn't get an invite to the debutante ball?"

C. J. gave him the finger before turning back around to face her laptop.

She could ignore the note, pretend like she had never seen it, but she knew the writer well enough that he wouldn't let this go ignored. He would follow through with his threat to let everyone at *Chesterton Times* know who she really was, and she had worked so hard to escape the scandal and drama of her past. No, there was no avoiding this. It looked like she would have to make a trip to the Aston Ministries Headquarters in North Carolina. It looked like she was finally heading back home.

C. J. slammed shut the door to her Honda Civic. She leaned her head back and squinted, holding up her hands over her eyes to block out the blinding light coming off the mirror-like exterior of the towering building in front of her. The building was one of many churches owned and operated by Aston Ministries. It was certainly one of its largest. The immense church was flanked on both sides by immaculate landscaping and a series of water fountains rivaling those found at Versailles. The church itself took up several football fields. It not only housed a sanctuary that could accommodate several thousand people, but also enough lighting, electronics, and pyrotechnics for a Las Vegas show. It operated as the headquarters of the religious conglomerate that had been founded by her father, the Honorable Reverend Pete Aston.

The sanctuary itself always looked amazing on television and her father took full advantage of it during his thunderous sermons, which were shown on cable as well as the three Jumbotron screens that hung over the pulpit. C. J. remembered being a young girl and sitting in rapture with the rest of the parishioners in the audience as she watched her father preach, feeling as if she was watching a grand performance. C. J. didn't realize until she was older that she *was* watching a performance— the greatest performance of all—because there was no way her father was the sanctified man he pretended to be. He certainly wasn't that man behind closed doors. She was sure his many mistresses would agree with her.

C. J. walked across the parking lot to a series of glass doors near the rear of the building that led to the offices of the Aston Ministries leadership. Her father's office was here and so was her brother Victor's. She would be seeing Victor today per his note instruction.

C. J. tugged one of the glass doors open and walked into the carpeted lobby. She paused and gazed around her apprehensively, hoping no one recognized her. It was a good chance no one did. She certainly looked different than when she had run away from everything she knew five years ago. She no longer looked like the prim and proper reverend's daughter. No more expensive dresses and suits that were just the right length and cut to be the perfect mix between demur and attractive. No more pressed and artfully styled hair. Today she wore jeans and a T-shirt along with a casual blazer. Her curly tendrils were pulled back in a ponytail under a baseball cap. She pulled the brim of the cap low over her eyes in a futile attempt to hide her face.

C. J. stared at the receptionist desk. Behind the woman sitting at the desk was a flat-screen television showing one of her father's sermons.

"Excuse me," C. J. said softly, making the receptionist raise her head. "I have an appointment with—"

"Courtney?" a familiar voice called from behind her.

At the sound of the voice, she stilled. She slowly turned and found a man gazing at her.

Oh God, she thought with panic. *He's still here?*

She had been under the misguided belief that he would have left the church, that the disgrace of what had happened would have made him move on to another flock. But no, Shaun Clancy was still here. And of all the people she had to run into today, it had to be him.

He was wearing a gray suit and blue tie. She knew that it was the European cut he preferred because it showed off the slim physique he had spent years perfecting in the gym and in track and field. A gold pendant with the Aston Enterprises emblem was pinned to his lapel. He squinted dark eyes at her, then blinked, as if he was seeing an apparition. His brown face creased into a frown.

"Court? Is . . . is that you?" he asked again, taking a tentative step toward her.

"Yeah, it's me." She pursed her lips and tugged at her leather satchel. "It's great to see you, Shaun." She smiled anxiously. "How have you been?"

"How have I been?" His face morphed from amazement to thinly veiled fury. He laughed coldly as he shoved his hands into his pants pockets. "Well, uh . . . let me think. I've been fairly good . . . considering how you left me standing at the altar five years ago."

C. J. lowered her eyes. She should have anticipated this, but she had been avoiding Shaun and the mess she had left behind for too long. "Shaun, I'm—"

"Who sends someone a text fifteen minutes before their wedding, telling them they can't get married? Huh? *Who does that?* Then, when I tried to talk to you . . . to ask you why you would do that, why you would walk out and humiliate me and break my heart, you refused to answer any of my phone calls or texts or e-mails."

"I'm sorry. I am so, *so* sorry." She took a deep breath and raised her eyes, feeling shame and regret curdle in her stomach. "I know there are no excuses for what I did. But believe me when I say I didn't want to hurt you. I had my reasons, but—"

"Finally," he continued undaunted, taking another step toward her, "after basically writing you off for dead, I had to learn to move on. With a lot of counseling and prayer, I managed to do it. I started dating again. I fell in love with someone—a good Christian girl with a good heart. I was able to forgive you, Court."

"I'm . . . I'm happy to hear that."

And she genuinely was happy to hear it. She had wanted him to fall in love with someone else and move on. Shaun had been a sweet guy, an innocent bystander in the mess that had been her life back then. It pained her to know what she had done to him.

"I forgave you, Court . . . but I can't forget." He glared at her and she saw so much rage in his eyes that she had to take a cautious step back from him. "I will *never* forget that mess you pulled."

She held up her hands. "Look, I said I was sorry. I know that I—"

"*Sorry?* Sorry!" he yelled, making the receptionist look up and stare at them in shock. "You think that makes it better?"

"No, I don't. But I wanted to explain why—"

"I thought we had something! I thought we were going to be together forever! I was prepared to pledge before God that—"

"Pastor Clancy," Victor called out, "not here."

C. J. turned to find her brother standing on the other side of the lobby, looking at them. He was even more immaculately dressed than Shaun, with his gold cuff links and Prada loafers—the best that Aston Ministries had to buy. His stony facial expression made them both fall silent. "Not here. This isn't the time or the place. All right?"

She watched as Shaun suddenly turned on his heel and stomped toward the glass doors. He yanked the door open before stalking off to somewhere unseen. Now badly shaken, C. J. turned to face her brother.

"Welcome back, Court," he said, before walking toward her. He wrapped his arms around her and she stiffly accepted his embrace. "We missed you," he whispered into her ear. "Good to have you home."

"Have a seat. Would you like some coffee? Tea?" Victor asked as he strode into his sunlit office and she trailed behind him. She sat down in one of the leather armchairs facing the office windows that overlooked one of the property's many gardens. "You used to always drink green tea. Is that still your thing?"

Victor didn't wait for her to answer him. He suddenly turned to a young man with flawless skin and sculpted cheekbones who waited silently near his desk. The young man had been standing there when she entered, looking ill at ease, like he wasn't quite sure what to do with himself. He looked like he belonged in an Abercrombie & Fitch catalog with his tight-fitting polo shirt and khakis—not working in a ministry office.

"Brian, can you get Court some green tea, please?" Victor asked as he sat down in the chair behind his immense desk.

The young man blinked. "Oh! Oh yeah. Sure, I can do that." He nodded, walked across the room and paused in front of the coffeemaker. He began to scan the Keurig cups.

"Not there, Brian," Victor said, his fake smile tightening. "The tea is in the cabinet overhead. Remember?"

Brian blinked again, this time in confusion. "In the . . . in the cabinet?"

Victor slowly nodded. "The teacups are there, too."

"Really, that's okay," C. J. said quickly just as Brian reached for the cabinet door handle. "I don't want any tea. I don't want anything. Thanks."

The young man paused and turned to look at Victor expectantly, as if to double-check with him that it was acceptable for her not to have anything to drink.

"It's all right, Brian," Victor said. "Just shut the door behind you, will you? I'll call you if I need you."

"Sure, honey," Brian said before getting a censuring glare from his boss. "I mean, yes, M-M-Mr. Aston," Brian stuttered. "I'll . . . I'll be right outside." He then rushed to the office door and shut it behind him.

"He's new. Just started here a couple of months ago," Victor explained.

C. J. nodded.

"It's so hard to find good staff these days," he said with a soft chuckle. He then adjusted a series of framed photos on his desk: one of his wife, Bethany, and the other of their son, Victor Jr.

"Especially in the places where *you* look," C. J. muttered, making Victor do a double take.

"Excuse me?" He raised an eyebrow.

"Nothing," she murmured, not wanting to get into it with him. She focused over his shoulder at the water fountain in the distance, not meeting his discerning gaze. "I didn't say anything."

It was evident that Victor hadn't hired Brian because of his office skills. Since she was a preteen, C. J. had heard rumors about her brother, Victor . . . how he snuck off to the city to dance clubs frequented by gay men, how he had dated men secretly for years, right under their father's nose. His marriage to Bethany didn't seem to stop his escapades. It only made him even sneakier, hence putting his boy toys on staff at Aston Ministries, Inc. She wondered how many young men who worked around the building had been recommended for a job by her dear, sweet brother, Victor.

"Look, you told me to come here today. Why did you invite me here?" she asked. "Nice touch with the letter, by the way. You couldn't send an e-mail like a normal person?"

"You know me, Court. I like to do things with a flourish," he said smugly, leaning back in his chair.

She crossed her arms over her chest. "My name isn't Court. It's C. J. now."

"Oh no, honey. You are Courtney Jocelyn Aston. That isn't going to change . . . no matter how many times you change your name, move to other parts of the country, or throw on those cheap clothes," he said, gesturing toward her outfit. "You can't hide who you are, Courtney. You thought you could just disappear and no one would notice? You thought we wouldn't ever find you after the stunt you pulled?"

"I didn't pull a stunt! I just didn't want to go forward with a lie because Dad sanctioned it."

Her father had chosen Shaun for her and had basically bullied her into marrying him. He had seen him as a second son and was grooming him to eventually take over as reverend of the church and help Victor head Aston Ministries someday. She had known her father's plans and the role he had expected her to play in them—and she wanted nothing to do with it.

"You ran away from a church filled with three hundred people, Court! You left that poor boy standing at the altar. You drove off in Dad's Benz, which he still considers to be stolen, by the way. You didn't think you would have to answer for your actions?"

"I'd rather have run away than continue lying! I didn't love Shaun. He deserved better . . . someone who really cared for him."

Victor snorted with contempt. "Oh please. Spare me the melodramatics!"

"I'm not like you. I'm not good at pretending."

Her brother inclined his head. "What the hell is that supposed to mean?"

"I don't know. Why don't you ask your *assistant*, Brian?" she spat out.

C. J. watched as a myriad of expressions crossed over her brother's face: shock, rage, maybe a little shame, then back to rage again. He rose from his chair and stalked around his desk so that he was standing in front of her. She sat upright, ready for anything.

If her father judged her with silent condemnation, Victor had always been the enforcer. He knew how to break a person, how to hit you where it hurt.

"All right, Courtney," he said, snatching off her cap, making her hands fly to her head. He tossed it onto his ebony desk. "Let's cut the bullshit."

He sat on the edge of his desk and smiled at her, though she wasn't fooled. Victor's body practically radiated the message, *"If I could wrap my hands around your neck, choke you right now, and not get caught, I totally would do it."*

"Do you *really* want to know the reason I asked you here today?" His smile widened. "I'll tell you. Dad asked me to invite you. So, of course, the next question is, if Dad wanted you here, why not talk to you himself? The reason he gave me was pretty simple: He couldn't stand to look at you." Victor sneered gleefully. "Neither can Mom. They're done with you, Courtney, or C. J., or whatever the fuck you want to call yourself these days! Your whole life you've been a spoiled little brat who's never understood the meaning of family or sacrifice. Dad built this church from the ground up and all he wanted was his family's love, support, and *allegiance* in that endeavor. But you were always willing to take and never willing to give back in return, weren't you?"

"That's *not* true," she said, clenching her fists in her lap. "I just didn't want to—"

"But they understand. Mom and Dad have accepted that you are what you are, Courtney. No one can change you. We get it now." He held up his hands in capitulation. "But Dad does have plans . . . plans even bigger than Aston Ministries and we need to make sure you're on board."

Here it comes, she thought.

What did her family need her to do? What lies did they need her to tell this time?

"He's considering getting into politics . . . a run for Congress," Victor continued. "The Republicans think he has a real chance with black voters and conservatives. We don't want your active participation in the family or the brand anymore. But we do need to know that if any reporters come sniffing around, asking questions about rumors surrounding Dad, surrounding *us* . . . you know what to say."

"What rumors?" she asked with mock innocence. "I don't know—"

"Don't play fucking games with me, Court!" he bellowed as he charged toward her chair and clamped his hands down on both arms. His face was only inches away from hers. His eyes seemed to catch on fire. Despite herself, she started to tremble. "I've had enough of your shit! You know what rumors I'm talking about. Keep your goddamn mouth shut! If any of the press calls you and asks you questions, you tell them you don't know. You tell them we're the perfect family. *Understood?*"

She swallowed and nodded.

"Understood?" he repeated. "I want you to answer me with words. I want to hear you say it."

"U-u-understood," she stuttered, feeling her throat go dry.

Her brother abruptly pulled back from her, and she felt like she could breathe again.

"Good," he said. "I'm glad we could come to an understanding." He put back on his pleasant façade, stood upright, and buttoned his suit jacket. "So, are you heading back home today? Are you going to stop in town?"

She slowly shook her head and rose from her chair. She looked down at her hands. They were still shaking. "Uh . . . no . . . I'm heading back to Chesterton. I have to . . . to get back to work. I have an event to cover tonight."

"Well, drive safely." He leaned forward and kissed her cheek. She flinched without realizing it. "I'll be in touch."

I bet you will, she thought before rushing to escape his office.

She pushed open the door and immediately collided with Shaun.

"I'm sorry," she said breathlessly, and his face instantly hardened at her words. "I-I'm sorry for running into you, I mean. I . . . I . . . I have to go," she whispered.

She then ran toward the lobby, not looking back.

Chapter 11
Terrence

Terrence gazed at the ballroom just steps beyond the entryway, where a hundred or so people sat at the banquet tables and danced on the parquet floor while the twelve-piece band played an acoustic version of The Commodores' "Easy."

He took a slow, deep, steadying breath, then glanced at his brother, who stood at his side. Evan was shifting restlessly from one foot to the other and tugging at his tuxedo tie. Terrence wasn't sure who was more nervous about tonight's outing: him or Evan.

"Are we all good?" Evan asked, shouting over the music and looking between Terrence and Leila. "Everybody's feeling okay?"

Leila, who looked dazzling in her ruby-red halter-topped, sequined gown, looped her arm through Evan's and smiled. "I'm fine."

"I'm fine, too," Terrence said, though his heart was starting to race.

He hadn't been at an event this public since before the accident. He hadn't been in a room with this many people, either. He felt hot and tense. Pinpricks of sweat were starting to form on his brow and beneath his armpits and it wasn't just from the strain of balancing himself on his new sleek wooden cane. As his heart continued to pound at a breakneck speed, Terrence thought he might be on the verge of having a real panic attack. But he told himself to calm down and to practice the breathing exercises that Dr. Sweeney—or as he called her, Dr. "How do you feel about that?"—had taught him during one of their previous sessions. He was seeing her twice a week now, an intensive therapy regime that she thought was warranted considering his depression and—he suspected— his ability to pay all those billable hours. Terrence was slowly getting better, but he still had setbacks on occasion. He reminded himself that the voices of pity and judgment were only in his head; it was just a manifestation of his own sense of inadequacy.

"Well, if we're all fine, then I guess we should head to our table," Evan announced.

Leila nodded. Terrence nodded—reluctantly.

Evan cleared his throat and took a step over the threshold into the ballroom with Leila on his arm. Terrence pulled up the rear, slowly walking behind him with his cane.

"Hey, Evan! Hey, Terry, good to see you back, man!" someone called out as they passed by.

"Hey, how're you doing?" Evan called back, waving.

Terrence forced himself to smile in greeting, then returned his focus to the back of Evan's head. A few more people shouted out their hellos and well wishes as the Murdochs made their way to their banquet table. Terrence told himself those weren't lingering gazes that he felt boring into him, or whispers that he heard coming from over his shoulder as he limped through the crowd of partygoers.

People aren't staring at your eye patch or your leg, Terry, he told himself. *They're just surprised to see you. You haven't been out in a while. That's all!*

But that didn't stop him from exhaling with relief when he finally fell into the chair at their table and set aside his cane. Sitting down in a crowd of people, he felt a lot less conspicuous. He no longer felt like a spotlight was following him around the room.

Once one of the waiters offered them a platter of hors d'oeuvres and another brought a platter covered with flutes of complimentary champagne, Terrence settled in even more. If before he felt only 20 percent like the "old, normal Terrence," now he felt closer to 40 percent. When one of their tablemates made a joke, Terrence even laughed without forcing himself to do it.

"Oh God," Leila murmured thirty minutes later. Her eyes went wide with panic. "Ugh, I have to go to the ladies' room."

"Are you okay?" Evan asked, frowning as she suddenly shot up from the table and shoved back her Chiavari chair.

She nodded and tossed onto the tablecloth the linen napkin that was on her lap. "Be right back," she garbled before clamping her hand over her mouth, raising the hem of her gown and racing in her high heels through the throng to the ballroom doors.

"Is she all right?" Terrence asked. He lowered his half-filled champagne glass back to the table as he watched his future sister-in-law's retreating back.

"She's fine. Just a little nauseated," Evan said with a winsome smile.

"Nauseated?" Terrence stared at his brother in confusion. That didn't seem like something to smile about. Terrence furrowed his brows and glanced at Leila's plate, where only a few skewers remained. "Was it the caviar deviled eggs? I thought they tasted kinda funny."

Evan quickly shook his head and leaned toward Terrence's ear. "Leila's pregnant," he whispered.

This time Terrence's eyes went wide. "She's *pregnant?*" he shouted.

"Sssshhh!" Evan said, raising a finger to his lips. "Don't tell the whole goddamn room!"

Evan sounded angry, but Terrence knew that he wasn't. His older brother was beaming.

"Congratulations, man!" Terrence whispered, thumping Evan on his shoulder. "Why didn't you tell me?"

"Well, she's still early in the pregnancy and we didn't want too many people to know yet. Lots of women miscarry in the first trimester."

Evan's smile faded. He went somber. Back when Evan and Charisse had been in their slightly better days, she had successfully gotten pregnant a few times herself—only to lose the baby each time. Evan, understandably, had taken the miscarriages pretty hard. Their marriage, which had been on shaky ground, suffered even more with each loss.

"I also didn't tell you," Evan continued, "because I didn't want to bring up something like this while you were going through your . . . your *thing*. You know? It didn't seem appropriate."

"What thing would ever make you think I wouldn't want to know about something like this?"

Evan pursed his lips. "You've been in a dark place, Terry. For a while I couldn't talk to you. None of us could."

Had he really been so wrapped up in feeling sorry for himself, in being so angry at the world, that his own brother hadn't felt comfortable telling him that he and his fiancée were going to have a baby? A new life was on the way and Evan had felt it better to keep it a secret from him? Was he really that bad off?

"I'm sorry," Terrence muttered.

"You don't have to apologize," Evan insisted, holding up his hand. "I know how—"

"No, I'm sorry." His voice was stronger now. He met his brother's eyes. "I'm sorry for being so bogged down in my own shit that I forgot other people existed."

After some time, Evan nodded. "I accept your apology."

Terrence nudged his shoulder. "Go ahead and check on Leila. Make sure she's okay and that she didn't throw up on the marble floors out there."

"Are you sure?" Evan asked, now gazing at him

worriedly. "You're going to be all right in here by yourself?"

Terrence nodded. "I'll be fine. I'm a big boy."

When Evan still lingered, Terrence nudged him again. "Go on. I'll throw up the bat signal if I need your help."

Gradually, Evan pushed back his chair and rose to his feet. "I'll be back in five minutes, tops. Okay?"

Terrence rolled his eyes and made a shooing motion. Finally, Evan pushed his chair back to the table, turned, and left.

Terrence raised his flute of champagne back to his lips and gazed around the room. He watched as people flitted from table to table, flirting and hobnobbing with the best that Chesterton had to offer. As the band kicked up a slow song, he watched as couples embraced on the dance floor, gazing into one another's eyes as they slowly turned in circles. He would probably never be able to dance like that again. But it wasn't the end of the world. He was still alive, still breathing. He had to stop feeling sorry for himself.

"Terry?" a female voice said behind him.

Terrence turned to find Monique, the psycho who had been stalking him for months, standing behind him, holding a glass of champagne. She was wearing a black velvet minidress and silver stilettos. A look of sheer horror was now on Monique's face as she stared at Terrence.

Of all the people to run into right now, why did it have to be her?

"Hello, Monique," he answered, resigned.

"Oh my . . . oh my *God!*" she cried, dropping her

red nails to her ample chest. She looked and sounded mildly drunk. "I heard you were in an accident. But I didn't know . . . I didn't know it was *this* bad! What happened to you, Terry?"

"Nothing happened." His jaw tightened to the point that he felt like he would crush his molars. He started to feel hot again. Sweat began to form under the collar of his tuxedo shirt. "I got injured. I'm getting better. It's not that big of a—"

"But your eye!" she yelled. Her false eyelashes opened and closed like black window shades as she blinked dramatically. "Is that . . . is that a cane I'm seeing? Are you walking with a cane now, too?"

He couldn't take this. Just when he had felt himself getting better, he had to encounter his worst nightmare: outright pity.

"Yes, it's my cane," he muttered before grabbing the carved wooden handle and slowly rising to his feet. "And now I'm using it to walk away. It was nice seeing you again, Monique," he lied.

He then shoved past her.

"Hey!" she yelled with outrage. "When did you get so rude?"

He didn't answer her. Instead he continued to make his way to the bar across the room, or to the ballroom doors; he didn't care where he went. He just wanted to get away from her.

"Karma's a bitch, isn't it, Terry!" she shouted after him, making his shoulders and back go rigid. "You treat people the way you do and life has a way of getting you back!"

He still didn't respond; instead he continued on his path, deciding to head to one of the many exit doors after all.

Five minutes later, Terrence leaned against the wall of a long corridor where only a few people lingered. He waited for his anxiety to wane and for his heartbeat to slow its rapid pace. He stared out the window at the enclosed atrium with a trickling water fountain that was lit by a few floodlights. It looked vaguely like a Hawaiian sanctuary. Behind the glass were vibrantly hued birds of paradise, red ginger, and yellow heliconia caribaea.

I shouldn't have let that chick get to me, he thought as he gazed at the flowers. He knew that Monique had wanted to piss him off, to exact her last revenge. But that still didn't prevent the shame and hurt from slicing their way through his chest. Would he always be vulnerable to people like that?

Terrence watched absently in the reflection of the atrium window as a woman walked by him with a notepad and pen in hand. She was wearing a pale gray chiffon gown that draped over her sumptuous curves. Its spaghetti straps revealed slender, nutmeg-toned shoulders. A nest of wiry curls was piled on top of her head in a hasty updo. As she passed, she glanced at him and slowed. Her brown eyes widened. She openly gaped.

Terrence rolled his eye. He had come out here to avoid the stares, but they had followed him anyway.

Enough of this shit, he thought.

"Can I help you?" he asked irritably, turning around to face her.

She closed her gaping mouth. "Uh, no. No! I-I . . . uh . . . I didn't . . . You're Terrence Murdoch, right?" she stuttered before pointing at him.

He took a long, tired breath and slowly nodded. "The one and only, honey."

"I didn't expect to see you here!" she cried, breaking into a smile. "I knew about your accident and that . . . that you were in recovery, but . . . but . . . Wow!"

He cocked an eyebrow. *Wow?*

"I mean, you . . . you look so . . . so . . ."

When will this agony end? Terrence pushed himself away from the wall, preparing to retreat again. Maybe he would head back to the ballroom. He would stop by the cash bar and get a drink—a stiff one.

"You look so good!" she shouted, still grinning. "You look great!"

That gave him pause. He narrowed his eye at her. "What?"

"I mean, I can barely tell what happened to you! Well, besides the . . . you know." She pointed to her own left eye. "But otherwise, you look amazing! It's great to see you like this."

Amazing? He didn't know if that was a word he would use to describe his current state. But she didn't seem to be lying. Her effusive compliments seemed genuine. He inclined his head. "I'm sorry, but . . . do I know you?"

"No. No, you don't. But I've heard about you and your family." She held up her notepad and pen. "I work for the local paper . . . the *Chesterton Times*. I'm covering tonight's event." She offered her hand to him for a shake, taking on a more formal tone. "My name is C. J. Aston. It's a pleasure to meet you, Mr. Murdoch."

He shook her soft hand and the instant he did,

an electric charge traveled up his arm. It caught him by surprise. He hadn't felt a charge like that in quite a while. Suddenly, the "old, normal Terrence" increased by another fifteen percentage points.

"Please, call me Terrence. And it's a pleasure to meet you, too," he said, now smiling.

"So, are you enjoying yourself tonight, Terrence?" she asked, drawing back her hand and flipping to a blank page in her notepad. "I know tonight's event is supposed to raise funds for leukemia research. Your family is involved with this charity, isn't it?"

"Yeah, we've donated a few times, but we . . ." He paused when she began to scribble on her notepad. He squinted. "Are you writing this down?"

She nodded. "So you said the Murdochs have donated a few times. Any personal relationship to the cause? I know some attendees said that they had people in their families who suffered from—"

"Don't do that," he said, shaking his head.

She looked up from her page and gazed at him quizzically. Her pen stopped midstroke. "I'm sorry. Don't do what?"

"Don't quote me. I thought we were having a conversation. I didn't want this to go in the paper."

"Oh." She lowered her notepad and anxiously cleared her throat. "I'm s-sorry. I didn't know. We were talking so . . . I-I assumed . . ." Her words drifted off. She gnawed her glossy lower lip.

"Don't men just talk to you sometimes?" He chuckled. "You know . . . playful banter or boring conversations about the weather or sports or politics?"

Her cheeks reddened as she tucked her notepad

into the satin purse that dangled on her shoulder. "Not in quite a while," she mumbled.

"Not in a while?" He smirked. "Oh, come on! You really expect me to believe that?" He let his appreciative gaze travel over her, settling for a second too long on the cleavage peeking over her heart-shaped neckline. "A beautiful woman like you . . . I would think men would go out of their way to strike up a conversation with you."

She slowly raised her eyes to stare at him. She crossed her arms over her chest. "Are you flirting with me, Mr. Murdoch?"

He laughed again. "I told you to call me Terrence. And I guess I'm not flirting very well if you have to ask."

She joined him in his laughter. Terrence thought she had a lovely laugh. It sounded almost melodic, like tinkling piano keys. "Oh, you're doing better than you think!" she muttered before giving him a rueful grin.

They continued to talk and he continued to flirt, emboldened with each blush that painted her cheeks. After a while, he grew tired of standing with his cane, so he sat on the windowsill facing the atrium and motioned for her to take the space on the ledge beside him. She hesitated briefly before accepting his invitation. Their shoulders brushed as she sat down and Terrence felt a slow heat surge through him that he hadn't felt in months. He wasn't just attracted to this woman with the dark eyes and musical laugh, but he actively desired her. He slowly realized this as they spoke about Chesterton and movies and the trials of his recovery from the accident. He fought to tear his gaze from her sumptuous lips and the curve of her breasts. Her intoxicating smell made his mouth water and every time she threw back her head and laughed, he wanted to lean over and kiss her.

He wondered what Dr. "How do you feel about that?" would think about all of this.

Suddenly, C. J. looked up and gazed around her as if waking up from a daze. "Hmm, where did everybody go?"

Terrence followed her gaze. The corridor was nearly deserted. "I don't know," he muttered.

And frankly, I don't care. He was happy to be alone with her.

"How long have we been out here?" she asked, furrowing her delicate brows. She reached into her purse and pulled out her cell phone. She gazed at the screen and gasped. "Oh, wow! It's almost midnight."

He frowned. "That can't be right."

She showed him her phone. The screen read 11:56. They had been talking for more than two hours and he hadn't even noticed.

She quickly rose to her feet and tossed the strap of her purse over her shoulder. "I should be going. I can't believe I've been back here so long!"

"Why leave now? Is your carriage about to turn into a pumpkin?"

She stared at him in confusion. "Huh?"

"Nothing." He shook his head. "I was just making a bad Cinderella joke."

"Cute," she said flatly, then laughed. "No, I'm not worried about my carriage, but I do think my Honda Civic is illegally parked. I hope I don't get towed." She glanced down at her notepad and began to randomly flip pages. "Hell, I've only gotten quotes from, like, two people! My editor is going to be so pissed, but . . . oh well." She shrugged and looked at Terrence. "I'm sorry for monopolizing all your time tonight."

"No need to apologize," he said softly. "I enjoyed myself."

"I did, too. My day started off bad, to say the least, but this was a vast improvement." She sighed and stared at the double doors leading back to the ballroom. "Well, I really should get going. I have to cover a court hearing that starts bright and early at eight a.m. I should head out now if I want to get a few hours of sleep. You have a good night, Terrence."

She began to walk down the corridor toward the exit sign, but Terrence grabbed his cane and pushed himself to his feet. "Hey, C. J.!" he called after her, making her pause.

She turned to face him. "Yes?"

"Would you . . ." He hesitated.

He couldn't get the words out of his mouth. He wanted to ask her out on a date, but the voices of doubt were shouting in his head again. Why would a woman like her want to date a broken man like him? Why should he set himself up for this type of rejection?

"Would I what?" she asked.

"Do you . . ." He took a deep breath, telling the voices to shut up for once. "Do you have any plans for Saturday? Maybe we could meet up . . . you know, get some coffee."

"Are you . . . are you asking me out?"

"Well . . . yeah." Apprehension crept over him again as she stared at him. Was she going to tell him no? "I mean, if you're not interested, then—"

"I'd love to. I just thought that . . . well, never mind." She reached into her purse and pulled out a business card. "My cell number is on there." She handed it to him, then paused. "You're serious, right?"

"Of course I'm serious! Why wouldn't I be?"

She shook her head again. "Nothing. Nothing. I just . . . wondered."

He gazed down at the laminated card and smiled at her. "I'll call you tomorrow."

"You'd better," she muttered before turning away and walking down the hall.

He watched her until she disappeared behind the double doors.

"The old, normal Terrence is now at one hundred percent," he whispered before tucking her card into his suit jacket pocket.

Chapter 12

Evan

"When should I come back to get you, sir?" Evan's driver, Bill, asked from the front seat. "Would you like me to wait for you in the driveway?"

Evan swallowed two aspirins, tiredly opened his eyes, and gazed at the stately colonial outside of the town car's tinted windows. A dull ache spread across his temples. He now regretted staying out so late at the charity banquet, dancing the night away with Leila on the dance floor. He also regretted breaking his "no alcohol" rule and drinking one champagne too many. But he had been so happy to see his brother, Terrence, finally cheer up, to see him confident again—that he had thrown caution to the wind last night. He was paying the price for that decision now.

"No, don't wait for me, Bill. Unfortunately, this might run a bit long," he murmured. "Just come back in an hour. If I need you sooner, I'll call you."

Less than a minute later, Evan stood at the end of a brick walkway that was bordered on both sides by a kelly-green lawn and blossoming daffodils. A birdbath sat not too far away. He remembered walking this same path six years ago with Charisse on his arm.

"Don't be nervous," she had assured with a mischievous grin as she tugged him to the red oak door to meet her parents for the first time. "Mom and Dad are going to *love* you, Ev!"

Unfortunately, Charisse's mother and her now-deceased father *hadn't* loved him. Her mother had at least remained awkwardly polite though gracious throughout the entire dinner, but her father had radiated no warmth. He barely had spoken and rarely seemed to address Evan directly.

Evan wasn't sure if the reason her parents had seemed so withdrawn, even downright standoffish, was because he was black. He didn't know what else it could be. He was educated; he had a master's from the Wharton School of Business, for God's sake! He wasn't poor. He came from one of the wealthier families in the D.C. region, which was one of the wealthiest regions in the country. The Murdochs certainly had more money than Charisse's family. So, why else had Charisse's mother been so stiff? Why else had her father behaved so rudely, if it wasn't because their future son-in-law was black?

Evan had posed the question to Charisse, but she had been clueless.

"What do you mean?" Charisse had asked as he drove her back to her condo all those years ago. "I thought the dinner went *well,* quite frankly."

He guessed he would never get a straight answer to his question, but at this point, it no longer mattered. He and Charisse were no longer together, and with today's meeting, he hoped they were finally on their way to solidifying their divorce. Evan had had to reschedule with her over the past month, perhaps subconsciously hoping that she would call off the meeting and send him the signed divorce papers anyway, but no such luck. She had stuck to her guns. She wanted to talk.

He walked the length of the brick walkway, climbed a short flight of stairs, then reached the front door. He rang the bell and heard the discreet chime that played inside the house. A few seconds later, Charisse's mother, Agatha, stood in the doorway.

She was a more mature version of her daughter, though petite. Her blond hair had long ago faded to a pale white that made it look almost platinum. Today she wore it in an understated chignon. Agatha and Charisse's figures were similar—trim enough to be appealing, but not so slim that they looked emaciated. She was wearing a simple white blouse and gray slacks on her slender frame. A yellow cardigan was tied around her shoulders. He had never seen pictures of an older Grace Kelly, but Evan imagined that Agatha resembled the screen queen in her later years.

"Hello, Evan," Agatha said, gesturing for him to come inside.

"Hello, Agatha," he said, taking on the formal tone that he often did with his in-law.

"Charisse is in the sunroom waiting for you." She pursed her wrinkled lips. "She wanted to smoke and it's the only place in the house where I'll allow her to do it. She smokes all the time now."

He nodded and turned toward the room that he had been to a few times over the course of the past six years. He paused when he felt Agatha suddenly reach out and clamp a firm hand around his arm. He stared at her in amazement. She had never touched him before except when she had given him a stiff hug on his and Charisse's wedding day.

"I wish you two all the luck in the world," she had whispered in his ear that day, though he never believed she had meant it.

"Please hear her out," Agatha said quietly. "Give her a chance to explain herself." She let go of his arm. "I've never been one for rehab. Those television shows make it look so silly with people sitting around in circles, crying about their lives. Why can't they just stop using drugs or alcohol? Why make such a big fuss about it? That's what I always thought." She adjusted the cardigan around her neck. "Why do they feel so sorry for themselves? Why the excuses? But I think it's done wonders for Charisse. I think it's helped her to get better, Evan. She's . . . she's a changed woman."

He frowned. He highly doubted that. No amount of detox or therapy would suddenly make Charisse an angel. Besides, even if she had finally gone cold turkey and let go of the booze, his problems with her went deeper than alcohol. Their relationship had been dysfunctional for years and had finally imploded. He hoped today's meeting wasn't a misguided attempt to salvage their marriage. If it was, he'd let her know that was out of the question. He was in love with Leila. They were going to have a baby. He was moving on.

He didn't respond to Agatha. Instead, he silently followed the series of hallways to the sunroom toward the back of the house. When he opened the glass door, he found Charisse sitting on one of the wicker sofas with one leg dangling over the terracotta tile and the other on the sofa, her knee propping up an arm. A lit cigarette dangled from her fingertips and she anxiously seemed to scan her phone in her other hand. When he shut the door behind him, she looked up.

"Ev!" she said, suddenly hopping to her feet. She leaned down and extinguished her cigarette in a nearby glass ashtray. "You came!"

In the old days, even when she had her worst hangovers, she had always looked immaculate and impeccably dressed. But today she was disheveled. Her blond hair—which had grown longer in the past several months—was in a haphazard ponytail atop her head. She wore a T-shirt that was so loose it hung off one shoulder. She had on blue yoga pants and floppy sandals. She wasn't wearing makeup, but her face looked healthy—freshly scrubbed and glistening, making her seem younger than her thirty-two years.

Agatha had been right. Charisse certainly had changed—on the outside, anyway.

"Of course I came. I told you I would," he answered bluntly.

She lowered her blue eyes. "You're right. You did. It's just . . . you had rescheduled so many times that I wasn't sure if you were just going to . . . Oh, never mind." She waved her hand dismissively and gestured to an adjacent sofa. "Have a seat."

He did as she ordered. She fell back on the other sofa. The sunroom descended into an awkward silence as they gazed at one another.

Evan raised his eyebrows expectantly. "You said you wanted to talk."

"I did." She looked down at her hands and licked her lips. "I-I do want to talk . . . to you about . . . about things."

He drummed his fingers on the arm of the sofa with impatience. "What *things*, Charisse?"

"Well, part of my counseling for alcohol addiction involved coming to terms with mistakes we've made in the past. We're . . . we're not supposed to dwell on them. We can't change what's been done, but we have to acknowledge it . . . acknowledge the people we've wronged in the course of our addiction." She cleared her throat and finally raised her eyes to look at him again. "I've . . . I've wronged you, Ev."

That is the understatement of the year, he thought.

"And I'm sorry."

An apology? He stopped drumming his fingers.

Charisse had been completely unapologetic during their marriage, blaming him for her shortcomings, saying that he was the reason she was miserable. He was shocked to hear her finally take some responsibility.

"And I'm not just sorry for having an affair with Dante or being a drunk and such a shitty wife. I should have been more honest with you. That's what husbands and wives are supposed to do. I never really gave our marriage a fair chance. I hope . . . I hope you can forgive me for all that I've done."

He leaned back and sighed. "That's a lot to ask, Charisse."

"I know. I know! I don't expect you to do it overnight, b-but I don't want us to hate each other anymore. I certainly don't hate you, Ev."

He leaned forward and gazed at her. "Look, I don't hate you, either . . . not anymore, anyway. I'm past that point. I just want us to heal, get better, and move on."

"*Move on?*" She grabbed for her pack of cigarettes again and a lighter from the glass coffee table. "You mean you want to start all over again with that woman?"

"Her name is Leila," he said tightly.

She lit her cigarette and shoved it into her mouth. "You told me she was just your secretary. That nothing was going on between you."

"And there *was* nothing going on between us . . . at the time."

"At the time." She laughed coldly and took a drag from her cigarette. "But she was well on her way to becoming your mistress, right? So I called it a week early. So what!"

"And I was under the impression that you and Dante weren't fucking each other, but I was wrong, now, wasn't I?" he said bitterly. "What's your point?"

She blew smoke from the side of her mouth in an angry gust. "The point is, *Evan*, that yes, I cheated. But you cheated, too," she said, pointing her finger at him.

"You know what I did was different."

"How the hell is it different?" she shouted.

"Because I *love* her! She and I struggled with what we were doing! I bet you didn't even think twice before you fucked him. You didn't give a shit about me or our marriage! You told me so yourself!"

"Fine! Fine, Ev." She took another drag from her cigarette and blew out another gust of smoke. "You're right. Is that what you want to hear? I didn't care. I didn't think twice about being with Dante . . . but I told you, I was wrong! I know that now. But so were you! I just don't understand why it means we have to . . ."

Her words faded and he inclined his head. "It means we have to what?"

"Why it means we . . . we have to give up on each other," she said softly, making him roll his eyes. "Why can't we try to make this work?"

"Okay." He rose from the sofa, buttoning his suit jacket and shaking his head in disgust. "So that's what this is really about? You want to try to reconcile? Are you *insane*? Do you remember what our marriage was like? It was pure hell!"

"It wasn't always that way!" she cried, shooting to her feet. "We were happy once! Don't deny it! We were—"

"For a very brief period of time . . . *yes,* we were happy. But there's too much that's gone on. And damn it, I told you, I've found someone else! I'm in love with her. Leila and I are getting married!"

"You can't marry her!" she screeched, dropping her cigarette to the tiled floor. Tears pooled in her eyes. Her face flushed crimson. "You can't marry her, Evan, because you're still married to me!

You're still *my* husband, even if that bitch wants to pretend like you're not. Even if *you* want to pretend like you're not!"

His jaw clenched. She wasn't going to sign the papers. She wasn't ready to move on. He could see it on her face now. Coming here had been a total waste of time. He turned on his heel to head back to the sunroom door, but he was stopped when she suddenly grabbed the back of his jacket and then his arm.

"Evan, please! Please wait! Listen to me!"

"There's nothing to listen to," he muttered, shoving her away, but she grabbed for him again.

"When we got married, we didn't have a chance because I was messed up! I was broken!" she cried, clutching at him. She tugged at his jacket lapels and he tried to pry her thin fingers away from the fabric but her grip was unyielding. "I couldn't be a wife. I was barely a human being! I *had* to drink! I had to make myself feel better."

Oh Jesus Christ, he thought, now beyond exhausted. And now his hangover headache was worse despite the aspirin he had swallowed. How had he walked into this ambush? Why had he come here?

"Evan, I couldn't stand to look at myself. I hated everything about me! I couldn't believe I let him touch me like that. I let him do those things to me for all those years!"

Evan paused. "What the hell are you talking about? Who's *he*? Who touched you?"

"My father!" she choked, her voice hitching in her throat. "Since I was five years old . . . since I was a little girl, he abused me. He did things to me a father should . . . should never do."

Evan stilled. He stared at his wife in shock.

She finally dropped her hands from his lapels and covered her face, which was now clouded with grief and humiliation.

"It happened for years," she whispered behind her hands. "He told me not to tell Mom. He told me it was our secret. That's how we . . . That's how we bonded. He wouldn't touch me any other way. He never hugged me. Never kissed me on the cheek. But in my bedroom he would finally show me affection, so . . . so I let him. I kept our secret. Every time I'd feel so dirty afterward. *So* dirty!" She suddenly burst into fresh sobs. Her shoulders shook with each cry and she seemed to double over with them.

Evan stared at her, unsure of what to do. He started to reach for her, then felt himself being shoved aside. Agatha had swung open the sunroom door and rushed into the room. She wrapped her arms around her sobbing daughter.

"It's okay, honey," she whispered into her ear, clutching her like she was an infant. "It's okay."

Evan stared at the two women, feeling like his feet were rooted in place. Finally, he eased toward the sunroom door. They didn't seem to notice. Charisse continued to cry and Agatha continued to coo reassuring words into her ear. He stepped through the doorway and softly shut the door behind him, feeling as if a sledgehammer had just been dropped onto his head.

For the first time in a long time, Evan had no plans to go back to the office after a midday excursion. Work still awaited him on his laptop and his desk. He had a meeting scheduled with the company auditor that would have to be canceled. His mind was unfocused now, more riddled with holes than Swiss cheese. He would be useless back at the office.

After his meeting with Charisse, he stood outside Agatha McPhee's home under her portico, leaning against one of the Ionic-style columns, patiently waiting for Bill to return. He was too shaken even to make the phone call to tell Bill to come to get him earlier than planned. He finally walked toward the town car a little after two o'clock as Bill held the door open for him.

"I didn't know you had been waiting, sir." Bill's easy smile faded as he looked at his boss more closely. "Is . . . is everything okay, Mr. Murdoch?"

"Everything is fine," Evan lied before climbing inside.

He slumped into the leather car seat and stared at the car's ceiling, reflecting on everything Charisse had told him today.

He now saw her father's standoffishness toward him in a new light. Thomas McPhee hadn't been cold to Evan for years because he had thought he wasn't good enough for his daughter; it was because he had seen Evan as a competing lover. Just the thought made Evan feel nauseated. How had Charisse kept this secret for all these years? Why hadn't she told anyone? He tried to think back, to consider moments when he should have seen the signs that something was amiss between her and her father: a hand that lingered too long, a look that seemed far from fatherly, or Charisse flinch-

ing away from Tom's touch. But Evan could remember none of that. Their relationship had
seemed normal; far from warm or loving, but considering his own family background and his relationship with his own father, it hadn't raised any
alarm bells.

Worst of all, Evan felt guilt—crippling guilt.
Charisse had suffered alone, unable to confess
even to him—her husband—her shocking secret.
He had been so cruel to her, so dismissive of her
drunkenness and her behavior. He had never considered that she was self-medicating. He had never
thought she was really hurting inside.

"That still isn't the reason your marriage fell
apart," the voice in his head insisted. "Her being
abused had nothing to do with her coldness toward you or her cheating."

But did it really? Was that true? If she hadn't en-
dured those horrible things in the past, would
their marriage have turned out better?

He arrived at the Murdoch Mansion thirty minutes later and went directly to his bedroom, barely
acknowledging the greeting from his housekeeper
or the questioning look Leila's mother gave him as
he passed her in the corridor. When he entered
his bedroom, he tiredly stripped off his jacket and
tie, tossing both onto the bed. Just as he kicked off
his shoes and was about to make his way to his
walk-in closet, Leila stepped into the bedroom and
stopped midstride, looking surprised.

"Oh," she said, a smile brightening her face, "I
didn't know you were home! What are you doing
here so early?"

Leila was wearing a blouse and tweed skirt and

clutching a large leather binder. He surmised she had probably just finished a meeting with one of her new clients.

Leila was putting her graphic arts training to good use and had recently started a custom wedding invitation and stationery boutique studio, working out of an office in the guest house. Though she no longer needed to work, Leila insisted she wanted to do something productive, to earn her own money.

"I can't just sit around on my hands all day," she told him four months ago when she started the business. "I have to keep busy!"

Evan secretly suspected Leila didn't want to become a housewife again like she had been with her ex-husband. She didn't want to be financially dependent on Evan like she had been with Brad—and run the risk of having the rug pulled out from under her again.

Leila now walked toward him and lightly kissed him. He didn't return her kiss. Instead he stood immobile, like a statue.

She stepped back and stared up at him apprehensively. "What's wrong? Rough day?"

He nodded and slowly walked into his closet, turning on the overhead lights and revealing row upon row of suits, shoes, coats, and shirts. The cedar shelving seemed to tower above him, filling the space with its pungent though calming scent.

Leila tossed her binder onto the bed and followed him into his closet. She leaned against the doorframe. "What happened?" she asked softly. "Is something going on with Terry again? *Paulette?*"

He shook his head.

"There's not some big shake-up at Murdoch Conglomerated, is there?"

"No, nothing like that," he mumbled, unbuttoning his shirt.

"So, tell me!" She stepped farther into the closet and wrapped her arms around him. "Tell me what's wrong, Ev. You're never home this early, and you look so down. This isn't like you."

"I met . . ." He cleared his throat. "I met with Charisse today and . . . and she told me something I hadn't expected."

Leila furrowed her brows. She took a step back, releasing him. "Wait! You went to see Charisse today? You mean Charisse, *your wife?*"

He nodded and watched as her facial expression changed. The brightness disappeared. Her eyes went flat. She crossed her arms over her chest.

"You didn't tell me you were going to see her today."

He took off his dress shirt, revealing the white tank top underneath. He tossed it into a nearby hamper. "I didn't know I had to tell you."

"You went to see *your wife* and you didn't feel the need to tell your fiancée that?"

"You don't tell me every time you pick up the phone to talk to Brad, do you?"

She narrowed her eyes at him. She was getting pissed, but frankly so was he. Evan had come home to find solace, not to start another argument. He was too tired to argue.

"Look, Lee, it wasn't like I was taking her out for a romantic dinner, okay? I just went to see her because she wanted to talk. She's been sitting on our divorce papers, refusing to sign them because she said she needed to talk to me first. That's all! It's no big deal."

Leila sucked her teeth and glared at him, as if silently saying, "*I'll be the judge of that.*" Evan ignored her and continued to undress, removing the belt from around his waist and walking to one of the drawers in a dresser positioned in the center of the closet.

"So what did she say?" Leila cocked an eyebrow. "Did she tell you she wanted to get back together?"

He suddenly whipped around from the drawer he had just opened and stared at her. "Why'd . . . why'd you ask me that?"

"I'm not an idiot, Ev. If she hasn't signed the divorce papers yet and she keeps putting it off, it's a pretty safe assumption that she's not ready to let you go. She still wants to keep her hooks in you." She snorted. "She just can't let go of that Murdoch money, can she?"

"It's not like that! She has her own money. You know that."

"Are you . . . are you actually *defending* her?"

"I'm not defending her!" he shouted, slamming the drawer shut, startling Leila. "I'm just saying she never—"

"That woman tortured you, Ev! You said yourself that she has total contempt for you. I saw myself how she treated you. She cheated on you with Dante, for God's sake—your own brother!"

"And I cheated on her with you! I'm no better than she is."

The walk-in closet fell silent. Leila continued to stare at him in disbelief.

"Oh my God!" She lowered her arms to her

sides. She slowly shook her head. "You're having second thoughts, aren't you?"

"What? What the hell are you talking about?"

"I can see it in your eyes, Ev! You went to see Charisse and you didn't even tell me! You're defending her! Now you're claiming that you're no better than she is, which is just . . . just bullshit! You're thinking about going back to her, aren't you? Just say it!"

"Lee, you're being paranoid and delusional. You're reading shit into this that isn't there! Maybe it's your pregnancy hormones talking, because you're not making any sense!"

"I told you in the beginning that I won't go back to being anyone's mistress!" she shouted like she could no longer hear him.

"And I'm not asking you to!"

Her face contorted with pain. Her eyes began to redden, though she held back her tears. Her bottom lip began to quiver, so she tucked it into her mouth and bit down hard on the flesh. She stoically pushed back her shoulders. "If you want to leave, then *leave,* Ev. It doesn't matter that we're engaged or that I'm pregnant—"

"Lee, stop!" He grabbed her shoulders and shook her, something he had never done before, but he couldn't take this. This was his worst nightmare. "Just stop, all right? You're talking crazy!"

"I'm not talking crazy! If you want to get back with Charisse," she continued, unable to hold back the tears any longer, "I won't hold you back! Then go, goddamnit! You don't have to—"

He kissed her, hoping that would smother her

angry words, hoping that would quell her fury. He prepared himself for her to wrench her mouth from his. She would shove him away and indignantly storm out of their bedroom. But Leila didn't. Instead, she wrapped her arms around his neck and kissed him back with the same ferocity. They clung to each other, despite the anger, despite the tears. The kisses reminded them of why they were together. Not just because they loved each other— because Evan certainly loved Leila. He had since he was a boy who was too young to even articulate the emotions he felt whenever he was around her. Their fervent kisses also reminded them of the passion they shared, which was almost combustible.

Evan began to quickly undo the buttons of her blouse, popping off the bottom ones with a sharp tug when he became too impatient. She groped for his pants zipper. He shoved her skirt up her legs so that the tweed fabric was bunched at her waist.

Evan suddenly had the presence of mind to remember that both the closet door and the bedroom door were open. Leila's mother, or even Isabel, could walk into the room at any second and see them. He reached around Leila and slammed the closet door shut. He shifted them so that Leila's back was pressed firmly against the door and he was facing her. But with every step and every turn, his mouth did not leave hers.

He pushed her silk blouse from off her shoulders and let the garment fall to the floor. Rather than taking off her bra, he pulled down the straps and shoved the bra itself down to her waist, revealing her breasts. They were larger now due to the pregnancy—even the areolas. They were definitely more than a handful, and he loved it.

He caressed them, and she arched her back as they kissed, inviting his touch, pressing herself into his hands. He tugged at her panties and she took his cue—pushing them down her hips and knees and letting them slide to her ankles and fall at her feet. She kicked them aside and let them land somewhere unseen in his closet. He finished undoing his pants so that they pooled at his feet. His boxer-briefs soon followed and his erection pressed urgently against her thighs, begging to be let in.

Evan lifted one of her legs and she wrapped it around his waist. He hoisted her up a few more inches so that their torsos were level. He bore her weight as he braced her against the door for additional support. She wrapped her other leg around him, hooking her ankles together.

"Don't ever doubt that I love you," he whispered into her ear before taking her mouth in another hungry kiss. He then entered her with one swift thrust.

"Evan! Oh God!" she shouted out against his lips as he thrust into her again and again, feeling her wet warmth around him. The closet filled with their moans and shouts.

A maid who had come into the room toting a vacuum and a duster was the only person who heard them. Her heart-shaped face flushed with heat and her brown eyes widened at the sound of the tortured groans coming from Mr. Murdoch's closet and the rhythmic *thud* against the closet door, like someone was taking a battering ram to it. The maid immediately rushed out of the room, back into the west wing's corridor, almost tripping on the vacuum's electrical cord as she fled.

Twenty minutes later, both Evan and Leila sat mostly naked on the closet's carpeted floor, satiated and worn out. Leila rested her sweaty brow on Evan's shoulder.

"I'm sorry," she muttered, tiredly closing her eyes. "I shouldn't have said those things. I shouldn't have doubted you. You didn't deserve that."

Evan reached for her hand, brought it to his mouth, and kissed it. "And I should have told you that I was going to see Charisse today. I wasn't trying to keep it a secret. I just didn't . . . well, I just didn't think."

She opened her eyes and let her head rest back against the door. "Maybe it is the hormones from the pregnancy. I've been so . . . so emotional lately. But it's hard, Ev. All this stuff is really hard. I was hoping you'd be divorced in a couple of months and we could finally get married, but it doesn't look like that's going to happen. Charisse is going to drag this out. Now we'll have to postpone the wedding. Instead of your wife, I'll just be some rich guy's mistress *slash* baby mama."

"Please don't say that. Don't start that again. Charisse will grant me the divorce, Lee. She'll do it."

Eventually, he wanted to add, but didn't.

"And Izzy isn't taking any of this well. I thought she would get used to the changes, that she would grow to love her life here. I mean, we're throwing her that big birthday party next week. I thought she'd be happy, but . . ." Leila slowly shook her head. "I finally told her yesterday that we were going to have a baby . . . that she was going to be a big sister. You know what she told me?"

He pursed his lips. "I'm afraid to ask."

"'Can I go live with Daddy now since you guys will have a kid of your own?' Like the baby makes her unnecessary." Leila's face twisted with pain again. She sniffed. "Mama told me to just give her more time, not to take this stuff personally. But how could I not take it personally, Ev? My little girl would rather live on the other side of the country with that asshole than with me! I couldn't even tell her that there's no way in hell she could ever live with him since he'll probably get sentenced to jail time next month. He could be in some federal penitentiary by the end of the year."

"Then tell her that!"

Leila shook her head again. "I can't. Izzy idealizes her dad. I don't want to be the one to knock him off his pedestal. It would alienate her from me even more."

Evan disagreed. He thought Isabel should finally know how much her father had put her mother through before she finally had to leave him, how close he had pushed their little family to the precipice of bankruptcy and homelessness because of his dirty dealings and selfishness. But he knew Leila would never listen to him.

"*You're not a parent, Ev,*" she would argue. "*You don't understand.*"

So instead of pushing his opinion, he wrapped his arm around her. "Let's worry about the things we *can* control, then. Izzy may want to live with her dad, but she's still here. Maybe . . . maybe your mom is right." Something he secretly doubted. "We just have to give Izzy more time. And even if Charisse drags her feet on the divorce, I still love you. I still want you at my side no matter what. And let's not forget . . ." He dropped his hand to her bare stomach. "We're having a baby! I don't know about you, but I'm fucking ecstatic!"

For the first time, she laughed. She finally broke into a smile and his heart lightened. She gazed up at him. "Let's see if you're still 'fucking ecstatic' when that baby is screaming at the top of its lungs at two o'clock in the morning."

"I'm still excited," he whispered before lowering his mouth to hers for a kiss.

She kissed him back and for a blissful moment, all their worries went away.

Chapter 13
Paulette

Paulette walked out of the examination room with her head bowed and her shoulders slumped.

She was now going to the doctor once a week and undergoing ultrasound after ultrasound. She had done a stress test, undergone an amniocentesis, was seeing a nutrition specialist, and had orders to be on modified bed rest, but her little boy was still too small for his gestational age, the specialist had told her with a frown. To make matters worse, she had developed high blood pressure and was starting to show early signs of preeclampsia.

More bad news, she thought sadly.

Her life was already falling apart and now her body was starting to take a tumble off a cliff too.

"Paulette?" someone called to her as she stepped listlessly into the waiting room.

Paulette was startled out of her stupor. She

looked up and saw Leila waving her hand wildly and rising from one of the waiting room chairs.

"Hey, girl! What are you doing here?" Leila asked as she strode toward her.

Paulette forced a smile, fighting down her panic. She hadn't expected Leila to be here. "Uh, just . . . just going to the doctor," she mumbled as Leila hugged her and kissed her on the cheek.

Leila stepped back and laughed. "Well, that makes sense considering where we are! But what are you doing in *here?* I thought all the docs in this practice were obstetricians." Leila paused. Her eyes widened to the size of saucers. "Wait, are you . . . are you pregnant? You mean to tell me you're pregnant, *too?* That's so ex—"

"No!" Paulette's tense smile broadened. "No, of course not! I was just here for a . . . a checkup. I mean, I was consulting with one of the . . . one of the doctors to ask how I could get pregnant in the . . . uh . . . in the future. Just in case Tony and I want to . . . to try to get pregnant . . . someday, b-but not n-n-now!" she stuttered.

Leila's face fell. "Here I was thinking we were pregnant at the same time." She poked out her lip in an exaggerated pout and laughed again. "I already had visions of us pushing around running strollers together. I thought I finally had someone to commiserate with about morning sickness and sore boobs."

Paulette shook her head. "Sorry to disappoint you. Maybe I'll get pregnant soon, though."

"Oh, it's not a big deal!" Leila said, waving her hand. "Besides, you guys just got married last year. You've got plenty of time! There's no rush to—"

"Mrs. Williams," a nurse in periwinkle blue scrubs suddenly called out from the opened door leading back to the examination rooms, "you forgot this, ma'am!"

Both Paulette and Leila turned to find the nurse holding up what was quite clearly an ultrasound printout. Paulette's mouth fell open. She rushed across the waiting room and snatched the printout from the nurse's hand, hoping Leila hadn't seen what it was. She quickly shoved it into the depths of her leather hobo bag.

"Thank you," she mumbled to the nurse before turning back around to face Leila. When she saw the look on Leila's face, she knew that her hope that Leila hadn't noticed what was on the printed pages had been futile. Her surrogate big sister had definitely seen the ultrasound. Leila's face morphed from shock to confusion.

"I thought . . . I thought you said you weren't pregnant."

Paulette took a deep breath. "I did," she whispered.

"So whose ultrasound is that?"

Paulette slowly walked toward her. "Lee, let me explain."

"What is there to explain? You're pregnant and you're lying about it for some reason. *Why?*"

"Can we not talk about this right here . . . right *now?*" Paulette glanced anxiously at the other women in the waiting room. They were all staring at the duo, not bothering to pretend that they weren't watching. "I'll try to explain what I can, b-but just not here with all these people around."

Leila crossed her arms over her chest obstinately. "Fine. I was fifteen minutes early for my appointment. I've got some time. Where do you wanna go?"

Five minutes later Leila and Paulette walked into the complex's center courtyard. A brick walkway bordered by flowering dogwoods and planters filled with marigolds, geraniums, and ferns wound its way toward a man-made pond that trickled softly. The two women sat on a metal bench facing the pond. The sun was shining. A light breeze made the weather seem balmy. The space was beautiful, too, but none of this lightened Paulette's mood. She felt sick to her stomach. A burning formed in her chest and she was sure it wasn't indigestion from the pregnancy. She was terrified. She would finally have to reveal her secret to someone besides her doctors. Paulette stared at her lap, not knowing where to start.

"So, you're pregnant . . ." Leila began for her.

Paulette nodded, her eyes still focused on her lap.

"Does Tony know?"

Paulette hesitated, then shook her head.

"Well, when do you plan to tell him? Why haven't you at least told him, even if you're keeping it a secret from everyone else?"

Paulette didn't answer. She loudly swallowed instead.

"Honey, you can't keep this a secret forever. You know that! You're going to start showing soon!" Leila then narrowed her eyes at Paulette's stomach. "How far along are you, anyway? I couldn't even tell you were pregnant."

"I'm . . . I'm twenty-seven weeks."

"Twenty-seven weeks! So you're . . . what? Six months pregnant now?"

"Almost seven," Paulette whispered, clutching her stomach. The baby shifted, jutting either his little foot or elbow into her rib cage.

Leila stared at her in amazement. "How could you possibly be almost seven months? I was twice your size when I was pregnant with Izzy!"

"I've hidden it well, I guess," Paulette confessed, finally raising her gaze. "I've been wearing baggy clothes since the beginning of the pregnancy. Plus, the doctor says the baby is . . . he's running a little small. Well, more than just a little. I guess that's why I'm not showing that much."

"But why are you hiding your baby at all, Paulette? Why haven't you told anyone when you're this far along? I still don't understand!"

"Because I . . ." She pursed her lips. "Because I don't know who the father is. I don't know if it's Antonio's baby."

"Oh my God!" Leila slumped back onto the bench. "Are you kidding me? You're not trying to tell me that you think it might be that guy's . . . your ex-boyfriend . . . what's his face?"

"Marques," Paulette said, almost choking on his name.

She wished she could erase the name Marques Whitney from her memory, but she couldn't. He seemed to be omnipresent in her life even though he was long dead, and if she was carrying his baby, he would be a permanent presence, as well.

"I cannot believe I'm hearing this." Leila slowly shook her head in denial. "I knew it! I knew that guy was bad news! Damn it, Paulette, I wish you would have—"

"Listened to you when you warned me to tell the police he was blackmailing me? Listened to you when you told me to tell Marques to go to hell? Yes, Leila, I know now that was probably what I *should* have done, but none of that matters now, does it? What matters now is that I'm pregnant and you know that I'm pregnant. If you care about me . . . if you care about my marriage to Tony . . . you'll let me handle this *my* way. I'm doing this the best way that I can."

"*By what?* Waiting until you're ready to deliver to finally tell Antonio and everyone else the truth? That's ridiculous!"

"Will you or won't you keep my secret, Lee? I need to know."

Leila licked her lips, closed her eyes, and bowed her head. "No."

Paulette frowned. Had she heard Leila correctly? "Did you just say 'no'?"

Leila opened her eyes and nodded. She met Paulette's gaze. "Yes, I told you no. No, I'm not keeping this secret. The abortion you had when you were sixteen . . . the affair you had with Marques . . . the blackmailing . . . I didn't tell anyone because you begged me not to. But every secret I've kept has made things worse for you, Paulette, not better . . . and I've lived every day with the guilt that comes with that. It's isolated you from your brothers. It's alienating you from Tony. You're nearly seven months' pregnant and you're hiding it, for Christ's sake! I'm not doing this again!"

"But it could end my marriage, Lee! You don't understand everything that's happened! Antonio could—"

"No," Leila said firmly. "I said no! Either you 'fess up to everyone, or I will."

Paulette fell silent.

Leila glanced down at her watch. "Look, I have to get back upstairs, or I'll miss my appointment. I'll give you a little time to tell Tony first. But after that, I . . . I can't anymore."

Paulette continued to clutch her stomach protectively, feeling her baby shift yet again. Leila was going to tell everyone the truth. The prospect left Paulette frozen with terror. In her periphery she watched as Leila stood from the bench and began to follow the brick pathway back to the complex's entrance. Leila paused and turned back to face Paulette.

"Even if you hate me now, know that I'm doing this because I care about you," Leila called to her. "Please . . . just tell Tony the truth. Tell him everything. If he forgave you before, he'll do it again. Just give him a chance."

Leila then turned back around and rushed toward the automatic doors.

Paulette could feel her eyes dampen with tears. She had unburdened herself and told Antonio the truth before—and what had it gotten her? A marriage on the brink of divorce, a dead lover, and a husband who could possibly face murder charges someday.

But now, because Leila refused to keep her secret, Paulette would have to walk into the fire again. She raised her hands to her face and wept silently in the courtyard. She didn't know how she was going to do this, but it looked like she had no choice but to try.

As she drove home, Paulette practiced the words over and over again in her head.

"Tony, I have something to tell you. It's something I should have told you long ago, but I was so scared," she whispered as she turned the corner that led to their neighborhood. "I . . . I'm pregnant."

As she said the word *pregnant*, she braced herself inevitably for the next obvious question.

"*Is it mine?*" he would ask.

"*I don't know,*" she would have to answer.

Just envisioning the scene made her flinch at the imaginary hand Antonio would pull back and slap squarely across her face. He had never hit her before, but there was a first time for everything. She sighed. Even practicing it aloud didn't make having to do this any easier.

Paulette gazed out the windshield at the rows upon rows of orderly lawns, immaculate hedges, luxury cars parked in driveways, and three-story colonials that were almost mirror images of each other. She wondered as she drove if the people inside those houses had lives that were as complicated as her own, if her neighbors had secrets they were terrified to share with the world. How would they face a challenge like the one she faced today?

As Paulette made a right turn onto her block, she wondered if Antonio would arrive home on time from work. Or would she have to wait for him for hours, sitting alone in the house biting her nails, wondering if Leila had already told Evan and if Evan had already told Terry? Would she be left alone to wonder how long it would take for the news to make its way back to her husband?

Her house finally came into view. She instantly spotted Antonio's silver Mercedes sedan parked in the driveway and her heart began to race. Her grip on the steering wheel tightened.

"What the hell is he doing home this early?" a panicked voice in her head shouted.

She soon got her answer as she drew closer and realized another car was parked beside Antonio's, an unmarked navy blue Ford Taurus. From the license plate, she knew it was the car driven by Detective Nola—the detective who was investigating Marques's murder and who wanted to talk to Antonio.

Suddenly, revealing that she was pregnant became a low priority.

"Oh shit! Oh shit! Oh shit!" she muttered over and over again. She almost hit Antonio's rear bumper before remembering to slam on the brakes. Her car lurched to a stop and she narrowly missed hitting her chin on the steering wheel. She threw the car into Park and frantically began to remove her seatbelt. Less than a minute later, she was running as fast as her pregnant body would allow to her front door. She tried to unlock it, but she dropped her keys twice with a clatter, too flustered to hold the house key still enough to insert it into the lock. When she bent down to her welcome mat to retrieve them the second time, the door slowly swung open before her.

Paulette looked up to find Antonio and Detective Nola standing in the doorway.

"Thank you for your time, Mr. . . ." Detective Nola was in the middle of saying before he paused to stare at Paulette quizzically.

Antonio cocked an eyebrow. "What are you doing?"

"I dropped . . . I dropped my keys," she mumbled before blowing at the hair that had fallen into her eyes and slowly standing upright. Her gaze darted from the detective to Antonio and back again.

What had they talked about? What had Antonio told him? Did he tell Detective Nola that he couldn't confirm her alibi? Was she or her husband about to go to jail?

"Good to see you again, Mrs. Williams," Detective Nola said, all the while boring into her with those intense blue eyes.

"Good to see you, too," she whispered reflexively, though it was far from the truth.

He turned to look up at Antonio. "If I have any further questions, I'll be in touch."

Antonio nodded. "You know where to find us, Detective."

They both watched as Detective Nola made his way down their brick walkway to the driveway. He then opened his car door. Paulette's gaze stayed locked on the Ford Taurus until it finally pulled off. When it disappeared around the corner, she whipped around to look at her husband.

"What did you tell him?" she asked, unable to hide the alarm in her voice.

Antonio casually stepped back into the foyer.

"Why didn't you tell me a detective wanted to talk to me?" he asked in return instead of answering her question.

Paulette followed him inside and loudly swallowed. She shut the front door behind her.

The foyer lights were off. Only a shaft of light came from the kitchen and murky light filtered through the curtains of the windows along the foyer so that Antonio stood mostly in shadow. She could barely see his face. At that moment, he was a looming figure in the dark.

"I didn't . . . I didn't want to get you involved," she answered shakily.

"But I *am* involved, aren't I?" He took a step toward her. "That guy is dead and the police still don't know who killed him. They're trying to pin the blame on somebody. I'm surprised it took them this long to figure out your connection to him but"—he shrugged—"then again, I didn't figure it out either, did I? Makes me feel a lot less stupid if even the cops didn't realize you two were having an affair. I'm not the only fool around here."

She lowered her eyes. She guessed she deserved that jab.

"I didn't tell you that the detective wanted to talk to you because . . . because he needed you to verify that I was at home on the night of the murder. But I knew you . . ." Her words drifted off.

"You knew that I what?"

"I knew that you couldn't." She took a deep breath and raised her eyes. "You weren't home that night."

She watched as he inclined his head. "So . . . where do you think I was?"

"I . . . I have no idea. You wouldn't answer my phone calls."

"Do you think I was at that guy's apartment?"

She didn't answer him. She couldn't answer without lying to him again or accusing him of something that was too horrible to consider.

"You think I murdered him, don't you?" He took another step toward her and she took a step back, almost bumping into the front door.

That was all the answer he needed.

Antonio suddenly reached for her and she moaned. She shifted her purse to cover her baby. She turned her face away to prepare herself for the impending blow. But instead of hitting her, instead of even touching her, he flicked the metal switch near her shoulder. The foyer was illuminated with light from the overhead chandelier. She could clearly see Antonio's face now. He didn't look angry. Instead, he looked sad and hurt.

"Do you really want to know where I was that night, Paulette? I was at my mom's. I lay awake in that little-ass bed in my old room for hours, thinking about what had happened. I couldn't believe you had cheated on me . . . and not just once, but for *months!* How the hell could you do that? I loved you. I damn near *adored* you and you did that to me!"

Her eyes dampened with tears again. She dropped her purse from her stomach, feeling ashamed that she had thought he was going to hurt her. "I'm so sorry, Tony. I didn't—"

"And you cheated on me with some blackmailing, do-rag-wearing thug! You broke my goddamn heart for a sorry son of a bitch like that piece of shit! You stomped it into pieces! So that night I lay awake, deciding whether I would end our marriage or come home and try . . . *try* to make this work. I decided that, unlike you, I would stick to my vows—because I had promised to stick with you for better or for worse. I would try again. I came back." He glared at her. "*That's* where I was that night, Paulette. *That's* where I was when I wasn't answering my phone!"

It all made sense now. He went to stay at Reina's house and his mother had probably welcomed him with open arms.

"*What did that mean ol' bitch do to my boy?*" Reina would have asked.

Of course that was the first place Antonio would go if something went wrong in his life and he could no longer turn to his wife. How could Paulette have doubted him?

"So now you know where I was and why I came back. You know why I stayed, but what I can't figure out is why the hell you stay."

She frowned. "What do you mean?"

"Why the fuck are you still here if you think you're living with a murderer?" he shouted, then shook his head. "I saw the look on your face! You thought I was going to do something . . . that I was going to hurt you. How can you sleep in the same house with someone you're afraid of?"

She stared at him in amazement. Did he really have to ask her that question? Wasn't it obvious?

"Because . . . because I love you, Tony," she answered softly.

He took a step back. His eyes flooded with emotions—heartbreak, longing, and maybe even love—then they went flat again. His expression hardened.

"Yeah, I'd like to believe that, but if you really loved me, you wouldn't have done what you did, Paulette. You wouldn't have lied to me all that time." He turned around and headed to the staircase. "I left work early to do the interview with the detective, but I still have a few things to finish up. I'll be in my office."

He bounded up the stairs, taking them two at a time. He abruptly paused to look back at her. "I lied to the detective, by the way," he said over his shoulder. "I told him I was home the whole night. Your alibi is covered." He then continued to climb to the second floor.

When she heard his office door slam shut, Paulette let her purse drop to the floor and her head fall back against the door.

Chapter 14

Terrence

Terrence sat poolside, reclined on a beach chair, watching as more than a dozen or so kids splashed and yelled as they played and tossed beach balls into the water. One did a cannonball off the springboard. Another shot a double-barreled water gun at a little girl with cornrows who screamed with delight. Two sat on the edge of the pool, sucking from helium balloons and talking to each other in cartoonish voices.

Just as many adults stood along the edge of the Olympic-sized pool, mingling and enjoying hors d'oeuvres that Terrence suspected probably weren't usually served at eight-year-olds' birthday parties. He thought he could safely assume that boudin balls and charbroiled oysters weren't on the menu at Chuck E. Cheese's.

Most of the parents tried to look blasé and casual as the children played, though a few of the adults and kids stared at the sights around them, absolutely gobsmacked.

Terrence drank from his beer bottle and chuckled as he watched them. They had a right to look stunned. Even when he stepped through the doors of Murdoch Mansion and saw all the decorations and hubbub, his mouth had fallen open.

It looked like Evan and Leila had gone above and beyond for Isabel's party. In addition to more than a hundred or so helium balloons and streamers, there was also a hip-hop DJ blasting tunes, a three-foot-tall cupcake tower, a mini-carousel ride near the tennis courts, a clown, a juggler, and a mini petting zoo with a pony and donkey available for rides. They had also set up cabanas alongside the pool where the parents were served signature cocktails and lobster and the kids sampled corn-dogs and popcorn.

Terrence smiled and sucked his fingers as he finished the last of his lobster po'boy. His empty plate was promptly taken away by a waiter dressed like Jafar from the movie *Aladdin*. He hadn't seen a party this big since his sister's wedding. Terrence glanced to his side just as Evan plopped onto the beach chair next to him. His smile widened into a grin.

"You went all-out for this one, Ev," Terrence said, nudging his brother's shoulder. "Is a marching band going to show up next, or the Rockettes?"

"Who knows?" Evan muttered flippantly. "We've got everything just short of a marching band and the Rockettes, but my instructions were to give Isabel pretty much whatever she wanted for her birthday party."

Terrence narrowed his eyes. "Lee said that? *Leila Hawkins?*"

Evan nodded while still gazing at the throng. He took a sip from the water bottle he was holding. Even the bottle was emblazoned with Isabel's name and custom-made emblem.

"That doesn't sound like Lee. I thought she didn't believe in spoiling her kid."

Evan loudly grumbled, "Yeah, that used to be the case . . . but Isabel seems to have mastered the art of emotional blackmail. She told Leila the other day that she wants to live with her father from now on. That made Leila so terrified that she's on a mission to prove to Isabel that she'll be happier here living with us. Hence"—Evan gestured to the party around them—"kiddie lollapalooza."

"But Isabel can't live with him anyway, though, right? I thought he was going to prison soon."

"You know that. I know that. Hell, I think Leila even knows it on some level. But she still wants to make her daughter happy. I've stopped arguing or asking questions." He slid further down in his chair so that he was almost lying on his back. "I just write the checks."

"Well, okie dokie then," Terrence said over the sounds of squeals and laughter echoing off the room's vaulted ceilings. He watched as a seven-year-old back-flipped into the pool. "Speaking of writing checks . . . do you mind if I borrow your driver tomorrow night? I'll pay you back."

"He's my driver, not my slave, Terry. You pay him for his services, not me."

"But I wanted to check with you first . . . to make sure you didn't need him tomorrow if he and I can work something out."

"Nope, I don't need him." He then turned to Terrence. "Why do you need a driver tomorrow night? Where you headed?"

"I've got a date," Terrence said before taking another drink of his beer.

"*A date?* Is this with the same woman you mentioned before? The one you ran into at the charity banquet and met up with later for coffee?"

Terrence raised his brows. "I didn't know you were paying such close attention to my love life, Ev."

Evan chuckled. "Sorry, I'm not trying to be a mother hen. It's just that after the accident you pretty much stopped dating for a while. I'm glad to see you getting back out there." Evan sat upright. "So, is it the same woman?"

Terrence nodded. "Yeah, it's the same."

"So you *are* getting back into the game!" Evan's face brightened as he held his fist toward Terrence. Terrence reluctantly gave him a fist bump. "Good to hear you're back on the prowl, boy."

Terrence's smile stayed firmly in place, though Evan's comment made him uncomfortable. He didn't know if he would refer to his impending date with C. J. Aston as signaling he was "back on the prowl."

C. J. was different from the women he usually dated. She was just as sexy, if not in the typical runway beauty or video vixen sort of way. But she was also smart, funny, classy, and shy—and she seemed

to be completely unaware of how all that com-
bined to make her a real spell-caster. Terrence was
finding it hard getting her out of his mind. He still
remembered her laugh—like tinkling piano keys
that went up and down the scale—the way her eyes
crinkled when she smiled, and how she would twirl
a curl around her finger when she got anxious or
flustered. Frankly, he couldn't wait to see her again.

"I'll let Bill know you want to hire him for tomorrow night," Evan said. "I'm sure he'd be happy
to do it."

"Thanks," Terry said. He then turned to look toward the room's entrance, where their sister,
Paulette, now stood holding a giant silver gift box
with a pink bow on top. He caught her gaze and
waved at her. She waved back and smiled timidly.

Paulette had never been a particularly confident woman, but in the past year or so, she seemed
even less so. Her shoulders were always slumped
and her head always hung a little low. She didn't
wear that much makeup or style her hair like she
once did. Her clothes looked drab, little more
than potato sacks made out of expensive fabric.

Terrence knew that her marriage with Antonio
had gone through a rough period. Paulette had
cheated on him and confessed. But they were still together. They had worked it out—or at least, that's
what the rest of the family had assumed. Terrence
now wondered if what was going on between
Paulette and Antonio was the reason for her un-
usual behavior. Was that the reason for the change
in his little sister?

He watched as Leila walked toward her. Paulette's
smile faded. The two women started to talk. As they

did, Paulette's brows lowered. Her lips tightened. Leila's back was facing him so he couldn't see her face, but he could see the muscles in her back go rigid. Her fists were balled at her sides.

"Oh man," Terrence muttered. "What's going on over there?"

"Huh?" Evan turned and looked in the same direction where Terrence was looking. He frowned as he also watched Leila and Paulette's exchange. "I don't know. They aren't arguing, are they?"

It certainly looked like they were arguing. Suddenly, Paulette shoved the gift at Leila, almost knocking the other woman back a step. She turned on her heel and marched right back through the pool room's entryway into the corridor.

"What the hell . . ." Evan murmured just as Terrence grabbed his cane and hoisted himself to his feet.

Terrence rushed as fast as his bad leg would allow toward the entrance, almost getting sideswiped by three roughhousing boys along the way. Evan was right behind him. They both reached Leila, who glared down at the gift in her hands, looking like she was on the verge of tossing it into the pool.

"What happened?" Evan cried.

"Why'd Paulette leave?" Terrence asked at the same time.

Leila looked up at them both. Her eyes were pink and brimming with tears. She quickly shook her head. "Nothing. Paulette just . . . she said she couldn't stay," she mumbled before walking away, clutching the present in her arms.

Evan's face crumpled in confusion. He threw up his hands. "What the hell is going on?"

"You deal with Lee. I'll go talk to Paulette," Terrence said to Evan before walking into the corridor. He caught a glimpse of his sister just as she strode around the corner. "Hey, Sweet Pea . . . I mean, Paulette! Paulette, wait up!"

She didn't stop, making him roll his eye in exasperation. "I'm handicapped, damn it," he mumbled as he followed her. "Don't make me chase you."

He finally caught up with her just as she reached the front door. She waved away a complimentary gift bag that was being handed out to all the party guests. She was pulling her car keys from her purse when she noticed Terrence coming toward her.

"Paulette," he said, almost gasping. He bore his weight on his cane and paused to catch his breath. "Didn't you hear me calling you?"

She shook her head. "No, sorry, Terry. I was a little . . ." She flapped her arms helplessly. "I was a little distracted."

He took a step toward her. "Why'd you rush out like that? What's wrong?"

"Nothing's wrong! I just . . . I just wanted to drop off the gift for Isabel. I didn't have time to stay for the party. That's . . . that's all."

He could tell she was lying. It was written all over her face.

"Well, can you stay a bit longer to talk to your big bro? I haven't seen you in a while." He reached out and rubbed her shoulder. "Come back to the party and stay just for ten . . . maybe fifteen minutes. You can spare that, right?"

She pursed her lips and tugged her purse strap

further up her arm. She hesitated, like she was contemplating his offer, but she shook her head again. "I really should get going. I don't—"

"What's going on?" he asked, deciding to stop beating around the bush. "What were you and Leila arguing about? Is that why you want to leave?"

A panicked expression flashed across her face. She blinked rapidly. "We weren't . . . we weren't arguing about anything! I t-t-told you, n-nothing is going on, Terry."

"Yes, there is. Something has been going on with you for months now, and I want to know what it is."

Paulette hesitated again. She stared at him grimly. He saw so much pain in her dark eyes, like she was carrying the weight of the world on her diminutive shoulders and couldn't spare an ounce. He had seen the same look in his own eyes whenever he gazed into the mirror a month or so ago, before he started therapy. Some days he still saw it when he wondered if he would ever be the same man that he had once been.

Paulette opened her mouth and Terrence leaned forward to hear her, prepared for whatever she might say. But suddenly two little girls came screaming down the hall into the foyer. They rushed past Paulette and Terrence with their parents trailing behind them, holding the strings to helium balloons and reaching for one of the gift bags.

The opportunity had passed. Paulette's mask went up again. She forced a smile.

"Really, I'm okay, Terry. I just have to run a few

quick errands so I can get back home to freshen up. I'm supposed to meet Tony. We're . . . we're supposed to go out to dinner and a movie tonight."

Terrence slowly nodded. "Okay. I'll let you go, then. I won't hold you up."

"You're the best, Terry." She stood on the balls of her feet and kissed him lightly on the cheek. "I'll see you later." She then headed toward the front door.

"But if you need to talk, you know where to find me," he called out to her, making her pause.

"Of course I do," she said before stepping through the door.

"Penny for your thoughts," C. J. said as she reclined back on her elbows and gazed up at him.

Terrence turned away from the giant movie screen to look at her. The shadows from the screen's black and white film danced across her face. "Huh?" He absently waved away a gnat that had been buzzing around his ear.

"You're *way* too engrossed in this movie, Terry. It's good, but it's not *that* good." A smile spread across her full pink lips. She pushed herself up so they were sitting eye to eye. "What's on your mind?"

They were watching a movie on one of the Jumbotrons set up in one of the fields in Macon Park in Chesterton. It was part of a movie festival featuring old Hollywood films. When Terrence discovered C. J. was a film buff, he knew this would be a perfect date for them. He planned a romantic evening watching *Casablanca* and *From Here to Eternity* while they lay on a wool blanket drinking Cabernet, nibbling gourmet cheese and strawberries, and kissing beneath the twinkling stars. He had even chosen a secluded spot near an old maple tree, away from all the other couples and families, to give them a bit of privacy.

Unfortunately, Terrence seemed to be screwing up the date by allowing his mind to wander.

"I'm sorry." He reached for her hand and squeezed it. "I apologize for being so distracted. I'm just worried about my sister."

She frowned. "Is everything okay with her?"

"She's just . . . going through some stuff. Though she won't tell anyone what that stuff is. She tends to hold a lot of things inside, which isn't healthy. But I guess we all do it in our family. Our dad kinda taught us to."

C. J. slowly nodded. "I know what you mean. My dad's the same way." She adjusted her sweater and sipped from her wineglass. "He gives new meaning to the words *emotionally crippled.*"

"The same for my dad . . . and for all of us, really. To make things worse, Paulette's become pretty secretive lately. But I guess that's just how she deals with things."

"For some people it's just easier to keep secrets, Terry. It's nothing personal. It can get complicated when you put everything out in the open."

He narrowed his eye at her and smiled. "You sound like you're speaking from experience."

C. J. blinked. She loudly cleared her throat. "Uh, no! Not really. I'm just saying that I can see your sister's side . . . a little." She suddenly grabbed for a slice of Gouda and a cracker that sat on the plate between them and shoved both into her mouth.

"Well, therapy has taught me the opposite. In most cases, honesty is the best policy. I've learned to put stuff out in the open. It's worse when you keep shit bottled up inside."

She stopped chewing and stared at him. *"You're* in therapy?"

He laughed. "Why'd you say it like that? *Yes,* I am in therapy. Is that so hard to believe?"

"No, but . . ." She shrugged. "You just don't seem like that type of guy. I can't envision you sitting on a therapist's couch pouring your heart out. It just doesn't seem like . . . your type of thing."

He inclined his head and sighed before reaching for his wineglass and taking a drink. "It wasn't my thing—less than a year ago. But after the accident, I changed. I had to."

She slid across the blanket closer to him and he caught a whiff of her perfume. "Why did you have to change?"

"Before the accident, I wasn't a guy who delved too deeply into things, but frankly, I didn't have to. I thought I had everything I wanted. Hell, I *got* everything I wanted! Cars, clothes, women . . . I didn't even have to try very hard. I was rich. I was easy on the eyes. Stuff just . . . came to me." When he saw her raise her brows sardonically, he held up his hands in protest. "Hey, I'm not boasting! I'm just stating the God's honest truth. That's how my life was!"

"Oh, I believe you," she mumbled flatly. "Trust me."

"But after the accident," he explained, "things changed. I lost my left eye. It took some painful physical therapy to be able to walk again, even with a cane, and I've still got this damn limp. I got sued. I couldn't just throw money at my problems anymore and make everything better. My good looks didn't mean shit anymore. I went from being admired to being pitied, and my pride took a beating." He paused. "I was in a . . . a very dark place, C. J. I wouldn't leave my condo. I stopped talking to everyone. I just sat in the dark and drank and felt sorry for myself. I guess that's what happens to shallow people when their world falls apart. You don't know how to cope. I didn't put a gun to my head, but you might as well say I was just waiting around to die."

Her breath hitched audibly in her throat. She placed a hand on his shoulder.

"I'm so sorry, Terry," she whispered.

His skin tingled where she touched him. He wanted to turn and kiss her, but C. J. sometimes turned skittish whenever he tried to make a move on her. On their first date he had leaned in for a kiss and she had backed away in surprise. To cover it up, he gave her a halfhearted hug good-bye and walked away muttering to himself. He hadn't tried to kiss her since.

He didn't want to ruin the moment again by being too overeager.

"It's okay," he said, turning his gaze away from her mouth. "Ev gave me a wake-up call and I finally manned up and took responsibility for myself, for my life. I was diagnosed with depression. I started seeing a therapist. I got better . . . well, I'm *getting* better. I still have moments when . . ."

He couldn't finish.

His eyes shifted away from her and he gazed at the movie screen where Humphrey Bogart was staring at Ingrid Bergman with the same longing that Terrence now felt for the woman beside him.

Pace yourself, Rick, Terrence thought, warning Bogart's character. *You don't want to scare her off.*

"You still have moments when . . . what?" C. J. asked, drawing even closer to him. He felt the warmth radiating off of her now.

Terrence took a deep breath. "When I wonder if I'll ever feel normal or whole again."

They both fell silent.

This time Terrence was the one who was caught by surprise when C. J. raised a hand to his cheek. He turned to face her.

"Terry," she whispered, "I don't know what your definition of 'normal' or 'whole' is. But the guy you are now, I think is wonderful. I wouldn't change him. I hope you wouldn't, either."

She then brought her mouth to his for a soul-stirring kiss that would leave them both weak-kneed and breathless for minutes after.

Chapter 15

Dante

Dante finished the last of his Scotch, shook the glass so that the ice cubes tinkled like brass bells, slammed the glass back to the tabletop, and slid across the booth's leather seat. He had just finished a meeting with one of his clients—a slob who had slipped and fallen on a pool of pickle juice in a grocery store and displaced a disc in his spine. He was now on workman's comp and hobbling around on crutches.

"Haven't been able to show up to the factory for fuckin' three weeks!" the guy had exclaimed an hour ago before throwing back the Stella Artois that Dante had ordered for him. He had then let out a loud, rumbling belch. Several diners at the supper club had stared at the man in disgust.

Dante had ignored their stares. What did he care that his client had shown up to one of the best restaurants in D.C. with stains on his shirt? Or that he smelled of chicken grease and dirt or had the table manners of a bear cub? This guy was potentially worth a half million dollars in legal fees. Dante could put up with almost anything for that much money!

Dante now rose to his feet and began to weave his way through the dining tables back toward the restaurant entrance, but he paused when he spotted two familiar faces at a nearby table. It was his half-brothers, Evan and Terrence. He had no idea why they were in the city tonight or why they were dining at this particular restaurant. But the instant he saw them, he saw red.

He hadn't been in the same room with his brothers in more than six months, not since they had ambushed him at an empty coffee shop where he thought he was meeting Paulette to discuss the details of her selling her Murdoch Conglomerated shares to him. She had been there—but she hadn't come alone. Her two bouncers Terrence and Evan were in tow. The woman seemed incapable of doing anything or making any damn decisions on her own.

Evan had sat in the center of his siblings at the metal bistro table, looking like some drug lord, and he had read Dante the riot act, telling him to stay away from their family and never to come back again.

Dante now glared across the restaurant at his brothers, watching them as they talked and laughed, as they drank from their wineglasses and ate their entrées. He knew he should keep walking. Nothing could be accomplished by talking to them, by taunting them into an argument or a fight. But then he remembered Evan's last words to him: *"Take your 'poor me' routine and your chip on your shoulder and get the fuck out."* Evan had dismissed him much like their father had two years ago. Just thinking back to those words infuriated Dante all over again. What gave Evan the right? Who did he think he was? He wished he could knock the smile right off of Evan's smug face. He wished he could throttle him, stab him, beat him, and hold up his mangled body for everyone in the restaurant to see.

For those reasons Dante felt almost a magnetic pull drawing him toward their table. He bumped into a waiter carrying a tray of dishes and glasses and did not excuse himself. He pushed his way past an old woman who paused in rising from her chair to glare at him with outrage. Finally he reached his half-brothers' table and stood silently in front of them until Terrence turned and looked up. The younger man's laughter died on his lips at the sight of him.

"You're in a good mood for someone who's being sued for four million dollars," Dante said, pasting on a Cheshire cat grin.

Terrence didn't respond. He only lowered his wineglass back to the table along with the eye that wasn't covered with an eye patch. In contrast, Evan leaned back in his chair and glowered at Dante with unconcealed hatred.

"So, how have you been, Terry?" Dante asked, thumping him on the shoulder. "And where's Paulette?" He made a show of looking around the crowded restaurant. "I don't see her anywhere. I would think she would be here, too. I know how the Marvelous Murdochs like to travel in packs."

"What the fuck do you want?" Evan snarled.

Dante raised his brows and chuckled. "Oh, *language!* Language, Evan! You're in a nice establishment. Don't talk like that here! What would Leila think?" He clucked his tongue. "On second thought, she might not mind. Leila's no saint either." He winked at Evan. "We both know that, don't we?"

Dante had dated Leila briefly before she began her affair with Evan. She had broken it off with Dante before they had the chance to get serious—and before he had the chance to use her the way he'd intended. It still enraged him to this day. He hadn't slept with her, but he always loved the look on Evan's face when he insinuated that he had.

Evan angrily started to rise from the table, but Terrence stopped him by clamping a hand around his wrist, giving his older brother a warning look. "Don't let him do it, Ev. You know what his game is."

Dante's smile widened. "You should listen to him."

"I probably should," Evan muttered as he lowered himself back into his chair and Terrence released him, "but frankly, every time I see you, I can't decide between punching you in your face and recommending a good therapist to you."

"Oh, come on!" Dante rolled his eyes. "We all know you would never hit me. Guys like you don't get their hands dirty."

Evan balled his fists on the white linen tablecloth. A vein bulged along his temple. "You never know. I might surprise you."

"Look, man," Terrence interceded, staring up at Dante, "why don't you just move it the hell along and go somewhere else? Hell, go *anywhere* else! You're not going to bait us into any shit tonight! If you've got something to say to me, you can say it in the courtroom."

"You really want to take it that far? If a judge had to side with poor Mavis Upton or a self-entitled rich boy like yourself, who do you think he's going to choose?" Dante snickered. "That eye patch and cane aren't going to get you that much sympathy."

"Who said I wanted sympathy?" Terrence asked tightly.

"I'm just saying that you might want to consider settling out of court . . . if you're smart."

"Uh-huh," Terrence grunted. "Says the dude who stands to benefit the most from that settlement!"

"You really think I give a shit about making money off of this?" Dante asked, leaning against the table. "You Murdochs are so fucking predictable! You always think it's just about the money!"

Diners at neighboring tables began to look at the three men uneasily. A waiter paused to stare at them.

"Well, you aren't doing it because you care about ol' Miss Mavis. If you claim you are, you're a damn liar!" Terrence barked.

"Of course I don't care about her! I'm more interested in watching you dangle like a worm on a hook."

Terrence slowly shook his head in bemusement. "Man, what is your problem? Are you really this hell-bent on revenge? Revenge for shit that I didn't . . . that *none* of us did to you?"

While they spoke, Evan sat staring at Dante like a coiled snake ready to strike. But Dante wanted him to strike. He wanted everyone in the restaurant to know that Evan Murdoch wasn't the perfect, stately millionaire who always kept his cool. Dante wanted him to humiliate himself. But Evan continued to sit and watch silently, despite his earlier bravado.

Like the pussy that he is, Dante thought.

"It's not just about revenge." Dante inclined his head. "I want to teach you . . . *all* of you a lesson. This is the first time your family name, your connections, and your money can't get you out of something, and I've got a front-row seat. I want to break out a box of popcorn just to watch the show!"

"Because you're jealous of the family name, connections, and money, right?" Terrence asked. "It's not like we asked for that shit! We didn't ask for any of it."

Dante poked out his lower lip mockingly. "Oh, poor you! I should break out the violin."

"Fuck you, man," Terrence spat.

Dante started to laugh again—hard and loud. That's when Terrence's control finally started to unravel. He grabbed his cane and began to hoist himself to his feet, but Evan beat him to it. He pushed back his chair and marched around the table before grabbing Dante around the upper arm in a vise-like grip. He then began to yank and shove Dante across the restaurant.

"Let go of me!" Dante said. "Get your fuckin' hands off of me!"

Half of the restaurant seemed to fall silent. Several diners began to glance nervously at each other.

Dante attempted to yank his arm out of Evan's hold, but it was surprisingly strong. He twisted and turned, yelling threats. Both men drew stares from the maître d' as they passed the restaurant's wait desk. They made it through the glass door leading to the busy street outside. They walked past a smiling couple who were making their way inside the restaurant. Evan finally released Dante with a hard shove that almost sent him tumbling to the sidewalk face-first. He fell to one knee and shouted out in pain. He instantly sprang upward with his fists balled in front of him, ready to rumble. Instead, Evan gazed at him placidly.

"Don't you ever fucking put your hands on me like that again!" Dante shouted, charging toward him. He shoved Evan hard, almost sending him back through the restaurant door. He then got in his face. They were almost nose to nose. "You hear me? Don't you ever do that shit again!"

"And don't you ever come after my family again," Evan said, barely above a whisper. He didn't blink. "I've put up with all the shit I'm going to take from you. I dealt with you screwing Charisse and with you blackmailing Paulette. But if you go forward with this bullshit lawsuit against Terry . . . if you let this go to court, I will fucking *bury* you . . . literally. Understand?"

Dante took a step back. He wanted to spit in Evan's face. Instead, he chuckled. "Are you threatening me, Evan? Am I really supposed to believe that a pussy like you is going to have me killed?" He adjusted the lapels of his suit, which had become disheveled during their tussle. "Forgive me if I don't start trembling in my shoes. We both know you're not gonna do shit to me!"

"You keep saying that, but the truth is that you don't know what I'll do," Evan said menacingly, fixing him with a level gaze. "I'm giving you fair warning, and I'm not going to do it again. Back off or I will find a way to make you go away . . . and my solution will be a permanent one." He then turned back toward the restaurant door and pushed it open. "Remember what I said," he called over his shoulder just as the glass door swung shut behind him.

Dante stood silently for several seconds. He turned to find a cab driver staring at him with his mouth gaping open.

"What the fuck are you looking at?" he yelled.

"You!" the old cab driver yelled back from his lowered window. "It sounds like you're in for a world of hurt if you keep doing what you're doing, fella. Whatever it is!"

Dante sucked his teeth as he leaned down and wiped the dirt from his knees. "World of hurt, my ass," he muttered, glaring at the restaurant door again. "I'm not afraid of you, Evan, and I never will be, you son of a bitch."

Chapter 16
C. J.

**Can't wait to see you tonight. Can we
meet at my place?**

C. J. read the text on her phone screen and
couldn't resist breaking into a grin. She surrepti-
tiously looked around her, glancing at the other
reporters in the press box at the county commis-
sioner's meeting. She quickly typed Terrence a
message.

**Can't wait to see you too and sure! I'll be
there at 8.**

Her cheeks hurt from smiling so hard. She
pressed Send and dropped her cell phone back
into her satchel before returning her attention to
the meeting in progress, but she could no longer

concentrate on what any of the commissioners were saying. It was just an endless string of nonsensical syllables from that point onward. C. J.'s thoughts kept drifting back to Terrence and the date they were going to have that night. He was taking her out to dinner to one of the nicest restaurants in Chesterton—Le Bayou Bleu. They had gone on a few dates already and each date had been better than the last.

C. J. hadn't realized how many wrong assumptions she had made about Terrence Murdoch. She had thought he was a self-involved, rich pretty boy who had as much depth as a puddle on the side of the road. But that wasn't true at all. He was gorgeous, of course, and charming, and an amazing kisser, but he was also funny, witty, and complex. He still seemed to be struggling with his recovery from the car accident, battling the physical damage as well as the psychological aftermath. He was a man at odds with his new identity as a "disabled person," and it made him insecure and occasionally in need of reassurance that he was still a man, that he was still worthy. How could that not tug at her heartstrings? How could she not like him? In truth, she was starting to suspect she more than liked him. She was starting to suspect she was falling in love.

"Meeting adjourned," the board president said.

As soon as she heard the bang of the ceremonial gavel, C. J. leapt out of her seat and bolted from the press box. She almost ran out of the building and to her car. She wanted to head straight to Main Street in Chesterton to one of the local dress shops. She had raided her closet yesterday in search of something nice to wear that evening, but she hadn't managed to find anything. This would be the first time she had gone shopping for a new outfit in months.

Her phone buzzed again as she walked across the parking lot to her Honda Civic. She eagerly dug into her satchel to retrieve it, wondering if it was another message from Terrénce. Unfortunately, it wasn't.

A reporter from the Washington Post should be calling you soon about Dad and his run for congress. Behave yourself. Remember what I told you.

C. J. rolled her eyes the instant she read the text. It was from her brother, Victor. Of course he was checking in on her, just like he had in the old days, to make sure she stayed in line, that she remained the perfect little preacher's daughter. *Hypocrite,* she thought angrily.

Got it, she typed back before opening her car door.

Her reply was succinct, but no more needed to be said. She hated being dragged back into her family drama, but she didn't want everyone in town—especially the guys at the paper—to know about her past. They already called her "African queen" and "Your Royal Highness." She could only imagine what they would say if they found out she was actually the daughter of the esteemed Reverend Pete Aston. She wouldn't hear the end of it! So she'd play along with Victor and her father's wishes for now. She'd answer the reporters' questions to appease her folks. She would just refuse to do video interviews—that was the deal she'd made with Victor.

A half hour later C. J. stepped through the door of a high-end boutique in town, the type of store that she usually avoided. Her mother had loved shops like this, dragging her to them constantly when she was a teenager.

"A young woman should always look her best and ladylike, Courtney," her mother would admonish. "As God intended."

Well, she had no plans to look "ladylike" tonight, but she certainly wanted to look her best. She knew the type of woman that Terrence was used to dating and though she had no hope of competing with those model types, she planned to come as close as she could.

C. J. instantly zeroed in on a rack of dresses with simple but flattering designs.

"Hi, can I help you?" someone said behind her.

C. J. turned to find a beautiful woman standing near an adjacent rack. Her dark hair was upswept. She had on a white tank top that showed off her perfect cleavage and a short skirt in a vibrant print that displayed her long, tanned legs. She smiled at C. J. She looked like one of the women Terrence usually dated. She looked like she'd just stepped out of a fashion magazine.

"Looking for something in particular?" the salesgirl asked perkily.

"Uh, n-no. I mean . . . yes." C. J. laughed, feeling anxious all of a sudden. "I just . . . I just wanted to buy a dress."

The salesgirl tilted her head. "Is it for a special occasion?"

"Sort of. I . . . I have a date tonight and—"

"A date! Oh, then we have to find you something really, really nice." The salesgirl strode across the boutique, her high heels clicking on the gleaming cement floor. She passed the sales counter and a display table of hats and scarves before sauntering to another rack filled with sexy, alluring dresses that C. J. would never wear. "What are you? A size eight?" she shouted over her shoulder.

C. J. nodded. "Uh, yes I am. But . . ." *I really don't need any help*, she wanted to say.

"Oh, I have the *perfect* dress for you! Just perfect!" The salesgirl yanked a dress off the rack, then paused. "Wait. Is this a first date?"

C. J. shook her head. "No, it's the fourth, actually."

The salesgirl's blue eyes widened. *"The fourth!* Oh, sweetie! This won't do. Not for a fourth date!" She put the dress back on the rack and grabbed another one. "This one is better." She held it up in front of herself. It was a short, bronze bandage dress that looked like it would barely cover C. J.'s top and bottom. "I hope you have some sexy underwear to pair with it. If not, we have bras and thongs in the back."

Why was what underwear she wore important? C. J.'s only rule was that as long as her underwear matched, it was fine. And sometimes she even bent *that* rule!

"I'm not wearing any special underwear. It's not like I plan on anyone seeing it," she joked.

"But it's the *fourth date*," the salesgirl repeated, looking dire. "You know what that means!"

"Umm, no. What . . . what does it mean?"

"Well"—the salesgirl walked toward her and dropped her voice to a whisper—"if you guys haven't had sex already, that's usually when a man makes his move. I don't know. It's like a rule nowadays."

C. J.'s mouth fell open. "That's not true, is it?"

The salesgirl shrugged. "It's been true for every guy *I've* dated." She shoved the bronze dress at her again. "Go to the dressing room and try it on. I bet you'll look like a knockout!"

C. J. stared dumbly at the dress. It practically screamed, "*You can have me any way you want, boy!*" She couldn't wear that. She couldn't give Terrence the wrong impression about her. She wasn't ready to have sex with him. Not yet!

"You'll have to do it at some point," the voice in her head countered. "You've been a virgin for way too long."

C. J. cursed her conservative background and her hypocritical father's constant lectures about "keeping yourself pure for your future husband." She even used to wear a sterling silver chastity ring. The ring was long gone, but thanks to all her father's brainwashing, she was now a twenty-six-year-old virgin who was paralyzed with fear at the idea of sex. She had successfully managed to avoid it for years, dodging men's advances, never letting any of them get too close—but would she be able to do it tonight? She gnawed at her bottom lip, wondering what she was going to do.

* * *

C. J. stood on the welcome mat in front of Terrence's condo and fought the urge to nervously wring her hands. She glanced down at her low-cut sundress with its delicate spaghetti straps and the flowers around the hem—the same dress she had nearly talked herself out of buying because she had thought it was too sexy and just plain not "her," but the salesgirl had talked her into it. She raised her hand to ring the doorbell.

It's just a date, C. J., she told herself for the umpteenth time. *It's just a date, like the others we've already had.*

"No, it's the *fourth* date," a voice countered in her head. "Remember what the salesgirl said?"

It meant sex. It meant sweaty, athletic, swinging-from-the-rafters sex—knowing Terrence and the many women he had probably bedded over the years. There was no way C. J. was ready for that.

C. J.'s finger hovered over the doorbell, inches away from the silver button.

But maybe he doesn't want sex yet, she told herself desperately. *Maybe the salesgirl doesn't know what the hell she's talking about! Terrence has just had a car accident. He needs more time to heal. Maybe he's willing to wait longer.*

"Are you kidding?" The voice in her head laughed. "His leg, arm, and eye may have been hurt in the accident, baby girl, but I bet one appendage is working just fine! And he probably can't wait to use it . . . if he hasn't already."

She grimaced. If Terrence was dating other women—more experienced women—then she didn't stand a chance. She felt inferior enough with her average looks and lack of allure. She was painfully aware that she wasn't one of the glamazons he usually dated. How the hell could she also compete with women who knew more positions than the Kama Sutra, who were the embodiment of every man's sexual fantasy, when she was still a virgin?

I'm so in over my head with this, she thought, her shoulders slumping with glumness. *What the hell am I doing?*

Maybe it was better to just beg off, to gracefully walk away from her budding relationship with Terrence. They had lots of fun and of course she found him attractive, but it was so obvious that they weren't compatible. She was C. J. Aston, the disowned preacher's daughter who put on the bravado of being worldly but who was really still as innocent as a babe in the woods. And he was Terrence Murdoch, a rich playboy who could probably have just about any woman he wanted. So why on God's green earth did he want *her?*

She lowered her hand from the doorbell and let it rest at her side.

She hated these feelings of self-doubt. She had worked so hard to become more confident, to stop questioning herself. But it had only taken a few dates with this man to make her insecure.

C. J. took a step back from the door, contemplating making an excuse for not seeing him tonight. Just as she was about to turn on her heel, Terrence's front door opened. He stood in the doorway in black slacks and a simple white, button-down shirt. He couldn't have been more handsome.

"Hey," he said with a charming smile, and all her doubts instantly disappeared. "Where are you going?"

"Uh, no-nowhere! I was just about to knock," she lied, then began fiddling with her hair. When she realized she was twirling a curly lock around her finger like some dippy schoolgirl, she dropped her hands to her sides.

"Well, you're right on time." He stepped forward, looped an arm around her waist, and drew her close to him, making her breathe in sharply. "You look amazing, by the way."

"Thanks. You look nice t—"

Her words halted in her throat when he leaned down and kissed her. She melted, going mushier than a marshmallow on an open flame.

The feel of Terrence's full lips against hers, the tickle of his goatee against her chin, the sensation of his tongue in her mouth, and his warm, manly smell all joined to overwhelm her senses. She couldn't think straight. She looped her arms around his neck and pressed against his chest to steady herself. She heard his cane clatter to the floor as he wrapped his other arm around her. They fell back against the doorjamb and continued to kiss, almost panting with eagerness. C. J.'s heart was racing. A fire caught inside her and she could feel herself growing hotter and hotter. She could barely breathe. She had to come up for air. She abruptly wrenched her lips from his.

"So . . . uh . . . so, are we still heading to Le Bayou Bleu?" she asked.

Terrence slowly opened the eye that wasn't covered by his eye patch. "Huh?"

"Le . . . Le Bayou Bleu," she repeated, taking a step out of the embrace. She bent down and picked up his cane, which had fallen into the condo's hallway. She handed it back to him. "You know, the . . . the restaurant. Our dinner reservations."

"Oh! Oh yeah." He licked his lips, and she was momentarily reminded of their steamy kiss. "I forgot to tell you . . . I had to cancel the reservations."

She frowned in confusion. "Cancel them?"

"Yeah, I'm afraid my leg is acting up tonight," he said with a slight wince as he gripped his cane and shifted his weight onto it. "It happens from time to time."

She stared down at his leg, feeling disheartened. So all her agonizing had been pointless. They weren't even going on a fourth date tonight!

"I'm sorry you aren't feeling well," she said softly. "Is there anything you need me to get for you?"

He shook his head. "No, I'm good."

"Well . . . uh . . ." She twisted her satchel strap, trying her best to hide her disappointment, though she suspected she wasn't being very successful. She painted on a smile. "I guess I can come back another day. Maybe we can reschedule when you're feeling better."

"*Reschedule?*" He raised an eyebrow. "Why would we reschedule?"

C. J. fell silent, now even more confused. Was he saying he didn't want to see her again? Her cheeks flushed with embarrassment.

"You thought I was canceling the date, *too*?" He reached out and grabbed her hand. He leaned down and kissed her reddened cheek. "You really think I'd let you get away that easily? Hell no! I just canceled the dinner reservations. We're still having dinner, though." He stepped back from the door and gestured with his cane into the home's interior.

Her frown deepened as she peeked around his broad shoulder. The lights were turned down low in the living room so that she could only see the outline of his leather sectional sofa and armchairs. Beyond the living room was the dining area, where a table was set. It seemed to sit under a little spotlight in his vast condo. She could see from here the white tapered candles, a bouquet of white dahlias, and two table settings of fine china, silver dishes, and crystal set out on a white linen tablecloth. Two empty chairs also sat waiting for them.

When C. J. saw the setup, she blinked a few times as if to clear her vision. Was all this for her? Her mouth fell open in shock.

"Don't worry. No one is gonna die from food poisoning tonight. I didn't cook the dinner," he joked before tugging her inside and shutting the door behind her.

They walked across the hardwood floor and Terrence paused to lean down and grab a digital remote from his glass coffee table. He tapped a button and flames erupted in the glass-tiled fireplace a few feet behind them, making her jump in surprise. He tapped another button and music suddenly filled the room—a low, soothing instrumental jazz piece.

"I had the food delivered," he said as he lowered the remote back to the coffee table. He then guided her into the dining room. "And it's not takeout—a reputable chef made it for us."

He let go of her hand and pulled out one of the chairs at the dining room table. He then gestured for her to sit down and she fell back into the seat, too stunned to sit down gracefully.

He removed the silver lids from the plates sitting in front of her, revealing their dinner. "Escarole salad, beef tenderloin, puréed potatoes and leeks, sautéed spinach and caramelized onions, and a bomb dulce de leche cake is in the fridge," he said as he walked to the other side of the table. "I cheated and sampled some of it before you arrived." She watched as he sat down next to her and reached for the bottle of wine at the center of the table. "It was pretty good."

"No, *you're* the one who's good, Terrence Murdoch," the voice in her head murmured before laughing again.

He had canceled their dinner reservations and decided to give her an intimate, five-star dinner at his home. Part of her—the inquisitive, incredulous journalist part—wondered if he had embellished the story about his leg. Was all of this some orchestration on his part?

It is the fourth date, after all, she reminded herself yet again.

Terrence was a master player, the ultimate seducer. What better way to seduce a woman than pulling a grand romantic move like this one? C. J. should have seen a move like this coming from a mile away, but then again, why would she? Shaun was the last man she had seriously dated, and he was far from a lothario. She had no experience at this.

She watched as Terrence poured himself a glass of red wine, then held the bottle over the lip of her glass. "Would you like some?"

C. J. tore her gaze from the dining room table spread and stared at him in amazement. She dumbly nodded.

"I hope you aren't too disappointed about not going out tonight," he said as he poured.

"No. No! This is just as nice," she answered honestly, running her hand over the linen tablecloth. "It's even better!"

"I'm glad you think so, because I'll be honest"— he set down the bottle, reached across the table and held her hand—"this leg thing isn't fun, but I looked forward to the chance to have you all to myself."

Her face warmed again, this time for a very different reason.

He gently ran his thumb over her knuckles and she started to tingle. "It may sound corny as hell when I say this, but . . . I don't think I've ever met a woman like you before."

"What . . . what do you mean?"

"Well, you're smart. You definitely have a lot more going on in here"—he gestured to his forehead—"than I'm used to. You're funny. You're sexy as hell. You're quite a woman, C. J."

"You're . . . you're not so bad yourself," she said dully, trying her best to reconcile herself with the woman he was now describing.

"I'm glad I met you," he whispered before leaning toward her, raising a hand to cup her face, and kissing her again.

And that's when C. J. knew she was gone. There was no hope of walking away from Terrence or postponing any sexual advances he might make tonight or in the near future. She didn't know if his intentions were fake or legitimate, but it didn't matter anymore. She had officially fallen for this guy—*hard!*

They ate dinner and fell into the familiar warmness that she had gotten used to having with Terrence. They joked with one another. They laughed and talked about anything and everything. All the while he kept touching and kissing her. A dumb smile plastered itself to her face. She felt drunk and giggly and it wasn't just because of the red wine. Being with Terrence was intoxicating.

As it neared midnight, they had moved from the dining room table to the couch to watch old Hitchcock films while the fire glowed nearby. Their wineglasses sat on the coffee table in front of them, along with plates covered with crumbs and scraped icing from the dulce de leche cake. Terrence had been right; the cake had been the bomb.

"You know what I've never gotten about this damn movie?" Terrence announced as he lay across the sectional cushions. C. J. sat beside him with her elbow propped on the armrest. His head rested in her lap. "If they're really so scared of the damn birds, why not just walk around with bread and birdseed and start throwing that stuff as soon as the birds come at them? Do it to distract them."

She sipped her wine and grinned. "I guess because it would be a pretty short movie if the answer was as simple as throwing Wonder Bread."

"But it would be straight to the point. You wouldn't waste almost two hours of the movie ignoring the obvious."

She shrugged and stared at the flat screen, watching as Tippi Hedren screamed and batted away an angry seagull. "Maybe."

He looked up at her. "Don't you think 'straight to the point' is best?"

She tore her eyes away from the television to look down at him. Terrence's gaze had become a lot more heated. Were they still talking about the movie? "I guess it . . . it depends on the circumstances," she said, lowering her glass to the end table.

"Not to me." He slowly raised his head from her lap and sat upright. He then eased toward her on the sectional so that they were only inches apart. He snaked an arm around her. "I'm a guy who hates to beat around the bush." He lowered his head to place a series of butterfly kisses on her bare shoulder.

She loudly swallowed, feeling her heart pounding again. *Okay, we're definitely no longer talking about the movie,* she thought.

"For me, directness works every time," Terrence said as he nipped and flicked his tongue along her neck.

C. J. closed her eyes and fought back a moan.

"And believe me, I like to be direct," he whispered before bringing his mouth to hers.

This kiss wasn't like the others. They had all been passionate and steamy, but C. J. got the sensation that imaginary floodgates had been thrown open. The hunger that Terrence had been keeping at bay surged forth—and she was swept under the current. They fell back against the sofa cushions and Terrence shifted his mouth from her lips to her neck and collarbone, then descended lower, kissing her breasts through the cotton fabric of her dress. He eased the straps of her sundress off of her shoulders and shoved the hem of her dress upward, revealing her white lace panties underneath. C. J. felt a mix of overwhelming pleasure, anticipation—and sheer panic.

"Terry," she whispered as he nestled between her legs and opened the top two delicate pearl buttons of her dress. His leg pain miraculously seemed to be forgotten. "Terry," she muttered plaintively, but her words were drowned by another kiss.

He undid yet another button and her breasts were suddenly exposed to the warm air of the living room. She felt her underwear being eased over her hips. Of all her emotions, panic won out.

I can't do this, her mind screamed. *I can't do this!*

"Terry, stop!" she ordered, shoving hard at his chest. "Stop, damnit!"

He did as she ordered, shifting back so that he was no longer on top of her. He stared at her in confusion. "What? What's wrong?"

She scrambled to sit up and closed the panels of her sundress, covering her breasts. She shoved her disheveled hair back from her face.

"What *happened?* Why'd you tell me to stop?"

Her eyes stayed downcast as she buttoned her dress. She couldn't meet his gaze. "I'm sorry. I'm so sorry."

"Sorry about what?"

"I can't do this. I thought I might be able to . . . but I can't. I can't have sex with you. I'm sorry."

She finally looked up at him, expecting to see anger on his face. Instead, he looked hurt. "Okay. Okay, fine." He grabbed his cane and hoisted himself to his feet. "I get it."

"You . . . you get what?"

He shook his head and laughed bitingly, walking away from the sofa. "I told you I prefer directness. Thanks for being so direct, C. J." He turned to glare at her. "But you didn't have to drag this out. You didn't have to lead me on!"

"Lead you on?"

"I thought you just wanted to take things slow, but I guess I was wrong. If you weren't interested in me in that way, you just could have said so in the beginning!"

Her brows furrowed. "What are you talking about? What makes you think I'm not interested in you? I just said I couldn't have sex with you tonight. That's all!"

"I should have known, though," he continued, not hearing her. "You're the bleeding heart type, right? You thought I was some sympathy case you could indulge with a few dates. You saw the half-blind cripple as some charity case that—"

"Is that what you think? That I went out with you for sympathy?"

"But I'm nobody's charity, all right?" he shouted. "Next time you decide to help out the needy, you make a fucking donation to the Make-a-Wish Foundation! Don't waste my time!"

"Hey!" She angrily shot to her feet. "I went out

with you because I *wanted* to go out with you, Terry! Not because I pitied you, you . . . you ass-hole!"

"Yeah, okay," he mumbled. "Whatever."

"It's true! And if you really want to be direct . . . if you really want some real talk, let's talk about the fact that you probably never would have gone out with *me* if it wasn't for your accident, if you weren't so down on yourself. Let's talk about that!"

He paused and narrowed his eye at her. "What the hell is that supposed to mean?"

"It means that last month's banquet isn't the first time we've run into each other, Terry! You've met me before, but you never asked me out. *Why?* Because you were too preoccupied chasing after fucking supermodel lookalikes and women who could star in porn movies! You weren't interested in someone like me," she said, pointing at her chest. "You looked right past me!"

He slowly shook his head. "That's not . . . that's not true."

"Yes, it is!" She took a deep breath. The living room fell silent. "Look, your limp isn't going to be this bad forever. You aren't going to always need that cane, either. You can get a good prosthesis to cover your eye. One day, you're going to go back to normal and you'll . . ." Her cheeks warmed with embarrassment again. "I'm worried that you won't see me the same way that you do now. You'll look right past me again."

"I would never do that," he said softly.

Her throat tightened.

"I mean it!" He stepped forward and grabbed

her hand. "I like you. I wasn't bullshitting you when I told you that. I admit, before the accident I was one shallow son of a bitch, but I'm not completely blind! Only half-blind." He laughed and she couldn't help but join him. "But I can see what's right in front of me. I'm attracted to you, C. J. There's no doubt about that."

She dropped her gaze again.

"So is that why you didn't want to have sex? Because you thought one day I won't be attracted to you anymore?"

"A . . . a little," she answered honestly. "I also had . . . other reasons."

"What other reasons?"

She gnawed the inside of her mouth. She would have to tell him the truth. She would have to make yet another humiliating revelation tonight. Oh, this fourth date was turning out to be a monumental one, indeed!

"Please tell me," he said. His hold on her hand tightened. "It can't be that bad. What is it? Are you on your period?"

She shook her head.

"Embarrassed about being naked in front of someone?"

She paused. That hit a lot closer to home, but of course, that wasn't it, either. She shook her head again.

"Do you have an STD?" His face fell. "Are you HIV-positive?"

"No, it's nothing like that."

He sighed, seeming relieved.

"I'm . . . I'm a virgin," she answered quietly.

"What?" He looked legitimately shocked at that one. He barked out a laugh. "You're joking, right?"

"No. Afraid not." She cleared her throat and met his gaze. "I'm a virgin, Terry."

He let go of her hand and squinted at her. "But you're like . . . what . . . twenty-five? *Twenty-six years old?*"

"I know how old I am," she said tightly.

"I'm sorry . . . it's just . . . how . . . how the *hell* are you still a virgin?"

"I grew up in a religious family, all right?" she explained, now beyond mortified. "I've been taught since I was a little girl to save myself for marriage. And I thought that's what I was going to do until . . ."

Her words drifted off. She remembered herself the day of her wedding, running to her father's Mercedes-Benz in her voluminous white dress, prepared to disappear to parts unknown.

". . . until that plan didn't work out so well," she continued. "I didn't get married. I'm not saving myself anymore, but you get so used to saying no, to holding back. It's hard to just flip a switch and tell yourself that it's okay to do this. But I think I could do it . . . eventually," she quickly added, not wanting to give him the impression that she never planned to have sex with him.

"So you've never had sex with anyone? In any form?"

She shook her head.

"Not even blow jobs? *Hand jobs?*"

"No, Terry! Nothing!"

"Wow." He looked shell-shocked. "That's hard-core." He scanned her up and down, as if really seeing her for the first time. "So, you're really a virgin, huh?"

"Yes! For the hundredth time, I'm *really* a virgin . . . which is why I need you to be patient with me. I need to know that you'll be willing to ease into this a little slower than you're probably used to going."

He ran a hand over his face and released a beleaguered breath. "Well, it's definitely a challenge but"—he broke into his usual charming smile—"I'm never one to run away from a challenge." He shrugged. "Okay, I'm game."

This time she was the one who was mystified. "You're game for what?"

"To help you ease into this stuff." His smile broadened. "I humbly volunteer to be your sex tutor."

She burst into laughter. "My *sex tutor?*"

He nodded, stepped forward, and clasped his hands on both sides of her face. "Yep, and your first lesson starts tonight."

She was caught off guard when he started kissing her again. Hadn't he just heard what she'd said? C. J. shoved back from him and glared at him with unveiled outrage.

"Terry, damnit, what are you doing? I told you I couldn't have sex with you tonight!"

"And we're not having sex," he insisted as he began to undo the front buttons of her dress again with a slow deliberateness that made her quiver. "There are plenty of steps between this and doing the deed, C. J. Trust me. And I plan to show you each and every one."

He pulled open the dress panels, then took a

breast in each warm hand, making her gulp audibly as her nipples hardened.

"You ready?" he asked, not giving her the chance to respond before he lowered his mouth and devoured her whole.

Chapter 17

Terrence

"Good afternoon, Mr. Murdoch," she said from over his shoulder. "And how are you today?"

The instant Terrence heard C. J.'s voice, he started to tingle from his head to his toes. His heartbeat picked up its pace. His throat went dry. Even his dick started to rise to attention. But he kept his cool façade in place while she lightly swept her hand along his back and shoulder and walked around him. She took the wrought-iron chair facing him at the bistro table, pushed her sunglasses to the crown of her head, and grinned.

"Good afternoon, Miss Aston," he said, returning her smile and adjusting the dinner napkin over his lap to cover the now-conspicuous bulge.

Terrence couldn't help himself. C. J. might be dressed casually today, wearing an unassuming V-neck white T-shirt that showed off her brown shoulders and hinted to the swell of her cleavage underneath, and navy blue capris that hugged her hips, thighs, and round bottom. But when he looked at her, his mind instantly harkened back to her lying naked on his bed, moaning and writhing while his head was nestled between her thighs.

The sex lessons were going better than expected. For the past few weeks, Terrence had been "teaching" C. J. the A's to Z's of erotic play, which included almost everything short of doing the deed itself. From her screams and moans, C. J. seemed to be enjoying every minute they spent in bed together.

"That wasn't the first time you ever came, was it?" he had asked her with a wicked smile last week.

He had asked it after one particularly loud yelling fit that he was sure even his neighbors had heard. It had left C. J. so mortified afterward that she covered her face with her hands and refused to look at him.

"Seriously, was it?" he prodded when she remained silent.

"Yes," she murmured behind her fingers, like it was the most horrible revelation in the world. She then slowly lowered her hands to glare at him. "Don't you *dare* look smug about that, Terrence Murdoch!"

His smile broadened and she grabbed one of his pillows and hit him over the head with it before bursting into laughter.

But how could he *not* be smug? He was laying claim to uncharted territory, going places with this sexy woman that no man had gone before! He wished he could find enjoyment just in that, in helping C. J. realize all the pleasure a considerate lover could give. But the truth was, Terrence was far from considerate and he had realized that way too late.

"You're the one who told her you'd be willing to be her sex teacher," the voice in his head chided. "You jackass!"

But how was he supposed to know that it would involve so much selflessness and restraint? Every time C. J. left his home with a smile on her face and a hop in her step after one of their lessons, Terrence would shut the door behind her and start muttering to himself. The afterglow of stolen kisses and pillow talk would wear off, and he would be more bitter and sullen than Ebenezer Scrooge.

Sure, C. J. got foreplay and orgasms. Meanwhile, all Terrence got was hand lotion, a scroll through X-rated pics on his iPhone, and five fingers—and frankly, he was starting to get tired of the whole routine. But he didn't want to push her past her limits. He wasn't a total asshole, after all. She was fragile, and she had told him she needed to go slow and be eased into this stuff, but he was starting to wonder just how slow she planned to go.

Just how long was this "easing" supposed to last? And couldn't she please *him* just a little once in a while?

I'm not asking for the world, he would think angrily as he lay alone in bed at night. *Just some reciprocation! How hard would it be to do a five-minute hand job or suck a guy's dick once in a while?*

And the moment those angry thoughts crossed

his mind, Terrence felt like an asshole all over again.

He had contemplated calling up one of his old girlfriends to see if maybe she could help him with his current "predicament." He hadn't spoken to any of them in months—not since the accident—but they might forgive him for that transgression if he gave them a sob story. Maybe Georgette was back in town, or maybe Asia at that Cuban restaurant downtown was looking for company.

But for some reason, the idea of having sex with another woman felt like a betrayal or like he was cheating. Terrence had never told C. J. they were exclusive, and in the past he never would have agreed to such a thing, but this time it felt like he and C. J. had an implicit agreement not to see other people. He knew he certainly would be pissed off to find out she was taking "lessons" from some other guy.

No, he wouldn't go to another woman to put him out of his misery. He'd stick it out with C. J. because this was about more than just sex. He really liked her—more than he cared to admit.

"I can't stay long," C. J. announced, tugging her satchel strap over her head and setting the canvas satchel on the cobblestones beneath her feet. She grabbed one of the menus on the bistro table. "I have an assignment across town at one thirty."

Terrence's heart sank a little. He had looked forward to seeing her today and she was already rushing off? "If you had stuff going on and you needed to cancel lunch, you could have just told me," he muttered, trying his best to keep the disappointment out of his voice.

She looked up from her menu and frowned at him. "Of course I wouldn't cancel! I wanted to see you. I missed you!"

His sinking heart started to take flight again, but he had to keep his emotions in check. There was no way he would let C. J. know how happy he was to hear her say that. "Missed me?" he muttered casually. "Woman, you saw me on Tuesday!"

"Irrelevant." She grabbed her water glass and took a sip. "I can only go a couple of days before I need my Terry fix."

He smirked and proudly leaned back in his chair. "Yeah, well . . . my loving has a tendency to do that."

She snorted. "You can try to play Rico Suave if you want to, but I know the truth, Terry." She reached across the table, catching him off guard. She rested a hand on his cheek. "You're an amazing guy and even though your loving is all that and then some, it's *you* that I missed."

At those words, the old Terrence would have laughed in her face, but the new Terrence instead turned his mouth toward her palm and kissed it.

"Terry?"

Terrence jumped in surprise at the sound of his brother's voice, making C. J. yank her hand away like someone had rapped her on the knuckles with a ruler.

Terrence turned to find Evan striding along the sidewalk toward them. "Ev! Hey! What are you doing here?" He waved his brother forward.

"I was just picking up something for Lee at the jewelry store," Evan called back, holding up a gold gift bag with the emblem from one of the jewelers in Chesterton.

Terrence turned back to C. J. "I want you to meet my brother."

"We've met," she said softly, dropping her gaze to her lap.

"Ev, this is C. J. My . . . uh . . . my friend that I told you about." He winked at his brother, hoping Evan caught onto his meaning.

Evan whipped off his Ray-Bans and narrowed his eyes at her. His smile faded. "*This* is your friend?"

Terrence nodded, confused by his brother's tone. "Yeah, uh . . . I guess you guys have run into each other before?"

C. J. refused to look up and Evan seemed angry for some reason. Terrence's gaze shifted between the two. Why were they both acting so peculiar?

"So you finally managed to talk to my brother, huh?" Evan asked, glowering at C. J.'s lowered head. "Well, if I can say anything about you . . . C. J., is it? If I could say anything about you, C. J., it's that you're tenacious, though your ethics are highly questionable."

C. J. didn't respond. Instead the same look of mortification passed across her face that had appeared when she'd shouted out Terrence's name in bed.

"Is something wrong?" Terrence asked, still looking uneasily between the two.

"I'm not the right person to answer that question," Evan said coolly. "You should ask your *friend* here."

C. J. finally looked up. She took a deep breath and gazed at Evan. "Look, Mr. Murdoch . . . I mean, Evan . . . I think my work as a reporter has given you the wrong impression about me. You see, I don't—"

"No, I think I have *exactly* the right impression about you!" Evan took another step toward the table. "You're a harasser and a liar and if you think you can—"

"Whoa!" Terrence said, holding up his hands. "Whoa, Ev! What the hell, man . . . why are you talking to her like that? You don't even know her!"

"I know enough! Trust me. You don't want to have anything to do with this . . . this *woman!*"

He said the word *woman* with a curl in his lip and a look of sheer disgust, like C. J. didn't deserve to be called that. Terrence stared at his brother in disbelief and then that disbelief quickly morphed into fury. How dare Evan treat C. J. that way?

"I'm a grown-ass man, Ev! I'll be the judge of who I should and shouldn't talk to, all right?" Terrence barked, glaring up at his big brother.

C. J. snatched her satchel from the ground, pushed back her chair noisily, and started to rise to her feet. "Look, I'm not trying to cause any friction between you," she mumbled. "Terry, I'll just go. I'll see you—"

"No," he said firmly while grabbing her hand, "*you* stay. You're the one I invited to lunch today. To hell with him! *He* can go."

Terrence barely glanced at his brother when he

said it. He didn't have to look at Evan; he already knew the expression that would be on Evan's face, a look of shock and probably outrage. But at that moment, Terrence didn't give a damn. Evan was out of line. He had to be put in his place.

C. J. slowly sat down in her chair.

"Don't say I didn't warn you," Evan muttered before walking off.

Chapter 18

Evan

"Good meeting, Joe," Evan said as he escorted his COO to his office door. "Come up with a game plan and present it to me the next time we meet, all right?"

The older man smiled and nodded before stepping out of Evan's office into the adjoining area, where Evan's new secretary sat at her desk, clicking away on her computer. Evan shut the door behind Joe and walked back toward his desk—glancing at the floor-to-ceiling windows that overlooked the Potomac River, eager to fire off an e-mail to one of the other company executives to inform them of the new changes—but he paused when he heard a buzz. It was a call on his iPhone. He picked up his pace and jogged across the office, frowning as he did.

Few people called him on this phone. He had

only given out the number to family members, to Leila, and to his secretary with express instructions to call it only when all other numbers failed to reach him. When he finally stood in front of his desk, he grabbed the phone and stared down at the screen. Terrence's name appeared in white letters. Evan was surprised to see it.

He and Terrence hadn't talked in days, not since he had seen Terrence with that reporter at the bistro in Chesterton. In retrospect, Evan could have handled the encounter better, but he had been so shocked to find out that *she* was the one who had gotten Terrence back into the dating game, that *she* was the one whom Terrence had been asking to use Bill's services to escort her to dinner dates and picnics—that Evan hadn't been able to keep up a polite façade. How had this woman managed to weasel her way into Terrence's circle? She certainly wasn't much to look at— about average level of attractiveness, at best. But more importantly, what had she done to make Terrence take sides with her over his own brother?

Evan and Terrence had always been close. During their childhood, they knew they couldn't turn to their dad for guidance or affection. That man had all the warmth of the Snow Miser, and his advice had been so harsh and emotionless, it bordered on sociopathic. Their mother, Angela, had been a kind, gentle woman, but she was so browbeaten and wary of their father that she wouldn't even sneeze without George's approval. The Murdoch kids could turn to her for a warm hug and a kiss, but that was about it. No, if they *really* needed advice, if they really needed someone in their corner, they knew they had to look no further than each other. It had always been that way since he and Terrence were little boys.

So, to hear Terrence say, "No, *you* stay . . . To hell with him! *He* can go," had been like a punch to the gut to Evan. He had never felt so betrayed by Terrence in his life and they had certainly had some knock-out, drag-out fights in the past thirty years. Evan had been too hurt to call his brother to try to talk to him and make things right, and Terrence probably had been too stubborn to call Evan to do the same. So for three days, the two brothers had been at a stalemate. It looked like Terrence had caved first—to Evan's great relief.

Evan pressed the green button on the glass screen and raised his phone to his ear. "Hello?"

"So what the fuck was that about?" Terrence snarled.

At the sound of Terrence's voice, Evan smiled despite his brother's less than conciliatory tone.

"Hi, Terry, how are you?" he deadpanned before pulling his chair from his desk and sitting down.

"Why'd you go off on C. J. like that? What was that shit about me having nothing to do with her?"

Evan leaned back in his chair and loosened his necktie. "You are aware that she's a reporter for the *Chesterton Times*, right?"

"Yeah, *and*? So what?"

"She's written stories about Murdoch Conglomerated before. Less-than-flattering ones, in fact," Evan continued. "She hounded me for almost a year trying to get an interview. She even followed me to a lunch meeting. I had to threaten her with a restraining order to get her to leave me the hell alone!"

"Look, Ev, that's her job! Maybe C. J. gets . . . I don't know . . . a little overzealous sometimes, but that doesn't mean she—"

"She showed up at the hospital the day after your accident. She lied and told the desk nurse that she was your fiancée so that she could get in your room and interview you. Did she tell you that?"

Terrence fell silent.

"Yeah, I didn't think so. I can only imagine what story she planned to write about you that day . . . or what story she *still* plans to write. You need to be careful with her, Terry, with what you say to her. She might be gunning for you or our family."

"C. J. . . . C. J. wouldn't do that," Terrence argued, but Evan could already hear the hint of doubt in his brother's voice. "She's not like that."

"I'm sorry, but it's obvious to me that you don't know enough about this woman to make that call. She hasn't told you the full truth. I'm just saying, tread carefully . . . or better yet, whatever you have going on with her, cut it off now."

Terrence paused. Evan heard him anxiously clear his throat on the other end of the line, making Evan roll his eyes heavenward.

"Jesus, Terry, there are other woman in the world! Don't risk your reputation and public embarrassment for a piece of ass! Is she really that good in bed?" he asked sarcastically.

"I . . . I wouldn't know," Terrence mumbled.

Evan furrowed his brows in confusion. "What do you mean, you don't know?"

"I mean, we . . . she and I . . . we haven't had sex yet. We've come close . . . *real* close, but we haven't . . . done it."

"But you've been seeing her for more than a month. Since when do you take that long to have sex with someone?"

"Since now, goddamn it!" Terrence growled, making Evan pull his phone away from his ear. "*Since now!* You think I don't want to have sex with her? You think I haven't *tried?* I have! But she wants to take things slow and 'ease into it,' whatever the fuck that means! I didn't want to push her too hard, so I've been holding back and now every time she leaves I feel like I'm going to punch my fist through a brick wall. I haven't been this sexually frustrated since I was thirteen years old, beatin' off to *Black Tail* magazine!"

Evan laughed despite himself. "Well, that's even more of a reason to cut her off. Don't let her play these head games with you anymore. End it now!"

"I . . . I can't, Ev."

"What do you mean, you can't? Why the hell not?"

Terrence didn't answer him. He fell silent again, leaving Evan totally perplexed. Suddenly, a thought dawned in Evan's head. He slowly sat forward in his chair. His mouth fell open in shock.

"Are you in love with her?"

"No!" Terrence cried a little too quickly and too keenly. "Of . . . of course not!"

"Terry, be honest with me. Are you in love with her?" Evan repeated again more slowly.

"No! Well, I don't think . . . I am. B-but, you know . . . I haven't . . . well, I haven't—"

"Oh, you've got to be kidding me, Terry! Are you serious? You don't fall for anyone after all these years and then *this* is the woman you fall in love with—a reporter who could possibly bring down our entire family by putting all our shit in the newspaper?"

"I never said I was in love with her!" Terrence argued. "Look, I've got to go. I'll talk to C. J. and ask her about all this stuff. I'm sure there's a good explanation for it."

"Yeah, you do that," Evan muttered, still dumbfounded.

Terrence was in love. This was the same man who had once compared being in love to getting lobotomized, or who had said he could never envision himself being with one woman longer than a month, let alone for the rest of his life. This man was now in love with someone and he couldn't have picked a worse candidate to bestow those affections upon.

"I'll talk to you later," Terrence mumbled before hanging up, leaving Evan to hang up, too—in disgust. His desk phone rang and he quickly picked it up.

"Mr. Murdoch," his secretary said, "are you busy, sir?"

He blew out a slow gust of air before scrubbing his hand over his face tiredly. "No, Adrienne, I'm not busy. What is it?"

"Well, uh . . . you have a woman out here waiting for you, sir," she whispered. "She isn't on the schedule, but she . . . she insists that she must speak with you now."

Evan frowned. "What woman?"

"She says . . . she says she's your wife, sir."

Oh shit, Evan thought, closing his eyes.

If he hadn't spoken to Terrence in days, he hadn't spoken to his wife, Charisse, in weeks. Evan hadn't known how to respond to her tearful outburst or her revelation about her father. Even though the matter of their divorce still wasn't resolved, Evan hadn't called her to rectify it. It seemed callous, maybe even cruel, to bring up something like that in light of everything she had told him. He wanted to give her some time before he broached the topic of her finally signing their divorce papers.

"You can send her in," he said.

"Uh, y-yes, r-right away, sir," Adrienne replied, and he heard her murmur something just before he hung up.

Evan sat upright in his chair and adjusted his tie. He felt like he was meeting the CEO from another company, preparing for an arduous round of contract negotiations, but the truth was, this was actually a lot worse. His relationship with Leila and his own emotional well-being could be on the line if this continued to drag out with Charisse. He hoped she was here to finally say she was ready to move on and let him go.

The door opened and Adrienne gestured into his office, smiling politely. Charisse strode in behind her. She wasn't wearing the haphazard ponytail, flip-flops, and oversized shirt today. She looked a lot more like the Charisse he remembered from the old days: the one who bought racks' worth of dresses and suits from Neiman Marcus and Saks Fifth Avenue, who got weekly mani-pedis. She was wearing a frilly blouse and teal skirt today along with kitten heels. Her hair was down and her blond, glossy curls undulated in waves down her back and around her shoulders.

"Hello, Charisse," he said.

"Hello, Evan." She removed her Chanel purse from her shoulder and walked toward him. "Your secretary seemed surprised to discover you had a wife," she said with raised brows before sitting in one of the Bauhaus chairs facing his desk.

"She's new, and frankly, it's been a while since you've been around here. It was an honest mistake."

Charisse pursed her lips and crossed her legs. "Yeah, well, I hope to rectify that problem so a 'mistake' like that doesn't happen again."

Evan narrowed his eyes at her. "What does that mean?"

"Before I get into that . . . First, let me apologize for how I behaved the last time we saw each other. That's not . . ." She looked down at her lap. "That's not how I intended that conversation to go."

"It's quite all right," he said and he meant it. "You're allowed to get emotional about something like that. Anyone would. I'm sorry your father did that to you. I wish I would have known then maybe I would've . . ."

"Then maybe you would've what?"

Then maybe I would have acted differently, treated you differently, he wanted to say.

He shook his head instead. "Never mind."

"Well, anyway, I'm sorry for how I behaved, because it took me off track from what I really wanted to say to you that day. Evan, I meant it when I told you I wanted to try to make our marriage work. Give me a chance to be the wife I always wanted to be."

He loudly sighed. So she hadn't come here to tell him she was changing her mind after all. "Charisse, I told you that isn't possible. Leila and I are going to get married."

"But you're forgetting the little detail that you're already married to me."

"Look, I can't . . . you don't . . . Leila and I are going to have a baby, all right?" he blurted out. "She's pregnant."

Charisse's face drained of all color. Her gaze sprang from her lap when he said that, and in her big blue eyes he saw so much pain and anguish. He knew what she was thinking. They had tried to have their own baby years ago without success and now he was having one with someone else, with a woman she openly despised.

Charisse closed her eyes, cleared her throat, and slowly opened her eyes again. She pushed back her shoulders. "I'll . . . I'll accept whatever baby you have with her as . . . as my own," she said softly, making him stare at her in disbelief. "If she can give you the son or daughter you always wanted, I won't . . . I won't begrudge you that, but it still doesn't mean that you have to marry her, Ev. Men have babies with women all the time and they don't rush to the altar."

"I'm not marrying her because she's having my baby; I'm marrying her because I love her! I told you that!"

She pointed at her chest. "You also told me that you loved me!"

"I told you that *years* ago! But so much has happened that there's no way—"

"And when you said it, you were just as earnest," she charged. "So I'm supposed to believe that when you said it to me, you didn't mean it, but now you mean it when you say it to her?"

He rested his elbows on his glass desk and dropped his face into his hands. "Charisse, you're not hearing me," he murmured into his palms.

"No, I hear you loud and clear, Ev! You're not hearing *me*. So now I'll just have to state it plainly." She leaned forward in her chair. "I am not willing to give you a divorce and if you insist on pushing this issue, I'm going to have to play hardball."

He lowered his hands. *Hardball?*

"I don't want to do it, but you're leaving me with no choice. I already consulted a lawyer and he said that even though you and I may have both cheated, your affair predates mine, so that would put you—not me—in violation of our prenup. I could argue in court that I still get half of your estate, in addition to half of your shares in Murdoch Conglomerated, because of your transgression."

His disbelief evaporated and now flamed into anger. "That's . . . that's bullshit! You were fucking Dante long before Leila and I started seeing each other. You know that and I know that! You told me so yourself! You had been cheating with him for almost a year."

"No, as I recall, my relationship with Dante was very brief," she said, taking on a stilted tone like she had been coached.

Probably by her lawyer, Evan thought with annoyance.

"I only slept with Dante a few times," she continued. "I turned to him for comfort after I found out my husband was cheating on me with his then-secretary, Leila Hawkins. I was quite devastated. That and the alcohol Dante kept plying me with obviously impaired my judgment. If it wasn't for that, I never would have cheated on my husband." She smiled primly and adjusted the hem of her skirt.

He shook his head. "That's a nice performance, but no judge would believe it."

"Maybe. Maybe not. But while you're arguing your case and I'm arguing mine, our divorce won't be finalized. That baby of yours could be five years old before you could legally marry someone else."

Evan's jaw tightened. Now he could see the old Charisse reemerging: the bitter, manipulative, and vengeful woman who had made his life such a bleak place until Leila had come back to Chesterton and become the bright light to banish all that darkness.

"Okay, fine." He interlocked his fingers and gazed coolly at his wife. "What do you want? What's the end game? You and I both know you don't give a damn about owning part of Murdoch Conglomerated. Do you want the house? *The cars?* Do you want more alimony?"

"No, Evan, for the umpteenth time, I just want my husband back! I want my rightful place at your side as Mrs. Evan Murdoch. I'm not ceding my spot to anyone, *especially* her." She rose from her chair and wiped fussily at a wrinkle in her blouse. "I'll give you a few weeks to think it over. Let me know your decision."

He watched dumbfounded as Charisse turned, strode toward his office door, and opened it. She paused to turn and look back at him. "Believe it or not, Evan, I still love you. And I'm not giving up on us—*ever.*"

She then shut the door behind her.

Chapter 19

C. J.

C. J. stood in the hallway of Terrence's condo, fussing with her hair. She had spent almost an hour trying to do something with it, wrestling with the flat iron, hair spray, and styling spritz. Now, thanks to a late spring monsoon that hadn't been in the weekend forecast, all her hard work was for naught. Her hair was a mass of frizzy curls. But she guessed it didn't matter anyway. If things went the way she planned tonight, Terrence wouldn't care what her hair looked like. He'd be more concerned with . . . other things.

She took a deep, fortifying breath and pressed his doorbell.

As she waited for him to answer the door, she shivered a little in her raincoat. The air-conditioning in the hallway was giving her the chills, but she guessed it would, considering she wasn't wearing much underneath her coat. She had on a black lace bra, a thong, and a garter belt—and that was it. The lingerie had made her gasp when she saw it at the dress shop.

"It looks like pasties and dental floss! How does this qualify as underwear?" C. J. had lamented as the salesgirl shoved the padded hanger at her. It was the same salesgirl who had dressed her for the now-infamous "fourth date" with Terrence.

"It doesn't leave much to the imagination"—the salesgirl had said with a saucy wink—"but that's *the point.*"

C. J. supposed she was right, but unfortunately the getup also left her feeling naked and awkward.

"He's already seen you naked and you aren't awkward," a voice in her head insisted. "You're sexy! You're confident! You are finally going after what you want!"

That was right. She was finally going after what she wanted, and what she wanted was Terrence Murdoch.

She had secretly lusted after him from afar, like just about every other single woman in Chesterton, but now that he was a real person to her, that lust had bloomed into something more. They had only dated for two months, but the feelings she had for Terrence, she had never had for any other man before—including her ex-fiancé, Shaun Clancy. It wasn't just the sexual awakening Terrence had spurred inside her that caused her heart to go pitter-patter and made it impossible to get him out of her mind. She was in love with Terrence. She could admit that now. He had opened her heart and her mind to endless possibilities.

"And now you're about to open your legs to him in return?" the voice asked in her head.

Yeah, that sounds about right, C. J. thought as she heard Terrence unlock his front door.

"Hey!" she cried, feeling her pulse thrum at a breakneck speed and her palms begin to sweat when she saw him.

"Hey," Terrence replied softly. He was wearing a T-shirt and sweatpants. His feet were bare. She imagined that he had probably been lounging on his sofa when she rang the doorbell. "I wasn't expecting you tonight. What's up?"

"Oh, nothing! Nothing! I just decided to stop by." She kissed his cheek and then sauntered through the doorway into his living room. "I didn't catch you at a bad time, did I? Are you busy?"

She was speaking too loudly. Her voice sounded squeaky to her own ears.

"Tone it down, C. J.," the voice in her head warned. "Try not to sound so terrified!"

But she *was* terrified. She was a twenty-six-year-old virgin about to offer herself to a man for the first time and she was going to do it wearing only a raincoat and underwear. This was new territory for her.

Terrence's handsome face creased into a bemused frown as he shut the door behind her. He shook his head. "No, I wasn't busy. Actually, I was about to head off to bed, but since you're here, I—"

"You go to bed *this* early? I'm usually awake for about another hour," she rambled, shoving her hands into her coat pockets when she realized she was fidgeting again. "I watch the late night shows.

If I really can't sleep, I'll watch the late *late* night shows, though they aren't as good. I usually end up turning off the TV and reading a book until I finally drift off to sleep."

Terrence squinted at her. "Umm, okay. Well, anyway . . ." He paused to purse his lips. "It's a good thing you stopped by." He walked past her and farther into the living room. His head was bowed. His back was to her. "I've got to talk to you about something, C. J."

Talking? Not more talking! She'd be rambling all night if he got her started again.

"Do it! Do it now!" the voice in her head urged. "Do it before you lose your nerve."

C. J. quickly undid the belt and buttons of her raincoat, revealing the sexy ensemble underneath. She sucked in her stomach and stuck out her hip, trying her best to strike a seductive pose.

Terrence slowly turned to face her. "I don't know how to say this, but I talked to Ev today and I found out that—"

He stopped midsentence and stared at her in amazement like she had just performed a magician's trick.

"I want you, Terry," she blurted out.

She pushed her coat off her shoulders and down her arms and let it fall to the floor. In the cold air of his living room, her entire body sprouted goosebumps. She was shaking a little, too, but not just because of the chill in the air.

"No more lessons. You don't have to be my tutor anymore. I'm . . ." She cleared her throat and slowly walked toward him. "I-I'm ready."

The silence caught her off guard. She had just

offered herself to him. He didn't have anything to say?

Confused, C. J. followed the direction of his gaze, which was presently on her feet.

"Yeah," she muttered, looking down at her purple galoshes, "not the sexiest footwear, I know. I bought a pair of killer stilettos that would have looked a lot better. But with the rain and the mud, I didn't want to—"

Her words were abruptly smothered by his lips. Terrence had moved with record speed, nearly tossing aside his cane before he wrapped his arm around her waist and pulled her flat against him. He had done all that before she even had the chance to realize he was kissing her. By the time she did, his hand was already sliding down her back and cupping her bare bottom. His tongue was already in her mouth and moving with the languid ease that she loved.

He reached for her bra clasp and began to fumble with it. His other hand groped for her garter. He suddenly wrenched his mouth away.

"Shit! I can't do this standing up. Come on." He grabbed her hand and started to drag her toward the hall leading to his bedroom.

"*Wait!* Your cane," she said, leaning down to get it.

"Don't bother. Don't need it," he muttered, tugging her again, making her trip out of one of her galoshes.

Terrence was right. He didn't need it. He quickly made his way to the bedroom, pulling her the entire time. His limp was barely noticeable. She knew he'd been walking better, but she had no idea he had gotten this good!

I guess he just needed a little encouragement, C. J. thought with a naughty smile as he shoved open his bedroom door and turned on the overhead lights, revealing a bedroom that she knew all too well now considering the pleasurable hours she had spent here the past few weeks.

She hurriedly kicked off her remaining shoe as they walked through the door. He turned to her and started kissing her again. She tugged his bottom lip between her teeth and pulled his T-shirt over his head, revealing the broad muscled chest underneath. He eased her back onto the king-sized bed and landed on top of her and she savored the reassuring feel of his weight, of his body pressed against her own. He started to remove her bra and garters again, but this time with a lot less struggle. In less than a minute, one hand was skimming her breast. The other eased between her legs, moving the flimsy lace of her thong aside.

She parted her legs in ready invitation, responding almost automatically to his touch. She had definitely become a good student under his tutelage. Her body reacted without hesitation now. She arched her hips and pelvis toward his hand, urging him onward. His fingers moved nimbly until she was slick and wet. His tongue slid across her breasts before he took one of her nipples between his teeth and clamped down hard on the sensitive nub. At the dual sensations, C. J. closed her eyes and moaned. Her body writhed in a mix of agony and ecstasy.

She didn't know how Terrence had learned how to do this, how to play her body like an expert violinist, how to coax out every shout and whimper with ease. Years of practice with countless women, maybe? She tried not to think about that right now. Instead she let her body do the thinking for her and she was rewarded with a mind-blowing orgasm that made her toes curl and her eyes roll to the back of her head. She shouted over and over again until the tremors subsided. When they finally did, C. J. pushed back the hair that had fallen into her face and slowly opened her eyes to find Terrence grinning down at her.

"I *love* to watch you come," he whispered, making her chuckle.

"Only because it feeds your ego."

He shrugged. "Hey, a guy's gotta get his rocks off somehow!"

"Well," she said, licking her lips, "I can think of better ways."

C. J. then rose from the bed and climbed on top of him. She straddled him and felt his hard-on jutting between her thighs.

"Are you really ready to do this?" a voice in her head asked.

In reply, she lowered her mouth to his and kissed him again. Terrence fisted his hand in her hair and linked an arm around her, drawing her close. She tugged at the waistband of his sweatpants and his boxers. He took her cue and shoved them down his waist and hips so that they dangled around his knees. He then shifted her aside to grope for one of the night table drawers. A box of condoms sat inside of it. As he did that, she took off her thong and tossed it to the other side of the bed.

A minute later, Terrence was wearing a condom

and they were kissing again. C. J. told herself to stay in the moment, though her anxiety increased with each passing second. Despite her best efforts, the panic was starting to win.

What am I doing? What the hell am I doing? Should I tell him to stop?

"Don't be scared," the voice inside her urged as Terrence climbed on top of her and settled between her parted legs. "You can do this. It won't be as bad as you think."

Terrence left a trail of kisses along her neck and collarbone before gripping her hips and centering himself. He plunged forward without warning and sank into her with a throaty groan. Her eyes widened to the size of saucers. She shouted out again—this time in pain.

Oh Jesus! It *was* as bad as she thought it would be. Maybe even worse! Being impaled on a red-hot poker came to mind, or having a knife driven straight down her center. She gritted her teeth. Her nails dug into his back.

He plunged again with another grunt and she shouted out again. She felt like she was being split in half.

Terrence paused to gaze down at her. He frowned. "Are you okay?"

She couldn't talk. She couldn't breathe! God, the pain was so bad!

"Do we need to stop?"

His voice sounded like he was coming from the other end of a tunnel. She couldn't hear him over her frantic voice inside yelling, *Why did I do this? What was I thinking? Women do this voluntarily? Are they insane?*

"C. J., talk to me," he ordered.

She shook her head. "I'm fine," she whispered finally, closing her eyes. "Just . . . just give me a sec, okay? Don't . . . don't move."

He waited as she asked. Gradually the pain dulled from excruciating to somewhat bearable. She opened her eyes to find him staring at her worriedly.

"Okay, you can keep going."

His brows furrowed. "Are you sure?"

She quickly nodded and forced a smile. "I'm sure."

They resumed making love, but this time, Terrence was more tempered and tenuous with each thrust.

"I'm not hurting you, am I?" he would ask every other minute.

She would shake her head, her smile firmly in place.

When C. J. focused on the sensation of his warm, full lips, on the soapy smell of his skin, on the tickle of his goatee on her cheek, the pain wasn't quite so bad. Besides, love was the ultimate opiate, and she was pretty high on it right now. She could fight through the pain.

After a few minutes, Terrence's tempered pace suddenly increased in vigor. He stopped asking her if he was hurting her. Instead he closed his eyes and plunged forward again and again and again. He shouted out her name a few minutes later, then fell on top of her. He breathed heavily against her ear while she wrapped her arms around his wide shoulders.

C. J. stared at the ceiling in amazement.

I did it, she thought with bemusement.

She had given her body to a man she truly cared about, someone she had fallen for.

Her father had once told her that the only man whom she should ever share her body with was the man that she would marry, but she had instead chosen to do it with the man that she loved.

No regrets.

C. J. woke up the next morning bleary-eyed and alone in a massive bed. She frowned when she realized the pillow beside her was empty. She reached out and placed her hand on the imprint left behind on the fluffy cotton.

"Terry," she called out weakly, pushing herself to her elbows and squinting against the bright light. "Terry?"

He had been lying beside her a few hours ago. In the wee hours of the morning, before the sunlight had pierced his bedroom blinds, she had felt Terrence stir in bed. His hand had fallen on her hip. His lips had skimmed her neck and shoulder. She had felt his manhood nudge insistently against the back of her thighs, begging to be let in, and she had instantly turned and offered her mouth to him first, then her body. She hadn't hesitated and neither had he. They had made love a second time in the dark and quiet of his room.

C. J. still had to bite down hard on her bottom lip to stifle her whimper when he entered her. But at least the pain had been nothing like the first time. She had even managed to move her hips a little with each thrust, tentatively meeting him stroke for stroke. Besides, having Terrence's hands on her, having his warm lips against her skin, made up for the pain.

She wanted his hands and lips on her again— *right now*—but he was nowhere to be found.

C. J. threw back the sheets, tossed her legs over the edge of the bed, and quickly stood up. She winced a little at the dull throbbing between her thighs—her body's silent reminder that she wasn't a virgin anymore. She staggered toward the bedroom door and stuck her head into the hallway. The corridor was dark.

"Terry!" she called out. No one answered.

Save for her, the condo seemed to be empty, but that didn't make any sense. He wouldn't have gone somewhere without telling her he was leaving.

"Where the hell is he?" she grumbled before walking across the bedroom's hardwood floor to the en suite bathroom. She knocked gently on the door.

"Terry, are you in here?"

When she didn't get a response, she pushed the door open and stepped inside. She flicked on the lights.

The bathroom was huge and looked like something you would find at a swanky five-star hotel in New York or South Beach. Its twelve-foot ceilings were covered in black mosaic tile and a freestanding soaking bathtub that looked like it could fit a small family was the centerpiece of the room. It had an enclosed shower and a mini-sauna. She turned toward the double vanity and caught a glimpse of herself in one of the swivel mirrors and almost yelped.

"Oh God," she said, staring at her reflection, raising a hand to her face.

She looked horrible! The makeup she had carefully applied the night before was now a smudged amalgamation of raccoon eyes, smeared red lipstick, and caked eye shadow. Her hair was a matted mess. She couldn't let him see her like this!

She hopped into the shower and washed. When she stepped out ten minutes later, drying herself with a towel, she realized then that she hadn't come with a toothbrush, makeup, or even clothes to change into—anything that a more experienced woman who had had her share of morning-after encounters would have known to bring along.

Amateur, C. J. thought as she grabbed for Terrence's bottle of mouthwash. After that, she wrestled her hair into a ponytail.

C. J. searched frantically around his bedroom for something to wear and settled on one of his bathrobes. It was a little big—she had to roll up the sleeves—but at least it was something. Finally, she made her way down the hall toward the kitchen and living room.

She found Terrence in the kitchen, sitting on one of the bar stools like he had always been there. Two paper cups of coffee sat on the marble counter in front of him. He stared absently at the television across the room. The flat screen was tuned to some twenty-four-hour television news network. When she walked into the kitchen, he suddenly turned and looked at her.

"Hey," she said with a smile, feeling her chest warm at the sight of him, "I was wondering where you had gotten off to."

"I walked down the block to pick up breakfast." He slid a paper bag across the counter in her direction.

"That was sweet of you!"

C. J. hopped on the stool beside him and opened the paper bag. She grabbed eagerly for the toasted chocolate croissant inside and bit into it. She moaned with contentment, rolling the flaky crust around in her mouth, not realizing how famished she had been.

"Nice robe," he muttered, fingering the lapel of the bathrobe she was wearing.

C. J. chuckled and glanced down at herself. She reached for one of the coffee cups and took a quick sip. "Sorry, I had to borrow yours," she said between chews. "I realized I didn't bring any clothes with me. Hope you don't mind."

"Of course I don't mind." He wiped chocolate away from the edge of her mouth with his thumb. "It looks good on you." He then lowered his gaze to the countertop and restlessly tapped his fingers on the granite.

C. J. squinted at him. Something was wrong. She could sense it. Unrest practically radiated off of him.

"Is everything all right, Terry?"

He raised his eye to look at her. His expression was grim. "Actually . . . no, it isn't. We need to talk."

Oh no, she thought, dropping her half-eaten croissant back into its bag. Everything had been going so perfectly. She should have known something would happen to screw it up.

She wiped her hands on a paper napkin. "T-talk about w-what?"

"That day . . . that day that I had my car accident downtown, did you come to the hospital to interview me?" Terrence asked, fixing her with a steady gaze.

She hesitated. Where had this come from?

"Did you lie and tell the nurse that you were my fiancée to get into my room?"

She gnawed her lower lip. "Well . . . uh, y-yes. Yes, I did."

She watched as he clenched his jaw and his back stiffened. She held up her hands in protest.

"B-but I only told her that because they wouldn't let anyone but next of kin go into the hospital room."

"So you lied."

"What else could I do? I had to write the story, Terry! My questions were going to be straightforward . . . nothing out of line. I swear!"

Terry slowly shook his head and let out a cold laugh. He pushed his coffee cup and plate aside and glared at her. "So, Ev was right. You lied to get into my hospital room. You stalked him for almost a whole fucking year to get some other story."

She rolled her eyes. "Now that is definitely an exaggeration. I may have followed him, asking for a quote a few times, but—"

"You *lied,* C. J.!"

"I didn't lie! I didn't! Stop saying that!"

What the hell was happening? This was supposed to be their beautiful morning after. They were still supposed to be lost in the postcoital glow, lying in bed together, gazing into each other's eyes. Not yelling at each other.

"Look, I just . . . I just *omitted* some information, but that doesn't change anything."

"Yes, it does!" he boomed, making her wince. "I told you how I felt about honesty. I told you how I felt about laying all my shit out on the table. Here I was, defending you to my brother and he was right all along. And now he says you're just using me to get more information about me . . . about *our* family, to put embarrassing shit about us in your fucking newspaper!"

"But you know I would never do that," she insisted.

"No, I don't know! I don't know that, C. J., because I can't trust you. You lied to me. You made me look like an asshole to my brother! Don't you get that?"

She tightened her hands into fists in her lap. Tears pricked her eyes. "Well, if you felt that way . . . if you really think that way about me, why are you just saying this now? Why'd . . . why'd you have sex with me last night?"

He sat back on the stool. All the warmth had left his gaze. "I'm a red-blooded man who hasn't had sex in months. An attractive, half-naked woman offered herself to me."

A lump formed in her throat. "So . . . so you took it because I . . . I offered? That's it? It's that simple?"

"It was a piece of ass, C. J.! What else do you want me to say?" He shrugged casually. "I did what any normal guy would do."

That hurt. It hurt worse than if he had driven a steak knife into her chest.

The tears were threatening to pool over now. C. J. slowly pushed herself away from the counter, feeling sick to her stomach. She wasn't going to cry in front of him. She refused to do that. She slid off the bar stool and landed on her feet.

"Well, thanks for the breakfast," she muttered with eyes downcast before walking toward the living room. She grabbed her raincoat off the floor, where it had landed last night. She then walked toward the sofa, bent down, reached for one of her boots, and began to search for the other one.

He frowned. "What are you doing?"

"What does it look like I'm doing? I'm getting my shit and I'm going home," she spat out as she headed for the hallway. Where was that other damn shoe? "I thought that's what you wanted."

He loudly sighed, looking irritated.

"I'll make sure you get the robe back tomorrow. Like I said, I don't have any other clothes."

"C. J., I'm not . . . I'm not kicking you out!" He grabbed his cane and hopped off his stool. He followed her as she continued to search for her shoe in his bedroom. "Don't do this."

"You called me a liar, insinuated that I deceived you to gather information about your family, and told me you had sex with me because I was a half-naked, willing"—she paused to drop to her knees and peek underneath his bed in search of her boots—"piece of ass." She sat back on her heels. "Why should I assume you want me here?"

"I just want you to be honest with me!"

She rose to her feet and glowered at him. "Fine,

I'll be honest. Yes, I did go to your hospital room to interview you that day, but when I found out how badly you were injured, I felt like shit. I filed the story without your quote and left it at that. And yes, I stalked your brother a couple of times to get him to talk about Murdoch Bank's mortgage foreclosures—like any serious reporter would." She dropped her hands to her hips. "I didn't tell you any of that, not because I wanted to keep secrets, but because I didn't think it was important. Okay? And I didn't date you or sleep with you to pump you for information. I'm a reporter, Terry, not a gossip columnist! I have no interest in airing your family's dirty laundry. I'm here because I like you. Well"—she tilted her head and narrowed her eyes—"because I *liked* you . . . but now I'm not so sure."

"Why?" He took a step toward her. "Because I called you out?"

"No, because you told me that you didn't trust me, and you were cruel when you didn't have to be."

She finally spotted her shoe. It was behind his night table. She walked toward it.

Terrence closed his eye. His chest rose and fell as he exhaled a loud breath. He sat down on the bed, still clutching his cane.

"I'm sorry," he blurted out, catching her by surprise, making her pause. "You're right. I was . . . I was cruel. But I did it because . . . shit, C. J.! I did it because I was hurt!" He looked at her again. "I like you, too. I *still* do! I've bared a lot to you, girl. I've told you things I haven't told *anybody* else. When Evan sprang that shit on me yesterday, it made me feel like a fool. I want to trust you. I really do. I just need to know you're the girl you claim to be. That's all."

C. J. stared at him. His gaze wasn't cold anymore. She saw vulnerability there.

No, she hadn't meant to lie to Terrence about the things that she did for her reporting job, but she had lied to him in other ways. He didn't know who she really was. C. J. Aston was a false image—another lie by omission. Terrence didn't know she was really someone else, someone she had tried for years to leave behind.

C. J. walked back toward the bed and sat beside him. She took a deep breath. She would have to tell him the truth.

"My name's not really C. J.," she whispered, staring down at her lap.

His frown deepened. "What?"

"I said that my name isn't really C. J., Terry. It's Courtney Jocelyn Aston. I shortened it for work . . . well, that's not true. I really shortened it because I didn't want people to recognize my name. Most people wouldn't, but some might recognize it thanks to my father."

He slowly shook his head in bemusement. "I'm not following you."

"My father is Reverend Pete Aston. You know . . . of *Aston Ministries*."

Terrence blinked in amazement. "You mean the guy on TV? The one with all those self-help books! Isn't he . . . isn't he friends with Oprah?"

She laughed ruefully. Her father would certainly appreciate his name being connected with Ms. Winfrey's.

"Yes, that's the guy."

Terrence still looked amazed. "Wow! So you're Pete Aston's daughter."

"His *estranged* daughter," she quickly clarified. "I've been excommunicated from the family, so to speak."

"Why? What did you do?"

"I embarrassed him and . . . and ruined his plans. Almost five years ago, I was supposed to get married to this guy who Dad had handpicked for me. Dad told me that it was what the family wanted . . . what God had *ordained* for me."

She raised her hand to her face in exasperation, thinking back to those days. It sounded so ridiculous now, but her father's words had been impossible to dismiss or ignore back then.

"I couldn't go through with it, though. I didn't love Shaun. It didn't feel right. So the day of our wedding, while everyone was in the next room waiting for me to finish dressing, I stole the keys from my mother's purse, snuck out of the church in my wedding gown, ran to the parking lot, and made my getaway." She lowered her hand and gazed at Terrence. "I didn't look back. I knew what my dad would say: '*Honor thy mother and father.*' If I couldn't follow that commandment, I couldn't live in his house anymore."

"So you haven't spoken to him?"

"Sort of. I did it through my brother. I was summoned down to North Carolina two months ago to have a 'talk,' but it wasn't a grand *happy* reunion. My parents still want nothing to do with me, but they need my help now. Dad's considering a run for office. He needs us to look like the perfect little family even if we aren't." She made a face. "I told them I'd answer any press questions when they came. I'd stick to the talking points. That's all." She shook her head. "But I can't go back to being their 'Court' anymore. I got tired of playing that damn role. I prefer to be C. J."

"And you shouldn't have to be her if you don't want to. I'd rather have C. J. anyway."

He reached out and grabbed her hand. She didn't pull away. Instead, she stared down at their interlocked fingers.

"Have her in what way, Terry?" she whispered.

He furrowed his brows. "What do you mean?"

"You know what I mean. I was high after what happened last night, but then after what happened this morning . . . I just can't do it. I don't want to be hurt like that again. Other women might be used to this type of stuff, but I'm not. It's all new to me. I need to know what's happening here before we go any further."

He chuckled anxiously. "You're really going to put me on the spot like this?"

"I love you, Terry. I'm being totally honest with you. I love you."

"Uh . . ." He loudly cleared his throat. He looked utterly terrified. "Uh . . ."

She watched as he fell silent and her heart broke a little.

C. J. didn't want to force him to say something he didn't feel. But she couldn't stay. She had allowed herself to get wrapped up in a whirlwind of emotions these past months or so. She had given this man her virginity, for Chrissake! It was time to take a step back. She pulled her hand away from his, rose from the bed, and kissed his cheek.

"I should go," she whispered into his ear.

He stared at her dumbly.

"I'll stop by tomorrow to bring you back your robe." She then reached down and grabbed her other boot and headed for the bedroom door. "Good-bye, Terry."

"Shit! *Shit!*" he yelled. "I love you, too! All right?"

She stopped and turned to stare at him. He groused loudly to himself, looking defeated.

"Fuck it. I admit it! I love you, too."

Not the most romantic declaration, but it still made C. J. smile.

Terrence patted the mattress tiredly. "Seriously, can we go back to bed now? All this confessing and arguing has made me tired as hell. Let's try this again in another hour."

"Do you really want to sleep?" She grinned and undid the belt of his robe as she walked back toward him.

He let his gaze travel languidly over her. "Well, not . . . not really."

C. J. straddled his lap and he cupped her bottom so that she could feel his manhood pressing eagerly through his sweatpants.

She wrapped her arms around his neck and placed a light kiss on his lips. "So, does this qualify as makeup sex?" she whispered.

"I'll call it whatever the hell you want just as long as you stay," he answered, pulling her close.

She lowered her mouth to his for another kiss just as the phone began to ring. She leaned back.

"You gotta be kidding me!" he lamented.

C. J. tilted her head. "If someone's calling this early, it has to be important, right?"

"Oh, come on!" he grumbled as she stood and reached for the phone on his night table. She then handed it to him before closing the robe again.

"Hello," he answered glumly and she resisted the urge to laugh. She watched as his face changed. His lips tightened. "Why are you calling here? Look, I'm sorry, lady. If you have something to say, you can say it to my lawyer."

C. J. frowned. "Who is it?" she whispered, and he shook his head in response.

"I'm sorry but . . . *what?*"

He fell silent and C. J. stared at him, desperate to know whom he was talking to and what he was talking about. Instead she had to decipher the flash of emotions spreading across his face. He looked angry then confused and finally he looked happy.

"Uh, no . . . n-no thank you," he said a few minutes later. "Yes. You . . . you have a good day, too." He hung up the phone and let it fall to the mattress.

"*Well?*" C. J. stared at him. "What was it? What happened?"

"It was the woman who was suing me," he said dazedly. He finally looked up at her. "She's calling off the lawsuit."

Chapter 20

Dante

Dante pounded his fist on the apartment door and angrily paced back and forth as he waited for the door to open. When it didn't happen within seconds, he banged on the door again.

He was past angry and beyond furious. He felt like steam was going to burst from his ears. He had gotten the call from Terrence Murdoch's lawyer this morning saying that he was happy to hear that Mavis Upton planned to withdraw her lawsuit and he looked forward to seeing the filing in court.

"I'm sorry, but you're mistaken," Dante had said into the phone, holding the handset so tightly that he felt as if he could crush it in his bare hand. "We are *not* withdrawing the case! We're still seeking punitive damages in the sum of—"

"Well, perhaps you should speak to your client, Mr. Turner," Terrence's lawyer had replied in clipped tones. "Terrence and I had a conference call with her yesterday and she told us quite plainly that those were her wishes. She even apologized for letting this drag on for so long."

Dante had frowned. "Wait . . . You had a conference call with her?"

"Yes, as I said, we had it yesterday." The lawyer had paused. "Ms. Upton *is* still your client, correct?"

"Of course she is!"

"Well, if that's the case, then I would think you would be privy to this information, Mr. Turner. I thought you would be the first to know she's withdrawing her lawsuit."

Dante couldn't believe Mavis had done it; not dim-witted, mushy-mouthed Mavis. She had gone behind his back and called Terrence. She even took it a step further and spoke to Terrence's lawyer, purposely cutting Dante out of the discussions.

Does this bitch know who she's fucking with? Dante thought as he paced the dirty, worn hallway carpet. If not, he was about to tell her. She was about to get a rude awakening!

Slowly, the door creaked open. Mavis peeked her head around the edge of the doorframe and gazed at him guardedly. "Hello, Mr. Turner."

"I need to talk to you *now*," he said tightly. Gone was the lawyerly, refined pretense he usually used with Mavis. At that moment, he frankly just wanted to choke a bitch.

"Now is not a good time. We were just about to have din—"

He shoved his way past her, shocking her and sending her almost stumbling backward against the adjacent wall. On the other side of the room, Renee and her daughter, Tasha, sat at a small dining table. A casserole dish filled with meat loaf sat at the center of the table along with a pitcher of fruit punch Kool-Aid. Renee was reaching for the pitcher. A fork laden with mashed potatoes hovered near Tasha's mouth. Both mother and daughter gaped at Dante as he stormed into Mavis's apartment.

"Dante," Renee said, quickly rising to her feet, "what . . . what are you doin' here?"

"Your mother called off the lawsuit!" he yelled before turning to glare at Mavis. "And she did that shit without consulting me, without telling me a damn thing!"

Renee stared at her mother, aghast. "Mama, tell me you didn't do that!"

Mavis clasped her hands in front of her. She pushed back her shoulders and met Renee's gaze evenly. "Yes, I did."

"But I thought we wanted to hold out for some money!" Renee cried. "I thought we were—"

"There is no 'we' in this, Renee. This all had to do with me and nobody else. It didn't feel comfortable in the beginning suing that boy. I said I couldn't remember what happened that night. I couldn't say for sure that I wasn't the one at fault. But I let y'all talk me into it." She reached for the gold cross dangling around her neck and patted it as she spoke. "I thought about it. I prayed on it. I talked to my pastor and"—she took a deep breath—"I changed my mind. It didn't feel right anymore. I decided I couldn't sue him."

"You changed your mind?" Dante repeated with

disbelief. He barked out a laugh. "You changed your fucking mind?"

Mavis raised her chin in defiance. "That's right, Mr. Turner. I changed my mind and no one—not even *you*—can make me change it again."

At that moment, he wanted to backhand her clear across her face. He took a menacing step toward her, feeling his hands itch to take a swing. "Now, you listen to me, you stupid old bitch, I'll be goddamned if—"

"Don't talk to my grandma that way!" Tasha suddenly shouted, leaping up from her chair at the dining room table. Her little face contorted with rage. Her tiny fists were balled at her sides. "Don't call my grandma that bad word!"

Dante gave the little girl a withering glance. "Shut up. Just drink your goddamn Kool-Aid."

"All right," Mavis said, marching up to Dante's chest, "you can call me out of my name as much as you want, but nobody speaks like that to my grandbaby!" She pointed to the door that still sat ajar. "You're going to have to get the hell out of here!"

The pot of rage was simmering and it was on the verge of bubbling over now. He could see it: him suddenly lunging forward and throttling Mavis within an inch of her life. The little girl would start screaming. Renee would shout for him to let her mother go, to let her breathe, but nothing would stop him until Mavis lay dead on her living room floor.

Dante cocked an eyebrow as he considered doing it anyway, but he acknowledged that he was too pretty for prison and he had no desire to serve twenty-to-life for killing this old cunt. With great reluctance, he slowly turned and walked toward her door.

"Wait, Dante! Wait! Don't go!" Renee shouted while running after him.

He strode through the door and she was at his heels, teetering in her knockoff Louboutins. "Dante, please! Baby, listen!" She grabbed his arm. "Don't walk out like this!"

He shoved her away as he stalked toward the apartment's elevators at the end of the hallway. "Where the fuck were you while she was making all these phone calls and talking to her pastor?" he shouted. "I could have used the heads-up!"

"I didn't know she called him! She didn't tell me!"

He reached the elevator doors, pressed the Down button, turned, and glared at Renee.

You are so goddamn useless, he thought, shaking his head. He had assumed she would be a reliable ally. Instead she had sat around on her ass, allowing him to get blindsided like this. He pressed the elevator button again, jabbing his finger so hard onto the plastic that his nail bed was starting to hurt.

"Please don't be mad at me, baby!" She grabbed his arm again. "Look, I'll talk to Mama! I'll . . . I'll get her to change her mind! Just don't leave like this!"

He rolled his eyes and yanked his arm out of her grasp.

"Okay, then forget Mama! Just don't let this affect what we have!"

"*What we have?*" He laughed, hard and loud. "Renee, what we had was a few sweaty hours in bed and a bunch of used condoms. That's all, honey!"

"What?" Her face crumpled. "You don't mean that! You told me you cared about me! You said . . . you said we were going to go to Barbados."

By the time the elevator doors dinged and opened, Dante was laughing even harder. After the day he had had, he needed a good laugh. Unfortunately, it was at Renee's expense and she didn't seem remotely amused.

"So you saying you don't love me?"

He walked inside the compartment and turned to face her. "I'm saying that question is so ridiculous it's not even worth answering." He then reached to press the button that would take him to the first level.

Her eyes narrowed into thin slits. Her ample chest started to heave like she was the Big Bad Wolf preparing to blow down some poor piglet's house.

"Fuck you, motherfucka!" she screeched. "Fuck you! You think you can treat me like some shit? I'ma show you, motherfucka! You're gonna—"

The doors shut, cutting her off mid-tirade.

Chapter 21
Paulette

Paulette gazed listlessly at the stacks of lettuce, kale, cucumbers, carrots, and leeks as she pushed her cart down the produce aisle. She paused on the glistening linoleum, closed her eyes, and rubbed her belly, wincing at the spasms of pain that wrapped their way from her spine to her navel in undulating lightning bolts. She breathed deeply in and out, her brown nostrils flaring as she waited for the pain to subside.

"Damn you, Braxton Hicks," Paulette muttered as she opened her eyes thirty seconds later and started to push the cart again, heading toward a mini-pyramid of navel oranges.

"Braxton Hicks," as in Braxton Hicks contractions, according to *What to Expect When You're Expecting*, the book she kept hidden in one of her bathroom drawers. It wasn't quite like contractions, the book said. Those would come closer to her delivery date. These were her uterus's way of prepping for delivery. Her body was practicing for its grand performance: ushering a baby into the world. Unfortunately, that "practicing" was starting to feel alarmingly real, from the pain that had plagued her since she had stood in the shower that morning, pressing her forehead against the tile as the lightning bolts struck. It had dragged on for a good three hours, coming at varying intervals. As soon as she would regain her breath and start going about her business, it would come in again like a tidal wave.

"Drink more water to make the pain go away," the book had advised. She had already downed four bottles today.

"Make sure you empty your bladder," she read next. Well, Paulette had that part covered. She peed all the time these days, thanks to her son using her bladder as his personal futon.

But the pain still hadn't gone away. To distract herself, she had driven to the grocery store to pick up magnesium supplements (another helpful suggestion for preventing Braxton Hicks contractions) and some badly needed food, since their fridge was getting alarmingly empty at home again.

Paulette now reached for a plastic bag on a dispenser hanging from a metal bar. She pulled the bag open with the tips of her fingernails. She then picked up an orange, examining it for dents. She dropped it into the bag and reached for another one.

"Mrs. Williams," someone said over her shoulder.

Paulette turned to find a man standing behind her, next to a stack of Gala apples. He was wearing a polo shirt and baggy khaki shorts. A Nationals baseball cap covered his bald head. He was even wearing leather sandals, though he had paired them with black dress socks for some reason. When she realized it was Detective Nola, her breath hitched in her throat. Her eyes widened.

"D-detective Nola, what . . . what are you doing here?"

He raised a bushy eyebrow and then the green plastic basket in his hand that was filled with bread, a six-pack of Budweiser, a box of saltines, and Cheese Whiz. "Just doing a bit of shopping, like yourself."

Paulette laughed nervously. "Uh, y-yes. I can see that. I'm just surprised to find you here in . . . in this grocery store, in particular. I-I didn't know you lived in Chesterton."

He nodded. "My place is only a half mile from here. I walk here all the time to pick up things I need around the house."

She continued to smile dumbly in response, squeezing the orange so hard in her hand that orange juice might begin to ooze between her fingers. She dropped the battered orange back on the stack.

"How are you doing, Mrs. Williams?"

"Oh, fine. Fine!" she cried, placing the bag filled with a solitary orange into her grocery cart, wondering how she could politely walk away from the detective without seeming like she was fleeing. She knew now that Antonio hadn't murdered Marques, but there was still something about the detective that made her uncomfortable. His discerning gaze, maybe? He stared at her like he could smell the guilt on her from a mile away, like he knew things that he shouldn't know.

The detective inclined his head. "And how is Mr. Williams?"

"He's also good. Thanks . . . thanks for asking."

"I appreciate you and your husband talking to me."

"Oh, it was no problem." Her eyes wandered to the end of the aisle. "Well, it was nice seeing you again, but I really should be going, D—"

"You know, we still haven't made much progress in the investigation into Mr. Whitney's murder."

She cleared her throat. Her smile teetered a little as tendrils of pain erupted again in her lower back. *Not now*, she thought, feeling another Braxton Hicks contraction coming on. "I'm sorry to hear that, Detective."

"It's quite all right. We're not taking it personally. It's often the case with a guy like Whitney who had lots of enemies, lots of people with the motivation to do him harm or get rid of him . . . however justified . . . You have so many suspects that you don't know which direction to look first." He raised his brows again. "In fact, I understand from one of Mr. Whitney's friends that in addition to making his money off of the selling of steroids and other drugs, Whitney wasn't above engaging in a little bit of blackmail to make some extra cash."

Paulette fought back a wince. It felt like a metal belt was being wrapped around her waist and someone was pulling it tighter and tighter. "Is that so?" she said through clenched teeth.

The detective nodded. "His friend told me that before Whitney died, he boasted about how he was making quite a lot of money off of one of his ex-girlfriends. He was blackmailing her. My understanding is that he managed to get more than two hundred thousand dollars out of her before all was said and done. He bought a new tricked-out car and everything."

"O-oh, r-really?"

She reached out and gripped the handrail of her cart, her fingers wrenching the smooth plastic so hard that she might rip it clear off its metal brackets.

The detective squinted his pale blue eyes at her. "You wouldn't happen to know anything about this ex-girlfriend, would you, Mrs. Williams?"

Breathe, girl, she told herself. *Breathe!*

But Paulette could feel her throat tightening despite her best efforts. The pain. It had turned from just a feeling into a living, malevolent being with claws that were dragging up and down her back and along her torso. She wanted to swat it away, to tell *it* and Detective Nola to leave her the hell alone, but she couldn't.

"N-no, I'm sorry," she managed to say between huffs. "I don't . . . I don't know, Detective."

He took a step toward her and she instinctively took a step back, bumping into the stack of oranges and sending one tumbling to the tile floor and bouncing beneath a table where bananas and plantains were arranged in a spiral under a grinning Chiquita banana placard.

"Are you all right, Mrs. Williams?" the detective asked.

Paulette quickly nodded. "Y-yes, I'm . . . I'm fine. I . . ."

She didn't finish. She dropped to her knees, doubled over with pain, and the detective rushed toward her.

"Mrs. Williams!" he shouted before dropping to one knee at her side. "Are you okay?"

She suddenly felt a clammy wetness between her thighs. She dazedly looked down and saw that she was kneeling in a murky puddle. Where had all the liquid come from?

Oh God, she thought, shaking with panic.

Her water broke. It had broken right here in the grocery store. That wasn't Braxton Hicks contractions she had been feeling all morning; it was the real thing. But it was too early . . . *way* too early! Her son wasn't due for another month and a half. But her body didn't seem to agree. Paulette fell to all fours as the pain doubled, tripled. Tears sprang to her eyes. She groaned in agony. She had never felt pain like this before.

"Mrs. Williams, tell me what's wrong!"

"I'm . . . I'm having my baby," she managed to whisper to the detective.

He blinked in surprise. "A baby? You mean you're . . . you're pregnant?"

She nodded before pressing her head down to the wet floor.

He turned and frantically waved down a produce boy who was pushing a cart of strawberries. "Call an ambulance! Call a goddamn ambulance! This woman needs help. She's about to deliver a baby!"

After that, the world around her seemed to lose all color and sound.

Chapter 22

Evan

Evan casually strolled from the conference room down the corridor leading back to his office. He adjusted the knot in his tie and glanced at his wristwatch. He sighed dejectedly, discovering that he had fewer minutes until his next meeting than he had hoped. He was going to have to have a talk with Morris, their quality assurance officer, about his long-windedness. Nothing like wasting an hour while a guy pontificated on the merits of coated versus uncoated food packaging. Evan was sure half of those assembled at the conference table had started to fall asleep midway through Morris's presentation.

Evan looked up to find his secretary, Adrienne, waving her arms wildly, making him pause.

He frowned quizzically and raised his hands in a *"What's wrong?"* gesture.

"Sir! Sir, you have a message from your brother,"

Adrienne said as he approached. Her petite body almost jittered with barely contained anxiety. "He's been trying to reach you, but you weren't answering your phone."

"He called me?" Evan instantly reached his hand inside his suit jacket to check the inner pocket. "Shit," he muttered. He had forgotten to bring his iPhone with him. "Is everything okay? What did Terrence say?"

"He said it was an emergency, but he wouldn't go into detail." She shrugged helplessly.

An emergency?

What possibly could have happened? Evan had spoken to Terrence only yesterday and his little brother had seemed almost euphoric.

"I've got good news and I've got bad news, Ev," Terrence had said over the phone. "Which do you want to hear first?"

"Well, it can't be that bad of news judging from how happy you sound. But I guess I'll start with the good news first. What is it?"

"That woman dropped her lawsuit against me," Terrence had said, making Evan almost leap out of his desk chair.

"What? Are you serious! When did you find that out?"

"Yesterday. She hasn't withdrawn it officially yet, but she pretty much said she doesn't give a shit what Dante does. She's done. She apologized and everything."

"That's amazing, Terry!" He had been grinning from ear to ear. "Well, I guess you can go ahead with the bad news since nothing could possibly compete with that."

"Well, it's not really bad news . . . though you might think it is."

Evan had squinted. "Huh? What does that mean?"

"I told . . ." Terrence had taken a deep breath. "I told C. J. that I was in love with her."

Evan had stilled.

"Look, I know how you . . . how you feel about her. I considered all of that. I confronted her with what you told me, Ev, and she explained everything. She said a lot more than I expected, honestly. I know that you're suspicious of her, but I'm telling you that you've got no reason to be. She doesn't mean us any harm."

Evan had remained silent.

"I love her. I admit that it snuck up on me, but I've got some really heavy feelings for her, man. I've fallen hard for this girl. It scares the shit out of me, but it is what it is, right?"

Evan had leaned back in his chair and sighed. "I just don't want you to get hurt, Terry."

"And I won't. I told you, I trust her."

"Well"—Evan had pursed his lips—"if you trust her, I guess I trust her, too," he had said grudgingly.

"Good! I'm glad to hear it, Ev!"

Evan now gazed at his assistant in bemusement. So how had Terrence gone from declarations of love to calling with an emergency?

"Your brother wouldn't give me more information," Adrienne continued. "He sounded really flustered. He just said to call him back as soon as you can. I'm . . . I'm so sorry, Mr. Murdoch. I'm sorry I can't be more helpful."

Evan shook his head. "It's all right. I'll give him a call back and find out what's going on."

Evan quickly strode into his office and grabbed his cell phone from his desk. He saw that Terrence had called him no less than half a dozen times. "What the hell is going on?" Evan muttered as he pressed the button on the glass screen to call his brother back.

"Ev!" Terrence shouted, picking up after the first ring. "Shit! Where the hell have you been, man?"

"Sorry, I was in a meeting all morning and I forgot to take my phone with me. What's wrong? What happened?"

"Paulette's at Chesterton General. I'm on my way to the hospital now. I had to catch a cab since I still feel weird driving."

The blood drained from Evan's head. He gripped the edge of his desk to steady himself. He suddenly got a flashback to that dreaded night when the police had called his home to tell him that Terrence had been in a car crash.

"What . . . what do you mean, she's at the hospital?" he shouted, his throat tightening with fright. "What's wrong? Did she have an accident?"

"No, nothing like that. Tony said she collapsed in some grocery store and the ambulance rushed her to the emergency room and then they took her to the maternity ward. I said, 'Why a goddamn maternity ward? She's not pregnant!' Tony said, according to the doctor, she's almost eight months along. Eight fucking months, Ev!"

Evan was starting to feel faint. He fell back into his desk chair. *"What?"*

"Yeah, my thoughts exactly! Our sister has been pregnant this *whole time* and she didn't tell anybody, not even her damn husband! I knew she was acting strange, that she was hiding something, but I had no idea it was this bad."

"Oh Jesus," Evan murmured just as his phone buzzed again. He glanced down at the screen and saw that Leila was on the other line. "Look, Terry, that's Lee calling me. Let me talk to her. We'll meet you at the hospital, all right?"

"Okay, bye," Terrence replied before hanging up.

Evan switched to the other line. "Lee?"

"Oh Evan! Thank God I caught you," Leila said, sounding like she was almost in tears. "I was hoping you were at your desk."

"If this is about Paulette, I already know."

Leila paused. "What about Paulette?"

"She was rushed to the hospital and is going into delivery. I just got off the phone with Terry. He said he's on his way to Chesterton General Hospital. Tony's already there."

"Paulette's about to deliver?" Leila sounded stunned. "Oh my . . . I didn't know! Oh God! It's way too early. The baby isn't due for several more weeks!"

Now Evan paused, shocked with what he was hearing. "Wait. You knew she was pregnant? *She told you?*"

Leila released a loud, impatient breath. "Yes, but she asked me not to tell you guys! I told her I couldn't keep yet another damn secret for her . . . that I'd give her some time to tell Tony, to do it her way first before I told everyone else. I guess she never did. But, Ev, that's not why I called. I—"

"What the hell, Lee!" he exploded. "Why wouldn't you tell me something like this? She could've—"

"Evan, please don't yell at me," Leila pled. He finally noticed that she was crying. "I can't take it right now. Not with what's happening. I don't know what to do!"

"What do you mean? What happened?"

"Izzy's missing. I went to her school, b-but they don't know anything. They said no one's seen her since before lunch period and they've checked the entire school . . . every room, every locker. I've called the little cell phone I gave Izzy for emergencies, but she's not answering. I don't . . . I don't know where she is. What if something really bad has happened to her?" She sobbed. "Please, I need you here. Come home!"

"I'm on my way," he said before hanging up his phone. He then leapt from his chair and raced toward his office door.

Evan arrived at Murdoch Mansion soon after three o'clock to find two deputies standing in the center of his three-story foyer, the beeps and static from the deputies' walkie-talkies echoing off the foyer's coffered ceiling. He knew that about a dozen more deputies were checking the mansion grounds and driving around town searching for Isabel. As Bill drove Evan from Murdoch Conglomerated Headquarters in Arlington back home to Chesterton—breaking several speed limits along the way, Evan had made a phone call to Chesterton's sheriff, asking him to pull out all his resources to find the missing little girl. Evan wasn't one to use the heavyweight of his family's reputation or the millions of dollars the Murdochs had invested in Chesterton to his advantage, but this time, he was willing to make an exception.

"Of course, Mr. Murdoch," the sheriff had assured him. "We're doing everything we can. We're canvassing the school and everything within town limits. We're putting out an Amber Alert. We're bringing the state police onboard to help in the search."

"Good to hear it," Evan had said. "And I'll be able to call you personally for updates?"

"Of course, Mr. Murdoch. You can reach me on my cell at any time of the day. Don't hesitate to call me."

But Evan knew ultimately that no amount of ass-kissing from the sheriff could ensure that Isabel would be found. Each hour that passed statistically lowered the chance that the cops would find her. Evan's stomach turned as he considered the many things that could have happened to Isabel. Had she run away? Was she abducted from the school playground by some deranged sexual predator? Was she still alive?

The housekeeper kept her head bowed as Evan stepped through the front door. When he did, the deputies turned to look at him. Leila, who had been sitting on one of the foyer's padded benches with her mother, Diane, at her side, suddenly looked up. Her eyes were puffy and almost entirely red. She wiped at her runny nose with a Kleenex and shakily rose to her feet.

"Ev, I-I . . . I can't . . ."

She broke down into sobs before she could finish whatever she was about to say, and Evan instantly reached for her. She collapsed against his shoulder and wrapped her arms around his neck, clinging to him as she cried.

"They're going to find our baby," Diane assured over the sound of Leila's strangled sobs. Tears were in the older woman's eyes, too. Her wrinkled cheeks were wet. "They're going to find Izzy. Don't worry, honey."

But Diane's promise seemed hollow. From what Evan understood after talking to the sheriff, the police weren't sure where to start in their search for Isabel. None of Isabel's classmates or teachers had seen her leave the school and none of the neighbors or businesses surrounding the elementary reported noticing a little girl wandering along the sidewalks. It was like she had just . . . vanished.

"It's all my fault," Leila moaned, finally calming down enough to articulate words. "She was so unhappy, Evan. I-I pushed her away! I made her feel like she wasn't wanted. No wonder she—"

"Shsssh," he whispered, rubbing her back. "You love Izzy and she knows that. You didn't push her away. That's ridiculous! I'm not letting you blame yourself for this."

"Are you Isabel's father, sir?" one of the deputies asked, squinting his green eyes at Evan.

Evan slowly shook his head. "No, I'm her . . . her stepfather—sort of. Her mother and I are engaged."

Though I'm still married to someone else, who refuses to give me a divorce, Evan thought but figured it better not to add that part.

"Has anyone spoken to her actual father?" the other deputy inquired. He was the shorter of the two and slighter in build. "We'd like to interview him, too, if that's possible."

"He's in California," Leila said, pulling away from Evan and dabbing at her eyes with her makeup-stained Kleenex. "He lives on the other side of the country. He wouldn't know anything about this."

Evan narrowed his eyes, wondering if that were true. If Isabel had indeed run away, her father would be the first person whom she would likely run to.

"I was hoping we'd find her before I had to tell him she was missing, since he'll . . ." Leila took a quivering breath. She wrapped her arms around herself and dropped her eyes to the floor. "He'll probably blame me."

"We should call him anyway," Evan said. "Maybe Isabel said something to him that might help us find her."

Leila raised her eyes and frowned at Evan. "You really think so?"

"At this point, anything is worth a try."

"He's right," Diane said, rising to her feet. "Call him, Lee. Call him now."

A few minutes later they all sat in the adjoining study in a semicircle around Leila, who sat at the oversized mahogany desk, dialing Brad's number on the desk phone.

Evan gazed around him. The room was a holdover from when his father, George, had been owner of Murdoch Mansion. Evan had never gotten a chance to redecorate in here, something he now regretted. The study was all wood paneling, green sconces, brass detailing, and thick velvet curtains that kept out most of the natural light. Leila had had to turn on a Tiffany lamp on the desk to be able to see the phone's dial pad because it was so dark. The room radiated no warmth and looked like it could be the setting of some gloomy Gothic novel.

This is not a place where you want to be when your daughter is missing, Evan thought. *All this gloom could make a person downright suicidal.*

One of the deputies stood off to the side as they waited, listening to Brad's line ring over and over again on the phone's speaker. Leila was wringing her hands and bouncing on the balls of her feet. Evan reached out and grabbed her hands, making her eyes dart up to look at him in surprise.

"*It'll be okay,*" he mouthed.

She nodded, though she still looked nervous.

"Hello?" a man answered. Booming music played in the background.

When Evan heard Brad's voice, his jaw tightened. He hadn't spoken to Brad in years, not since he was engaged to Leila. Whenever she had conversations with her ex-husband, which often would devolve into arguments, Evan would make it a habit to be out of the room. He didn't want to talk or listen to what that man had to say. He had never liked him, from the moment Leila had introduced him during a summer break from college. Time hadn't lessened Evan's dislike for Bradley Hawkins at all.

"Hey, Lee," Brad said, shouting over the music, "I'm driving and traffic is a real bitch. Can you call me back later?"

"No, Brad, I can't call you back," Leila said. "I need to talk to you *now*."

"If this is about your child support, I told you my check is going to be a little late this month since I'm short on cash. It's not like you need the fucking money anyway!" A car horn suddenly blared, making Evan wince. "Hey, watch it! Did you get your goddamn driver's license yesterday?" Brad yelled.

"This isn't about the check!" she shouted with annoyance, then closed her eyes. "Look, there's no easy way to say this. But . . . but Izzy is missing."

The music faded a little like Brad had turned down the volume. "She's missing, huh?"

Evan squinted, confused by Brad's tone. The man didn't sound alarmed or the least bit surprised to hear the news.

"What do you mean, she's missing?" Brad asked, finally sounding like a real father whose child had disappeared.

"I mean exactly what I said. Izzy . . . well, she went to school and didn't come home. They can't find her and we can't, either. She just . . . just disappeared. And we need your—"

"Oh, good job, Lee! Were you so busy sucking your sugar daddy's dick that you couldn't be bothered with watching over our daughter?"

The deputy, who had been scribbling onto a notepad, suddenly stopped mid–pen stroke. His eyes widened in astonishment. Diane sat upright in her chair, looking furious. Evan's fist clenched in barely controlled rage. Meanwhile Leila bit down hard on her bottom lip and pushed back her shoulders, putting on the mask of calm.

"Please don't start with me, Brad. I just called you to see if you could help us find Izzy, not to be abused."

"*Abused?* Oh Lee, baby, as far as I'm concerned, I'm going easy on you! You lost our goddamn daughter, you dumb b—"

"The police are here," she said quickly, trying to cut him off before he started another embarrassing tirade. "They're listening to our conversation, Brad. Please . . . we need your help. Did Izzy say anything to you the last time you spoke to her? Did she mention anything about running away?"

"Yeah, in fact, she mentioned that she hated you and hated living with you," Brad said. "She said, 'Come and get me, Daddy! I don't like it here.' I told her I couldn't take her because her mom railroaded me out of my rights as a daddy. She dragged my child thousands of miles away so she can live in some big house with a big shot while I have to live off of baked beans and tuna!"

Evan tensed in his chair. He clamped his mouth shut, forcing himself to remain silent. He didn't want to ruin the chance of them getting information from Brad that would help find Isabel, but it took all his control not to shout at Brad, not to want to reach through the phone and punch him in the face.

"Please," Leila said softly. Her eyes welled with tears again. "Please, just . . . just tell us if she said something. I don't—"

"Fuck you! You *stole* her from me and now you want my help in finding her because you lost her? Why don't you ask your sugar daddy for help, huh?"

Evan gazed at Leila as she dropped her head and started to cry openly.

He wanted her to scream at Brad, to tell him to go to hell. He wanted her to remind Brad of the years he had cheated on her with other women ... of how he had gambled away their livelihood and well-being with illegal pyramid schemes that landed him criminal charges ... how his selfishness had driven Leila away. Brad's egotistical behavior had forced her to put herself and her daughter first. That's why she had left him! That's why she had moved clear across the country and taken their daughter with her. She hadn't done it out of selfishness, but *selflessness*.

But Leila didn't say any of that; she didn't defend herself. She sat there silently and accepted his insults and yelling like it was her penance, like she deserved this flagellation because she had done something wrong. And what had she done wrong? She had the audacity to want to be happy. She wanted to be loved by someone who truly loved her back. She wanted to get married and have a baby in a stable home with a man who adored her. How dare she!

To hell with this shit, Evan thought.

Leila shouldn't have to apologize for falling in love and wanting to start a new life. And neither should Evan. They had served their time in abysmal relationships.

You don't owe him a damn thing, Lee.

"Why don't you write a check and buy a new kid?" Brad continued with maniacal glee. "Or hey, how about this? How about you give her name to the bastard baby you're having with him? So whenever the hell you guys find her bloody, mangled body somewhere, you can—"

"Enough," Evan said, reaching over to hang up the phone, cutting off Brad. "That's fucking enough." He turned to look at her, regretting that he was the one who had suggested she call Brad for help. He had given that sorry son of a bitch too much credit. "I'm sorry, baby. I'm so sorry."

She dropped her face into her hands and Evan held her as the dial tone echoed in the study and she wept on his shoulder.

Chapter 23

C. J.

C. J. knew something was wrong the instant she heard his voice. They hadn't been together long, but she knew him well enough that she could detect when he was antsy, angry, or worried and she heard all of that now in his simple greeting of "What's up, babe?" Her hold tightened on her cell phone and she grimaced, nervousness suddenly making the muscles in her stomach tighten.

"What happened?" C. J. asked, unable to keep her own alarm out of her voice.

"Oh, nothing," Terrence replied dryly. "Just the whole damn world has gone to hell."

She narrowed her eyes. "*What?* What does that mean?"

"My sister is giving birth to her baby . . . a baby I didn't even know existed since she decided to tell no one that she was pregnant. And my brother called about an hour ago to tell me that every deputy in the county is looking for his fiancée's daughter. The poor kid ran away or got kidnapped or . . ." His voice trailed off. "Hell, I don't know. I have no fucking clue what's going on anymore!"

C. J. fell into one of her kitchen dinette chairs in shock. "All of this happened *today?*"

"Pretty much. I'm starting to wonder whether it's Friday the thirteenth and no one told me."

She couldn't help but smile. "You're safe. It's still Thursday."

"Yeah, that's what I thought." Terrence sighed. "Well, needless to say, I don't think we'll be able to meet up tonight. I'm sorry, babe."

C. J. winced. She had expected him to say as much, but part of her hoped he might still want her to come over to his condo for a romantic evening and a repeat of the first night they had spent together. She ran her fingertip along the brown surface of the oak table, envisioning running it along his brown broad chest and rippled abs. She took a deep breath and clenched her legs together tightly.

Focus, C. J. Focus, she told herself. *His world is falling apart around him and you're thinking about having sex with him again.*

"Don't apologize, Terry. Really, it's . . . it's okay."

"Are you sure?"

"Definitely! You saved me from having to get all dolled up," she lied before glancing down at the clingy black dress she was wearing. She shifted in her chair and adjusted the lace thong beneath her dress. It was far from comfortable, but she had worn it just for Terrence—a surprise gift she knew he would enjoy. Now he wouldn't get to see it.

"You did me a favor. I can just lounge around in my pj's!"

"Well, don't act that damn excited not to see me! Way to make a brotha feel important!"

"Oh, stop! You big baby," she said with a laugh. "Go deal with your family stuff. I'll be fine. Just get back to me when everything settles down."

"Don't worry. I will."

"I guess I'll talk to you later, then," she said.

"Yeah, guess so. 'Bye, babe. Love you," he said, then hung up, not giving her a chance to respond.

He said the last part so quickly that she wondered if she had really heard it. *Love you.*

She smiled and hung up her cell phone, lowering it to the kitchen table, feeling warm all over.

Terrence Murdoch said he loved her and he had said it *twice!* Part of her wanted to break out into girlish giggles, but she resisted the urge. Instead she rose to her feet and began to lower the zipper on the side of her dress, preparing herself for a quiet evening at home alone.

Twenty minutes later, C. J. was removing a bag of popcorn from the microwave, carefully tugging open the seams of the bag so as to not burn her fingertips.

She had traded her slinky black dress for a baggy T-shirt and sweatpants. Her hair was piled into a crudely crafted bun atop her head. She set the steaming popcorn bag aside and walked to the other end of her counter to sample the bottle of Merlot she had picked up at the Chesterton supermarket a few days ago. She uncorked it and poured some wine into a coffee mug before carrying the mug and popcorn to her living room. The opening credits to *Imitation of Life*—one of her favorite old movies—appeared on-screen. She set the popcorn bag and mug on the coffee table before plopping onto her sofa. Just as she stuck her hand inside the bag and pulled out a fistful of popcorn kernels, she heard a knock at her apartment door. She raised her brows in surprise. Besides Terrence, she hadn't expected any visitors this evening.

C. J. shoved the buttery popcorn into her mouth, chewing it as she slowly walked to her front door. "Who is it?" she called out between chews.

C. J. stood on the balls of her feet and peered through the peephole. When she saw who was standing on the welcome mat in her hallway, she stumbled back in shock. Her hand flew to her chest, where her heart was beating so fast that she thought it might seize up and she'd die of a heart attack.

This can't be possible, she thought, absolutely stunned.

She threw open the deadbolt and unlocked the bottom lock before cracking open the door and peering into the hall, to prove to herself that she wasn't daydreaming.

"D-d-daddy?" she stuttered, barely above a whisper.

Her father gazed at her, looking staid and regal like an Ethiopian king. His face revealed no hint of emotion. He nodded curtly. "Courtney, how have you been?"

A tidal wave of emotions swept over C. J. She

hadn't seen her father in *years* and when she had last spoken to him she had been at an emotional low. She had been in tears, sobbing and telling him that there was no way possible she could marry Shaun Clancy.

"I can't do it, Daddy!" she had remembered crying to him on the eve of her wedding, speaking with him in his private study. "I don't love him! I can't marry a guy I don't love!"

"You can and you *will*," her father had said firmly, when all attempts to rationalize and cajole her had failed. "My children obey me. It is what you owe me as your father. 'Children, obey your parents in everything, for this pleases the Lord.' Colossians, chapter 3, verse 20."

C. J. had never forgiven him for how callous he had been, for quoting Bible verses and refusing to budge when she had poured her heart out to him. And how could he possibly quote Bible verses to her when she knew what he did behind closed doors, when she knew the double life he led?

But as she gazed at him now, she realized that even though she was hurt by her father and angry at him, she still missed him. A part of her still yearned for the man who had once called her his "precious jewel," who had once been the center of her universe.

She pushed the door open farther. Now she could see that the esteemed Reverend Pete Aston was not alone. Her mother and her brother, Victor, stood to the side. They both looked solemn.

"What . . . what are you guys doing here?" she asked, still stunned that her family was standing in her hallway. She wanted to reach out to touch her father and mother to assure herself that they were really there, but she fought back the impulse.

"We need your help, sweetheart," her mother said with her head bowed and her hands clasped in front of her plump frame.

She had gained weight since C. J. had last seen her. She looked like she had put on about thirty pounds. Her hair also had more gray strands than C. J. remembered. Her wheat-colored face had several more wrinkles.

It's only been five years, Mama! When did you get so old?

C. J. shifted her gaze to her mother. "What do you mean?"

"Look, can we come in, Court?" Victor asked, stepping forward. The dour expression didn't leave his face. "We've been driving for hours. I think Mom and Dad would like to sit down."

She instantly nodded and gestured for them to come inside her home. Her family silently walked through the doorway, her father taking the lead. After they stepped over the threshold, they peered around her apartment—staring at the space and the décor. The look of disdain that crossed all of their faces didn't surprise C. J. Her humble abode was nothing like her father's four-thousand-square-foot home back in North Carolina with its high ceilings, expensive knickknacks and artwork, and stately furniture. But she made no apologies for her plain existence. However, she did stiffen when her mother leaned down and scooped up C. J.'s half-filled coffee mug from the coffee table and sniffed its contents. The older woman raised her brows. Her heavy frown deepened even further, making C. J.'s cheeks warm with embarrassment.

"You're drinking liquor now?" her mother asked, turning to her, looking distraught. "Has the devil ensnared you in his evil ways?"

C. J. didn't answer her. What could she say? *"Yes, Mama, I drink now. I also haven't gone to church in years. And I had premarital sex and liked it. I hope to do it again as soon as I can. Maybe the devil has ensnared me, but compared to what Daddy and Victor do on the regular, I think I still have a long way to go on the grand scale of sinning!"*

Instead she gestured toward the sofa and armchairs. "Please have a seat."

Her mother slowly lowered herself onto the sofa, placing the cup back on the coffee table and shoving it away like it was arsenic, not red wine. Her father took a seat beside her. Victor sat in one of the armchairs and C. J. took the other. The living room fell into awkward silence. She could practically hear Victor's Movado watch ticking on his wrist.

"So," C. J. said when she couldn't take the silence anymore, "what brings you all here?"

Victor opened his mouth, then paused. He glanced at his father. The older man nodded his dark head, giving him approval to speak.

"We have a . . . a bit of a problem at Aston Ministries," Victor began.

"What problem?" C. J. asked. *And what does it have to do with me?*

"We've got wind of an impending lawsuit by a former employee. One of Dad's previous assistants—"

"The low-down hussy," C. J.'s mother spat. "I knew it the minute I laid eyes on her that she would be nothing but trouble! I could see it in her eyes. I heard the voice of the Lord whispering in my head telling me, *Watch out for that one, Sarah. She is the wolf in sheep's clothing*," her mother ranted. "She is the—"

Her mother immediately fell silent when her father placed his hand on top of hers and gave it a squeeze that looked affectionate at first glance, but C. J. knew it meant more than that.

Be quiet, Sarah, the squeeze said.

"Well, anyway," Victor continued, "she's making unsubstantiated allegations that could taint Dad's reputation, as well as the reputation of Aston Ministries. Her lawyer says he's going to go to the press with it if Dad doesn't agree to settle for a substantial sum. And it's coming at a very, *very* delicate time when Dad is seriously considering a run for office."

C. J. turned to her father. "What allegations?"

"She says he's the father of her bastard child!" her mother suddenly burst out, leaning forward on the sofa.

C. J. cringed.

"Can you believe that?" her mother yelled. "That hussy sinned and rutted with who knows what, and now she's trying to tarnish your daddy with this! She's trying to force him to take a DNA test after the baby is born. She should be ashamed of herself!"

"Sarah," her father began softly.

"No, Pete! You were nothing but kind to that gal—helping her pay her way through college and giving her a good wage to take care of the child she *already had* out of wedlock. You took her under your wing! And this is how she repays you?"

C. J. gazed at her father, feeling a mix of disillusionment and disgust. Though her mother was sure that her father was innocent, C. J. wasn't so certain. But the older woman had subsisted for decades on a buffet of denial and willful ignorance; C. J. couldn't stand to live on a similar diet. She knew about her father's dalliances and had even stumbled upon him in a heated embrace with one of his female parishioners back when she was nineteen years old. But he had never gotten any of his girlfriends pregnant before. Could he really have been so careless? *So stupid?*

"So what exactly do you expect *me* to do?" she asked, unable to hide her anger or distaste.

"We need to show a united front, Court." Victor leaned forward with his elbows perched on his knees. "I know you agreed before not to do any on-camera interviews—"

"And I still won't," she said firmly.

"But we plan to hold a press conference," Victor continued. "Dad wants to fight this lawsuit. And it will look strange if you're not there!"

"I don't care! No, I can't do it. I *won't* do it. I explained that to you in the beginning when you asked for my help . . . no, when you *bullied* me into helping the first time! I have a life here! A new life that I just won't toss aside because—"

"So you would let that woman send your daddy down the river because you want to keep your privacy?" her mother asked, looking horrified. "When did you get so selfish, girl?"

"Selfish? *Selfish?*" C. J. screeched, feeling decades' worth of anger suddenly erupt to the surface.

"Watch the volume and watch your tone," Victor ordered tightly, pointing his finger at her.

"No, Victor, I won't do that. And I won't keep silent anymore, either. I've been silent long enough." She turned back to her mother, feeling emboldened. "Mama, for twenty-one years I did everything . . . *everything* that you and Daddy told me to do! I was almost willing to marry a man I had no interest in marrying just to make you happy. But it was never good enough. Was it? You always wanted more and more and more and more!"

"Yes," her mother said with a nod, "the devil definitely has his hooks in you, because the sanctified girl I knew never would speak to her mother like this. How dare you yell at me!"

"No, Mama, how dare you—"

"That's it! That is it!" Victor shouted simultaneously, shooting to his feet. "I've had enough of this, you ungrateful little—"

"We will speak privately," her father suddenly boomed. "Nothing will get settled here with all of you barking and growling at each other like some . . . some rabid dogs." He walked toward the apartment's hallway leading to her bedroom and master bath, expecting her to wordlessly follow him.

C. J.'s heart thudded wildly in her chest. Her chest heaved. Her face felt like it was on fire.

He paused at the hall's entrance and turned to her. "Are you coming, Courtney?"

Old habits die hard. At her father's question, she rose to her feet and walked past him, leading the way to her bedroom. She pushed her bedroom door open and he followed her.

When he shut the door behind him, she turned to him expectantly.

"Have a seat," he said, gesturing to her bed.

She furrowed her brows and slowly sat down. He stood near the bed, looming over her like he loomed from the elevated pulpit at his church.

"I know you think me a . . . a proud man," her father began, pacing in front of her. "But I am not. I want to start off by humbling myself to you. I want to tell you, Courtney, that I am sorry."

She raised her brows in surprise. *An apology?* That wasn't what she had expected.

He lowered his eyes to his ebony, wrinkled hands. "I want to apologize for disappointing you, for not being the daddy I should have been. I should have listened when you turned to me for help. But I put my pride before my obligation, and I drove my precious jewel away. For that, I am deeply ashamed. Can you . . . can you forgive me?"

Her mouth fell open. Tears sprung to her eyes. She was at a loss for words. When he raised his dark eyes and stared at her expectantly, she quickly nodded.

"Of course, Daddy!" she said, her voice cracking with a well of emotion. "Of . . . of course, I forgive you."

"Thank you. I am glad to hear it." He sat on the bed beside her, reached for her hand, and held it. "I want us to be father and daughter again, Courtney. And I want it not just to have you standing beside me at a press conference, but standing beside me *period*. You're my child . . . flesh of my flesh, blood of my blood. It breaks my heart to have you so far away from me."

"I will always be your daughter, Daddy, but I can't lie anymore."

"And I would never ask you to lie."

Maybe. But in the past her father had had no problem asking her to pretend, which was the closest you could get to lying. Was he about to ask her to do it all over again? She needed to know the truth.

"So there's no way possible that you could be that baby's father? You never did anything with that woman?"

He dropped her hand and sat back, looking stunned by her question. "How could you even ask me that?"

"Daddy . . ." She paused. She couldn't meet his eyes anymore. "Daddy, I know everything. I know about the other women and . . . and about all the affairs. I know, okay? Please, just . . . just tell me the truth."

He narrowed his eyes. "I did not fornicate with that young woman. I saw her as a daughter, as a young lady with lots of potential who needed guidance and a helping hand. But she didn't seem to be of the same mind," he said ruefully. "She came to the house one day and tried to seduce me. I suppose she had gotten word of my . . . my past indiscretions that I had committed in a moment of weakness. But I prayed to God long ago for forgiveness for that sinfulness. I told Him I would never do it again. So I told her no and she became angry, belligerent." He shook his head. "I had to ask her to leave my home. The next day she told me she would be resigning her position as my assistant. Five months after that, I got a letter from her lawyer saying that she was pregnant and she was suing me for sexual harassment."

C. J. pursed her lips.

"Perhaps you see this as justice due for the sins I have committed, and perhaps you're right. I know I have been tainted, Courtney. 'Like a muddied spring or a polluted well are the righteous who give way to the wicked.' "

"From the Book of Proverbs," C. J. whispered.

Now her father was the one who looked surprised. A small smile crept to his lips. "That's right."

"Look, Daddy, I don't see any justice in what you're going through now. I never wanted bad things to happen to you or Mom or even Victor. You're my family . . . the only family I've ever known."

"You've never wished us ill will because you have a good heart," he said, placing a hand on her shoulder. "And I'm appealing to that good heart now, Courtney. Please, stand by my side. Show the world that you trust your father's word . . . that you believe me."

She sat silently for several seconds, knowing that if she agreed to this, she would no longer live in anonymity. The guys at the newspaper and everyone else in Chesterton would know who she really was. And once again she would have to play the role of the devout preacher's daughter. She would have to smile sweetly, dress primly, and reenter that claustrophobic world.

But Daddy's worked so hard, she told herself. *And he sounds like he's tried to change. It would only be temporary. I'll do this favor for him until the storm blows over. Until that woman's baby is born and she's proven to be the liar that she is.*

C. J. took a deep breath and slowly raised her eyes. "I'll do it," she said softly. "I'll do it for you, Daddy."

His smile widened. He threw his arms around her, almost with relief. "Thank you. Thank you, my precious jewel. Thank you from the bottom of my heart!"

Chapter 24

Evan

Evan watched as the police car pulled off. His eyes locked on the taillights as the deputies made their way down the driveway.

The deputies had finished asking questions of him, his family, and the staff. They had examined every inch of the mansion grounds and still saw no sign of Isabel. They were now going home for the day while the search continued elsewhere in Chesterton.

He had called Terrence to tell him about Isabel's disappearance and to get an update on Paulette. Terrence said mother and son were fine, though Little Nathan, who had been born several weeks' premature, was in the NICU recovering.

"But they're alive. They're okay," Terrence had assured him. "You just do what you have to do and take care of Lee."

Evan closed his front door and headed toward the staircase. He walked toward their bedroom, hoping to find Leila there. He hadn't seen her in hours, not since her disastrous phone conversation with Brad. He pushed his bedroom door open and leaned inside the room.

"Lee," he called out, but the bedroom was empty.

He walked along the west wing in search of her before finally heading to the east wing. He found her in Isabel's room, which was probably the first place he should have looked.

It was a little girl's perfect paradise with its soft pink walls, gauzy curtains, and silver details. Evan had outfitted it with a pearl gray armoire and dressing table, an oversized toy box, a wardrobe filled with costumes, and glass shelves covered with ballet figurines, unicorns, and Fabergé eggs. He had done it to impress Isabel, to make her feel like a little princess in a fairy tale.

Leila was sitting on Isabel's queen-sized bed, her face half-hidden by the bed's silk canopy. She was holding on her lap a framed photograph of her daughter, running her fingers over the glass and smiling at it lovingly.

She glanced up at Evan as he walked across the room toward her. Tears were in her eyes.

"I had this photo taken of her when she was two weeks old," she whispered. "She was so tiny and wrinkly. Her foot was about the size of my pinkie."

Evan silently sat on the bed beside her.

"I remember the day we brought her home from the hospital. Brad couldn't stay, of course," she said, rolling her eyes. "He said he had to get to some important networking function. Chances are he had to run off to go see one of his girlfriends. But either way, I was home alone with Izzy for most of the night." She touched the frame's glass again. Her tears spilled onto her cheeks. Evan rested a hand on her shoulder. "Izzy lay in her bassinet and I just stared at her, Ev. I did it for hours, watching her sleep, watching her breathe. I couldn't believe how perfect she was. I couldn't believe that I had helped make this beautiful little person. She was my own special little gift." She finally raised her gaze from the picture frame to look at him. He saw an ocean of pain in her dark eyes. "Now I feel like I've squandered that gift, like I let it get away from me."

"You didn't squander anything! We're going to find her, Lee," he said, leaning forward and kissing her cheek. "You *have* to believe that."

"I want to. And in some ways, I agree that I have to believe it. Because if anything happened to her, Ev." She started to choke up again. She closed her eyes and shook her head furiously, dropping the picture frame to the bed.

Evan's cell phone started to buzz in his pocket, but he ignored it.

"If . . . if *anything* has happened to my baby and she doesn't come home to me, I'm done."

He frowned uneasily at her. "What . . . what does that mean? What do you mean, you're done?"

"I mean I can't go on! I can't go about my life like everything is normal when I've failed at the most important thing in my life: being a mother and protecting my child. I don't . . . I don't want to be here! I don't *deserve* to be here, Ev!"

Evan felt like someone had reached inside his chest and wrenched out his heart. He shifted closer to Leila and cupped her face. He raised her chin so that she had to look at him. They were almost nose to nose.

"Now you listen to me. Listen to me, Lee, all right? Stop talking like this! I don't want to hear this shit come out of your mouth again!"

"I'm telling you the truth, Ev! I can't—"

"We are going to find Isabel! She is going to be okay!"

"You don't know that!"

"But even if by some far chance the worst-case scenario happens and we don't find her, Lee, you are going to continue to exist. You're going to continue to live because you have to."

She didn't answer him. She obstinately closed her eyes instead, like shutting out the sight of him was the equivalent of shutting out his words.

"Lee, I *need* you! Our baby needs you! Did you forget about the baby we're going to have in less than five months? What about *that* child? Are you telling me you don't owe it anything?"

He knew he had gotten through to her with that one. She slowly opened her eyes to stare at him.

"You're going to get through this. We're going to get through this together. Because we love each other. We depend on each other! And if you go, I go. Understood?"

He released her long enough so that she slowly nodded, though he could tell she did it reluctantly.

"We'll get through this," he whispered.

"Lee!" Diane shouted. "Lee, where are you?"

Evan dropped his hands from Leila's face and turned toward the opened door. "We're in here, Diane."

The older woman raced into the room, clutching at her chest, gasping for air. "They found her! They found Izzy! Praise the Lord! Thank You, Jesus!" Diane said, raising a lone hand to the ceiling.

They both stared at her in utter shock. Leila gradually rose to her feet, taking a hesitant step toward her mother.

"What did you say?" she whispered breathlessly.

"I said they found her!" Diane was beaming. "They found her at Dulles Airport—of all places! She was trying to catch a flight to Los Angeles. Can you believe that? She couldn't get through the checkpoint because she didn't have any ID on her or an adult with her, so she had been wandering around the airport for hours. Someone recognized her and took her to the airport police. I swear I could give that person a big ol' kiss right now!" Diane turned to Evan. "The sheriff said he's been calling you on your cell phone, trying to reach you, but you weren't answering."

So that's why my phone was buzzing, Evan thought, but his attention was abruptly drawn to Leila, who dropped to her knees in the center of the bedroom floor.

"Oh, thank You, God!" Leila screamed, weeping and rocking back and forth on her shins. "Oh, thank You! Thank You! Thank You!"

* * *

The ride from the airport was a quiet one. Because he had sent Bill home hours ago, Evan had to drive their small caravan from Dulles back to Chesterton in his Range Rover. He sat in the front with Diane while Leila and Isabel sat in the back-seat. As he drove, Evan stole glances at the rearview mirror, watching the mother/daughter reunion. Leila clung to Isabel like she was a new-born babe. She kissed the little girl's forehead and cheeks. She whispered to her as she rocked her in her arms. Isabel didn't say anything, seemingly too exhausted to speak. Her head drooped on her mother's shoulder listlessly.

"Why did you do that, baby?" Evan heard Leila ask. Her voice was fierce and passionate. "What got in your head to do such a thing?"

Evan had his suspicions. Though Isabel was pre-cocious for her age, he found it hard to believe that she had bought an airplane ticket to LAX all on her own—with a prepaid debit card, no less, according to police. He also wondered how an eight-year-old had managed to get a cab from Chesterton to Dulles Airport, which was twenty miles away. It wasn't like there were cabs driving around their small town. Isabel would have had to call a cab ser-vice to achieve such a feat.

Or he *would have had to call,* Evan thought as he drove, turning onto the road leading back to Mur-doch Mansion.

He remembered again how Brad had sounded when Leila told him that Isabel had disappeared. The man didn't seem surprised or alarmed. He had been more concerned with scolding Leila and making her feel worthless than he was about the safety of his own daughter. But why would he be concerned if he had known what was happening all along?

Brad, you son of a bitch, Evan thought as he pulled into his driveway. *You set up this whole thing, didn't you?*

"I'm sleeping in Izzy's room tonight," Leila announced as they climbed out of the car.

Evan nodded, knowing that there was no point in arguing. Leila wanted to keep her daughter close in light of what had just happened. He understood such a wish.

He watched as Leila, Diane, and Isabel slowly climbed the stone steps leading to the mansion doors with hands linked. He was relieved that Leila had gotten her happy ending, but a seed of discontent still sprouted within him. Something wasn't right about this. Evan could feel it in his bones.

About a half hour later—after he undressed and donned his robe—he headed to the east wing. He knocked on the closed door.

"Come in!" Leila called out.

He found her and Isabel in the queen-sized bed, munching on chocolate chip cookies and reclining on oversized pillows as they watched a cartoon on the wall-mounted television on the other side of the room. Isabel was in her pink pajamas. Leila had donned an oversized T-shirt and a pair of Evan's gym shorts. They looked like two girls enjoying a sleepover. When he saw them, he smiled.

"I just wanted to say goodnight," Evan said from the doorway.

"Good night!" Leila called.

"Night," Isabel mumbled, seeming to be entranced by her cartoon.

"I'll see you guys in the morning," he said as he drew the door shut but paused to push it open again. "You didn't need anything, did you?"

Leila shook her head. "No, I think we've got everything. Cookies, milk, popcorn . . ."

"We didn't get ice cream," Isabel piped. "You told me I could have ice cream if I wanted, Mommy."

Leila bolted upright. Her cheeks flushed pink. "Oh, I'm . . . I'm so sorry, honey! I guess the housekeeper forgot to bring it."

"She's probably in bed now," Evan said, breaking into their conversation.

The older woman usually was out like a light by ten p.m., but she had stayed up late because of all the household uproar. She had even given Isabel a kiss on the cheek when the little girl walked through the door.

"I'll go get you some ice cream myself then," Leila said, climbing off the bed. "I'll even make you a sundae! Just give me a—" She halted midway across the plush carpet, like she suddenly remembered something. Her hands fell to her sides. She turned back around to look at Isabel, who was still staring at the television while munching on a cookie.

Lee's too frightened to leave, Evan thought. *She's scared to let her out of her sight.*

"I'll stay," he said, making her whip around to look at him. "Go ahead and make the sundae. I'll watch her."

"Really? Are you sure? I thought you were headed to bed."

"It's no big deal. I can wait."

She ran toward him and kissed him on the cheek before darting through the door and down the hall, her bedroom slippers flapping softly on the marble tile floor. Evan waited until Leila disappeared around a corner before he turned back around to gaze at Isabel. The little girl seemed almost oblivious to his presence. Evan pasted on a polite smile.

"Today was pretty scary, huh?" he asked, talking loudly so he could be heard over the sound of the television. "Being in that big airport all by yourself."

Isabel glanced at him and shrugged. "I guess," she muttered before returning her attention to the TV.

"I heard that you were trying to catch a flight to Los Angeles."

He walked toward her, shoving his hands into his robe pockets, trying his best to keep his tone light and casual. She was a kid, after all. He didn't want to make her feel like she had done something wrong. "Were you trying to see your dad?"

"I miss my daddy," she mumbled between cookie bites.

Evan drew closer so that he was almost standing at the edge of her bed. He wanted to see her face when he said his next words.

"I know you do. I bet he misses you, too. I bet your dad was really happy to hear you were coming."

A grin sprouted on Isabel's face, revealing one of her missing front teeth. "He said he was going to give me cotton candy as soon as I got there," she said excitedly. "And then we were going to go to Disneyland and I could ride the Teacups! And we could stay there until it got dark and I could see the castle light up! Cinderella lives in the castle, you know. Everyone thinks it's the prince's castle, but it's really *hers!*"

Bingo, Evan thought. So his suspicions had been right. Brad had orchestrated this.

"So your daddy was the one who told you to run away?"

Isabel's smile disappeared. She removed the cookie from her mouth.

"He bought you the plane ticket, too. Didn't he?" Evan persisted.

The little girl lowered her head. Her eyes started to well up with tears. "He told me not to tell! Daddy said if I told, he would get in trouble. He said Mommy would be mad at me!" she sobbed, making her thin shoulders tremble.

"Don't cry." Evan reached for one of the linen napkins the housekeeper had left on Isabel's night table. He leaned down and dabbed the little girl's eyes with it. "Your mommy isn't mad at you. She was upset that you disappeared, that's all. It's because she loves you, Isabel, not because she was angry."

Isabel's sobs calmed a little. She sniffed and he handed her the napkin so that she could blow her nose. "Are you going to tell my mommy what my daddy did?"

Evan shook his head. "No, I think it would only upset your mother even more."

Leila would be furious. She would probably want to press charges against Brad, though it would serve no purpose. The man was already headed to jail.

"We'll make this our little secret. But I want you to do something. If your father ever asks you to do something like this again, you tell him no and you tell me. What your daddy asked you to do, he shouldn't have. Something could have happened to you out there. Don't put your mother through that again. Promise me you won't."

Isabel nodded solemnly. "I promise," she whispered.

Leila arrived back to the room ten minutes later, carrying a glass dish filled with two spoons and a gargantuan-sized sundae. By then, Isabel's tears had dried and Evan was sitting in a chair adjacent to the bed watching her cartoon with her. They were sharing a bowl of popcorn between them.

"I'm back!" Leila announced, licking chocolate syrup off her fingers. "I'll admit I got a little crazy with the whipped cream, but my excuse is I'm eating for two." She giggled then gazed at Evan and Isabel quizzically. "You two look chummy."

He shrugged and rose to his feet. "What can I say? We're both big fans of SpongeBob."

Leila squinted at him as he walked toward her. He gave her a quick peck, but she pulled back to stare up at him. "Something is going on, Evan Murdoch. I don't know what it is, but I get the feeling that—"

"It's nothing, Lee. Everything is fine," he said, before kissing her again. "You two have a good night. Enjoy your ice cream. I'll see you in the a.m., all right?"

He didn't give her the chance to respond. Instead, he walked out the bedroom door, shutting it behind him.

Chapter 25
Paulette

Paulette slowly walked down the staircase, gritting her teeth as she gripped the handrail. It had been almost a week—five days, to be exact—since her emergency C-section, but the pain around her midsection still lingered. It was sharp one moment and then sometimes it was a dull throb, like she had done one too many sit-ups and was suffering the aftermath. She didn't care about the pain, though. Only hell or high water would keep her from making the daily trips to the hospital to see her infant son.

She closed her eyes as she descended to the next riser, thinking back to the day she had delivered him. It had been so traumatic—the pain, the blood, and the feeling that things had spiraled so far out of control that she couldn't tell up from down anymore.

She remembered EMS easing her from the grocery store floor onto a stretcher, asking her so many questions that she could barely answer. She also remembered how Detective Nola's face had gone almost completely white as he watched her being carted down the produce aisle. Paulette would have been amused that she had managed to terrify a man who'd had her scared and looking over her shoulder for so many months if it hadn't been for the fact that she had been in mind-numbing agony at the time. She was then rushed by ambulance to the local hospital. During the ride there and after she arrived, she kept whimpering, "It's too early. It's too early. It's too early."

"None of that matters now," a nurse had whispered reassuringly to Paulette as she was wheeled into the operating room. "You're going to have your baby today. It's going to be okay."

And then she felt her son being pushed and tugged out of her. After the epidural, that was all she could feel—the pressure of the doctor's hands. And then she saw him—a mini-version of the baby she had anticipated. But instead of a fist-pumping, feet-kicking, screaming baby, his body was limp. He was quiet. There was another frantic rush as he was taken to the NICU.

Little Nathan was still there in the NICU. Her baby rested under a heat lamp to help him control his body temperature. He lay in a tight little ball—as he had when he was inside her tummy—with tubing down his throat and wires attached by clear tape all over his body. Every time she saw him her heart broke.

"I'm so sorry, Nate," she had whispered to him the last time she had seen him, gently rubbing his wrinkled arm, listening to the beep of the monitor. "Mommy is so, *so* sorry she did this to you."

She hadn't put her baby first. She had let her fears and worries dominate her decisions, when her focus should have been on preparing for Nate, on giving him all she had to give.

"I was so stupid, honey," she had told him.

Paulette now stepped onto the foyer floor and walked toward the door.

"Where are you going?" she heard Antonio ask over her shoulder.

She turned to find him walking down the staircase toward her.

They hadn't talked—really talked—since he arrived at the hospital and walked into her recovery room. His expression had been indecipherable as he stood near her hospital bed.

"So I hear I'm a dad now," he had said casually.

She had been unable to meet his eyes when he said that. Instead, she had stared down at her lap.

"When were you planning to tell me you were pregnant? Were you *ever* planning to tell me?"

She had opened her mouth to reply, then closed it. Her tongue had felt heavy, and not just because of the painkillers she had been given through her IV.

"You know, I don't get it, Paulette. All the lies . . . the betrayal. How much do you expect me to take, huh?"

She had closed her eyes in response.

In the face of her silence, Antonio had slowly

shaken his head and walked out of the hospital room, leaving her alone with her thoughts and her guilt.

He had driven her home from the hospital two days after her cesarean. He had deposited her in her bed, fluffing her pillows behind her head and setting a glass of water and the TV remote nearby.

"Tell me if you need anything," he had murmured before shutting her door behind him.

"Are you going to see Nate?" Antonio now asked as he walked toward her across the foyer.

Paulette nodded. "I haven't been to the hospital yet today. I try to do it before noon, but I'm moving a little slower than usual." She gave a pained smile before reaching for her sweater on one of the coat hooks and wincing at the dull throb that erupted along her stomach.

"I can drive you," Antonio said, stepping off the last riser.

She paused. "You . . . you don't have to do that."

"I know I don't have to. I *want* to. I want to see him. I haven't been to the hospital since he was born."

Paulette had noticed, but she hadn't faulted Antonio for keeping his distance from the baby. She had assumed Antonio hadn't gone back to the NICU because he doubted whether Nathan was his son. And in truth, he was right to doubt it.

"Come on," he said, walking across the foyer and retrieving his keys from the foyer's oak table. "Let's go."

Ten minutes later they rode in silence in his Mercedes to Chesterton General Hospital. Paulette remembered having a similar strained car ride with Antonio only months ago when they were driving to see Terrence in the ICU. That ride had been carried out in silence, too, though the whole time she had wanted to confess her feelings to Antonio, to tell him all her secrets and regrets. But she had held back. She wasn't going to do that again.

"I should have told you," she now said as he drove.

His eyes darted from the windshield and he glanced at her. "Huh?"

"I should have told you about the baby," she said in a louder voice, swallowing the lump that had lodged in her throat. "It was wrong of me to keep that secret from you . . . ridiculously wrong. But I was scared. I make the worst decisions when I'm scared. I know that now."

"Why were you scared?" he asked, reaching over to lower the volume of the radio.

She took a deep breath. This would be the hardest part. "Because I wanted for so long for us to have a baby, Tony. I had been hoping about it, dreaming about it. And then when I finally got pregnant, I . . . I couldn't say for sure if it was *our* baby."

"Our baby?" She watched as the muscle flexed along his mahogany-hued jaw. "You mean, you think it's his baby, then?"

"I don't know. I couldn't say for sure. And I know how you feel about the affair . . . how you feel about . . ." She was going to say his name but thought better of it. "I know how you feel about that man and I didn't want you to . . . I didn't want you to take it out on me and the baby," she whispered.

The car compartment fell silent again. Antonio's hands visibly tensed on the wheel.

"I wish you would give me more credit, Paulette. You make me out to be some monster."

"No, I make you out to be a normal man who's been through a lot, whose wife has pushed him to the point that any other guy might break or go crazy. But you haven't broken or gone crazy, Tony, and I'm in awe of you. You are a good man . . . a man who is *way* too good for someone like me."

He didn't respond. Instead he kept his eyes focused on the windshield, on the roadway in front of him.

"So if you want a divorce, I'll give it to you. I understand." She lowered her eyes. "I thought about it last night and I'm . . . I'm going to talk to Evan and ask him if I could stay at the mansion for a while, at least until Little Nate gets better. You can have the house all to yourself. It'll give you some peace, finally. I'll pack my things and—"

"No," Antonio suddenly said.

"Huh?" she asked, raising her eyes.

"I said, no, baby. I don't want to get a divorce. I told you I was in this for the long haul. And besides, I don't want my son being raised apart from me. That's not what I signed up for."

"But . . . but you don't know if he is—"

"He's my son," Antonio declared. There was so much resolution in his tone that she wouldn't dare argue with him. "I okayed my name being added to his birth certificate, didn't I? You don't think I realized what I was doing? No, Nathan Williams is *my* son. I don't care what any DNA test says. And my son will be raised with his father. And we will . . . we *will* work through this." He drew to a stop at a stoplight and turned to gaze at her. "I want to be with you, Paulette. I want to make this work."

Tears sprang to her eyes. After all this, he still wanted to be married to her. And he was willing to claim the baby as his own without question.

"You're too good," she squeaked, her throat tightening.

The light turned green and he accelerated. "I'm not perfect," he said. "By no means, but my family is important to me. *You're* important to me. I fight for what's mine."

They arrived at the hospital a few minutes later. In the elevator, Antonio reached out and grabbed her hand and she almost fainted from the feeling of relief and calm that washed over her. He hadn't held her hand in almost a year. He hadn't touched her. The feel of his warm palm against her skin was a sensation that she had sincerely missed.

They made their way down the hall of the maternity ward to the NICU. Paulette knew most of the nurses by name by now and greeted them when she entered. One blond nurse looked up at Antonio in surprise.

"Are you Little Nate's daddy?" she asked, a smile on her pink lips.

Antonio nodded. "That's me."

They walked to Nathan's incubator and Paulette watched as Antonio hesitated. "Can I touch him?"

he asked the nurse. For the first time, he seemed nervous.

The nurse nodded. "Of course!"

He then leaned his hand in and caressed a finger along Nathan's leg.

"Hey, buddy," he whispered, grinning from ear to ear. "It's your daddy."

Chapter 26

Terrence

"She's all yours, Mr. Murdoch," the car salesman said with a bleached-white grin as he rose from his desk and extended the keys toward Terrence.

Terrence slowly lowered the ballpoint pen to the salesman's desk, pushed away the stack of documents in front of him, and hesitated. He stared at the dangling keys like a recovering alcoholic would stare at a bottle of gin—with a mix of longing and fear. He wanted badly to take the keys, but he was scared he might regret it later.

"You don't have to be scared, Terry," Dr. "How Do You Feel About That?" had told him during his last therapy session earlier that week. "It's been several months now. Your doctor okayed you to drive again. Don't you think you're finally ready?"

Maybe he was, but still, he wished he had planned this better. He had purchased a new car on impulse after he saw a double-page ad in one of the men's

magazines he got in the mail. The new Porsche
Boxster GTS . . . not identical to the last car that
he had owned and totaled, but certainly a close
enough replica. The instant he saw it, he called
the car charter service that he had been using for
the past month and asked them to take him to the
Porsche dealership just outside of Chesterton. He
hadn't even bothered to test-drive the damn thing.
He didn't want to lose his nerve when he climbed
behind the wheel. Instead, he had pointed to the
car as soon as he stepped into the showroom.

"How can I help you, sir?" asked the salesman in
the sharkskin suit with his hair loaded with so
much gel that it glistened under the showroom's
lights. "Any particular vehicle you're interested in
today?"

"I want that one," Terrence had said boldly, still
pointing his index finger at the Boxster GTS.

"Wow! You're a man who knows what he wants,
huh?" The salesman had guffawed and slapped
him on his shoulder so hard that it stung.

"Yeah, I . . . I guess you could say that."

But now Terrence regretted his boldness.

What the hell was I thinking? he now wondered.

The salesman's grin started to wane when Terrence made no move to take the car keys. "Is something wrong, Mr. Murdoch?"

"Uh, no. No, everything's fine," Terence said
with a forced smile before finally reaching for the
keys. The cool metal and plastic felt heavy in his
hand. He reached for his cane and slowly rose to
his feet.

"Does your wife or girlfriend know you bought a
new car today?" the salesman asked.

Terrence stared down at the keys in his palm, transfixed by the Porsche emblem. "It's girlfriend and no . . . no, she doesn't know I bought a car."

"Ah, well! Then this will be a big surprise!"

Terrence nodded, though the truth was that C. J. wouldn't give a damn that he had bought a new Porsche. She would more likely chide him about it.

"*Your penis is fine, Terry,*" she would say dryly with a smirk once she saw the gleaming roadster. "*You don't have to drive around in a fake one.*"

But she would be proud of him for overcoming his fears, for finally taking the last step he needed to move on with his life, to prove that he had finally left that horrible accident and all the aftermath that came with it, behind him.

"It was a pleasure working with you, Mr. Murdoch," the salesman said, extending his hand for a shake.

"Thanks," Terrence mumbled before resting his cane on the edge of the table and shaking the salesman's hand distractedly.

When Terrence climbed onto the car's leather seat ten minutes later, inhaling the soothing new car fragrance, he felt a rush filled with a mix of excitement and anxiety. He buckled his seatbelt, checking the fastener once, twice, and then three times to make sure it was secure. He inserted his key and listened to the engine rumble to life. He ran his hands over the leather steering wheel and sat back in the driver's seat, staring out the windshield, working up the will to press the accelerator and pull out of the parking space.

"You can't sit here forever, Terry," the voice said in his head.

"I know that," he whispered fiercely, feeling the panic rise within him. His heart galloped. His grip on the steering wheel tightened. His breathing became shallower and shallower. The car's compartment started to feel smaller and smaller; it was like the roof and the side doors were pressing in on him.

What if he pulled off and made a wrong turn and sideswiped someone? What if the wheel spun out of his hands and he jumped the curb and hit some poor pedestrian, or he stopped at a stoplight and someone rear-ended him, sending him careening into oncoming traffic? He had lost an eye and fractured a leg in his last car accident. What if he lost his *life* this time around?

"*You'll be fine, Terry,*" C. J.'s voice suddenly whispered in his ear. "*I have every confidence in you.*"

At the thought of her, his breathing and his heartbeat slowed. His grip on the steering wheel loosened.

"*Now put the pedal to the metal and come and see me!*" her voice ordered huskily, making a reluctant smile spring to Terrence's lips.

Terrence did just that, shifting the roadster into drive and pulling out of the dealership's parking lot.

Twenty minutes later, Terrence pulled into the lot of C. J.'s apartment complex, gliding into one of the few empty spaces. He turned off the car engine and released a long breath. It hadn't been an easy drive. He had been tense for the first five minutes of the car ride, driving so slow that a woman who had to be in her eighties had blared her horn at him and passed him while giving him the evil eye. He finally started to relax as he drew closer to C. J.'s apartment, keeping a vision of her face in his mind the rest of the way.

As he opened the roadster's car door, he saw a vision of her again—this time in the flesh. Terrence squinted as he watched C. J. walk toward her Honda Civic, dragging a suitcase on rollers behind her. Or at least, he thought it was C. J. At this distance, he couldn't say for sure because she looked so different.

"C. J.?" he called to her as he climbed out of his Porsche.

She paused just as she opened her trunk. She turned her head to look in his direction. A smile brightened her face. "Terry, hey!" She waved.

He crossed the parking lot, all the while staring at her in confusion.

She was wearing a suit—a pale blue ensemble with pearl buttons down the front and along the cuffs and a skirt that fell just below her knees. She had finished the outfit with sensible heels of the same shade as her suit. She had straightened her hair, too. Gone were the corkscrew curls he knew and loved and in their place was a shag haircut that fell over her shoulders. She was even wearing makeup.

C. J. looked like someone had abducted her and forced her to undergo a makeover—the Stepford Wife edition.

"What the . . . what did you do to your hair?" he said, reaching out to run his fingers through her tresses.

"Nothing!" she cried, smacking his hand away. She smoothed her hair back into place, looking somewhat embarrassed. "I just got it flat-ironed. I used to wear my hair like this all the time until . . . well . . . a few years ago." She paused and gazed at him. "What? You don't like it?"

Terrence shrugged. "It's not bad, I guess. I just wasn't expecting it." He let his eye slowly travel over her. His focus settled on the suitcase leaning against her rear tire. "Are you going somewhere?"

She nodded almost apologetically. "I was heading to North Carolina. I didn't get the chance to tell you. I-I figured you were busy with your family stuff. I didn't want to bother you."

His newly minted girlfriend was disappearing somewhere and she didn't think she needed to tell him that? He couldn't help but be a little offended and irritated.

"You wouldn't be bothering me, babe. I'd want to know something like this. What if I showed up and found you had just . . . just *disappeared*? That wouldn't have been cool."

She lowered her eyes. "I know. I'm sorry. I should have told you. But honestly, Terry, I would have called from the road to tell you. Besides, I'll be back before you know it. It'll only be a couple of days. You'll barely notice that I'm gone."

Oh, he'd notice! It was alarming how quickly he had gotten addicted to this woman and her reassuring presence. But she was allowed to have a life. She was allowed to do things without him.

"So what's in North Carolina anyway? Are you headed to a news assignment?"

"No, nothing like that." She paused to toss her suitcase into the trunk. "My family is there. It's also the home base of Aston Ministries. They invited me to come down."

Terrence grinned. "That's great! So your dad is finally willing to talk to you? He wants to make up with you?"

She closed the trunk and pursed her lips. "Sort of."

"Sort of? What does that mean?"

"He wants to make up . . . but it kind of comes with strings attached."

Terrence's smile faded.

"There's some dustup within the church. It's bad, Terry. Really bad. And it's happening just when Dad is thinking about running for office. He wants us to show a united front, so he asked me if I would—"

"Go back to being Courtney Jocelyn Aston. Go back to pretending you're the perfect family," Terrence finished for her, slowly shaking his head. "Babe, I thought you told me you didn't want to do that anymore."

"I don't. And . . . and I'm not! I'm still going to be me. I'm not letting my dad and my brother pull the same manipulative bullshit that they used to, but I agreed to do a few press conferences and meet and greets . . . to stand smiling in the background while he or Victor talked. I'll do a few on-camera interviews. That's all."

So that's what the makeover was all about. Reverend Aston wanted his daughter to look prim, proper, and perfect on camera.

"Are you sure that's all?" Terrence asked, taking a step toward her. "Just look at you, C. J.! You even look like a different person. First you agreed to do phone interviews and now they're asking you to do TV press conferences. What's next? *Asking you to get engaged to that guy again to distract everyone from their latest church fiasco?*"

She impatiently sighed and rolled her eyes. "Terry, give me some credit!"

"They're asking you to lie! They're asking you to do the same stuff that—"

"No," she said steadfastly, "they're asking me for love without judgment. 'Do not judge others, and you will not be judged. Do not condemn others, or it will all come back against you. Forgive others, and you will be forgiven.' "

He raised his brows. "Oh, we're quoting the Bible now? Well, you'd better flip it open again, because I'm pretty sure there's plenty of shit in there about not bearing false witness."

"Terry, I'm doing this for something I know you consider even more sacred than the Bible: family loyalty. It's something I would think that you of all people would understand!"

"The stuff with my family is different. You know that!"

"*Oh, really?*" She took a step toward him. "How many times do you go to bat for your brother or sister, Terry? How many times did you look the other way or put on a brave face for *your* dad?"

He fell silent.

She stood on the balls of her feet, looped her arms around his neck, and kissed him. Despite his frustration, he wrapped his arms around her and kissed her back.

"Nothing will change, if that's what you're worried about," she said a minute later against his lips. "I'll still be C. J., even if I look different."

He pressed his forehead against hers. He wanted to believe it, but a gnawing in his stomach told him differently. This was a slippery slope of compromises in the name of family, and he feared that C. J. would be too far downhill before she realized what was happening, or how much she really would change.

She tugged away from him, seeming to do it with great reluctance. "I should get going. I told them I'd arrive there by tonight to do prep work for the conference."

A few minutes later, she was behind the wheel of the car and he was standing on the curb, watching as she put her key in the ignition.

"I'll see you in a couple of days," she said after lowering the car window and smiling up at him. "By then I'll probably be feenin' for my Terry fix." She laughed.

Tinkling piano keys, he thought, remembering the first time he heard her laugh at the charity banquet. That's what he thought her laugh sounded like, piano keys going up and down the scale.

"See you soon," she said with a wave, before driving off.

Terrence watched her until she pulled out of the parking lot and turned onto the roadway.

Chapter 27

Evan

Evan leaned back against the elevator wall and gazed at Leila as she paced back and forth in front of him.

"I'll be back home in about an hour, Mama," she said into her cell phone as the elevator ascended to the hospital's sixth floor. "Two hours tops . . . So how's it going? Is everything okay? . . . Izzy's all right?"

Though Leila wasn't quite the emotional wreck she had been while Isabel had been missing, she still was more tightly wound than a violin string. He noticed it from the way her lips were taut as she talked to her mother, from the way she clenched her cell phone in her hand to the point her knuckles almost were white. He hoped over the next few months she would return back to the Leila he knew and loved—at least, for their baby's sake.

"So you know for sure she's in her room, right?"

Leila asked. "You checked on her, I mean . . . Yes . . . Yes, I know we told her we weren't going to hover but I just . . . I just want to make sure Izzy is okay . . . that she's there."

Evan shifted his gaze to Leila's stomach. Her torso was no longer relatively flat. A noticeable potbelly poked out over the top of her linen pants, pushing against the waistband, straining the pants button. She was four and a half months along now. It was about time she started to show! Evan smiled a little at the thought of Leila round and swollen with their baby in a few months. He never could have imagined this more than a year ago.

She paused mid-conversation and glanced at him quizzically. Leila followed the path of his gaze. Her cheeks reddened and she quickly tugged down her shirt to cover the exposed skin. His smile widened as he took a step toward her and placed a hand lovingly on her stomach.

"Don't cover up the Buddha belly. I like it," he whispered. She rolled her eyes and slapped his hand away but not before smiling at him.

"So you do know *for sure* Izzy is in her room, right?" she asked her mother again a second later as the elevator doors opened. "Oh, you're in her room right now?"

Evan stepped out of the elevator into the maternity ward hallway. Leila trailed after him.

"Sure, you can put her on the phone, Mama. Thanks . . . Hey! Hi, Izzy!" Leila said with an unnatural chirpiness, the same voice you would use with a cooing infant. "It's Mommy! I just wanted to say hi and tell you that I'll be back real soon, okay?"

Evan grabbed her arm, making her stop as she strode past him. She stared at him in surprise.

"What?" she mouthed and he silently pointed up to the sign showing a drawing of a cell phone with a giant red *X* crossed through it.

She quickly nodded. "Look, honey, Mommy has to go," she said into her phone. "I'm at the hospital and I can't talk on my phone here. Hospital rules . . . No. No, I'm not sick! . . . Evan and I are here to see a baby." Leila laughed and Evan's heart melted a little. "Yes, exactly! . . . I will see you soon. Okay? Love you, honey. 'Bye." She hung up, dropped her phone into her purse, and turned to Evan, still grinning. "She wanted to know if we were here to help give you some practice with babies. I told her yes."

He reached for Leila's hand and held it. They continued their way down the corridor. A nurse walked past them, holding a clipboard. "I'm glad you had the chance to talk to her. I hope it made you feel better," Evan said.

Leila's smile faded a little and she rubbed her stomach absently. She did that a lot nowadays. "I just still worry about her, you know? Every now and then I'll flash back to that day when Mom called me and said Izzy didn't come home from school and I just—"

"It's not going to happen again." He squeezed her hand tighter. "I talked to Izzy. We have an agreement."

Leila narrowed her eyes at him. "I wish you would tell me what you said to her."

"I told you the gist of it."

"The gist, but not—"

"Trust me. It was nothing out of line. I wouldn't do that."

"I know." Leila took a deep breath and nodded again. "I . . . I trust you, Ev."

They rounded the corner and he saw Paulette and Antonio standing near the end of the hall. The couple turned away from the window they had been gazing into, looked up at Evan and Leila, and waved.

Evan didn't know when was the last time he had seen Paulette and her husband together, let alone together *smiling*. It was a relief. They had been through so much and yet they were still making their marriage work. It was definitely a testimony to the belief that true love could endure just about anything because Paulette and Antonio certainly had faced some severe trials and tribulations lately— from an affair and now, the unexpected birth of their son. Evan still couldn't believe that his sister had lied that long about her pregnancy, that she had let it go that far—to the point that she had actually delivered her baby before she was willing to tell anyone the truth. But then again, Evan didn't have much room to talk; he was keeping his own secrets now. He still hadn't told Leila about Charisse showing up at his office and giving him that ultimatum. But Leila had enough to worry about with Isabel and her own pregnancy. He didn't want to burden her with that right now.

"I'm so glad you guys could make it," Paulette called out as she walked toward them with Antonio at her side.

"Of course we made it," Evan said, hugging his sister. He turned to Antonio and shook his hand.

"In fact, we would have been here to see Little Nate sooner but . . . well . . . stuff happened."

Antonio nodded. "Yeah, I heard." He gazed down at Leila. "How is your daughter doing, by the way?"

"My baby's home. She's safe, which is all that really matters, right?"

"I agree," Paulette said.

The two women stared at one another and Evan felt something pass between them, a secret message, perhaps, or unspoken words that only they could decipher.

Evan knew that Paulette had once viewed Leila as somewhat of a big sister and Leila had reciprocated those feelings, loving and protecting Paulette as fiercely as Evan or Terrence would. The two women had once been close. But lately, a tension seemed to radiate between them. At that moment, Evan felt the tension dissipate.

The two women stepped forward simultaneously and fell into an embrace. They cried softly on each other's shoulders.

"I'm so sorry, Lee," Paulette said between hiccups.

"No, *I'm* sorry," Leila whimpered.

Meanwhile, Evan and Antonio stood awkwardly off to the side, watching them.

"Give them their moment," Antonio whispered with a chuckle.

The two women continued mumbling heartfelt apologies for another five minutes or so until Paulette pulled away, wiping her eyes with the backs of her hands. "Do you want to go in the NICU to see Nate?"

Leila's teary eyes widened. "Of course! I would love to! B-but would they let me in there?"

"I'd like to see them try to keep you out!" Paulette proclaimed with a grin before dragging Leila toward the NICU's metal door.

"I'll be right back," Leila called over her shoulder as both women rushed through the entrance.

Evan watched them with bemusement.

"Glad to see them finally make up," Antonio said.

"Me too."

He and Antonio strolled toward the glass window at the end of the corridor, where Antonio and Paulette had been standing earlier. Evan now realized that it was a window leading to the NICU. Two blinds were drawn over the double-paned glass but one blind was open. Evan could see Paulette and Leila a few feet away from the window, gazing down at one of the incubators. A tiny infant lay inside it. The baby's skin was almost translucent, revealing a web of veins, and was covered with a fine layer of dark hair. Wires were attached to thin legs and arms. A foam bandage was over his eyes. Paulette reached a hand inside the incubator and gently rubbed the baby's torso. Her eyes filled with tears. Leila placed a hand on Paulette's shoulder and whispered something into her ear.

"Nate doesn't look great now, but the doc says he's actually doing pretty good," Antonio said over Evan's shoulder, making him turn to look at him. "He's off the respirator. He's breathing on his own. She said if he keeps this up, they'll be able to move him out of the NICU. He might even be able to go home with us in a month or so, when he can feed on his own and puts on more weight." Antonio shrugged. "Of course, Paulette wants to take him home *now*, but she knows that it would be best to let the doctors and nurses do what they do. It's the best thing for Nate to be here . . . for now anyway."

Evan slowly shook his head. "I'll tell you, Tony, you're handling all of this a hell of a lot better than I would. I've had *months* to adjust to the idea of becoming a dad and I'm still freaking out a little. You had a couple of hours. And now you have to deal with all this." He gestured to the glass.

"Trust me. I've been through worse," Antonio said dryly, though Evan couldn't fathom what could possibly be worse than this.

"I'm just happy our son is going to pull through and that Paulette didn't die in childbirth," Antonio continued. "Granted, I'm still pissed that she thought she could keep something like this from me, but you know, Ev, I'm tired of being angry. *This* is our happy ending, as far as I'm concerned."

Evan slumped against the wall and nodded. "I feel you, Tony. There are so many things you can't control. At some point, you just have to throw in the towel and say, 'To hell with it! If this is the best it's going to get, I'll accept it.' " He pursed his lips. "And you know . . . if it weren't for a few people fucking things up, life would be pretty damn perfect."

Antonio furrowed his brows. "Any people in particular?"

"Leila's ex-husband and my wife, for example," Evan muttered ruefully.

Though he felt like he had the situation with Brad in hand, he wasn't so sure about Charisse.

She was definitely a wild card now. He thought back to how Charisse had looked in his office more than a week ago, so stubborn and filled with self-righteousness. He knew that he was in for a battle with her, but his conflicted emotions about their relationship made him less than willing to engage in an all-out war.

"And our damn brother, Dante," he said. His voice lowered an octave. He had no ambivalence about his feelings for Dante; he hated that bastard. "Dante's had it out for us from the beginning. He's hell-bent on revenge and nothing seems to stop him. He's gone after me, Terry, even Paulette. He—"

"When the hell did he go after Paulette?"

"Last year," Evan said, returning his gaze to the NICU window.

The nurse had opened the incubator and now Leila was holding Little Nate against her chest, gazing at the infant lovingly. She waved at Evan. Evan waved back.

"Dante tried to blackmail Paulette into selling her shares in Murdoch Conglomerated," Evan continued. "He found out about her . . ." He paused and glanced at Antonio, unsure if he wanted to bring up the topic of her past affair right now. "Well, anyway . . . Dante found out delicate information about Paulette. He basically told her he'd let the secret out if she didn't cooperate with him."

"*What?*" Antonio's face darkened. He balled his fists at his sides. "She never told me that!"

Evan loudly cleared his throat, hoping that their conversation wasn't reopening old wounds. "There wasn't anything to tell, Tony. He didn't get a chance to blackmail her. We confronted him. We handled it and he backed off, but . . . I have a feeling he's going to try something again. I just don't know what it is."

"Guys like that never stop on their own accord, Ev," Antonio said quietly. "You know that. I know that. They've got to *be* stopped."

"Yeah, well, short of putting a bullet in that asshole, I'm not sure what else would work."

In his darker moments, Evan had fantasized about killing Dante. He dreamed of marching up to him, pulling out a .38, and holding it up to his temple before pulling the trigger. But Evan wasn't capable of murder—for now anyway. If Dante pushed him hard enough, he could start researching the going rate for putting out a hit these days.

Mark my words, Evan thought.

"It wouldn't necessarily take a bullet to solve your problem." Antonio crossed his arms over his broad chest. "There are more simple ways."

"I'm all ears," Evan said sarcastically. He watched as Leila handed Nate back to the maternity ward nurse.

"I could do it for you," Antonio said.

"Do what?" Evan was barely paying attention now. He watched as the nurse stepped forward to lower Nate gently back onto his bed. She raised the plastic door to close the incubator.

"Take care of him. I've done it before. Paulette had a problem just like this one. I knew it wouldn't go away on its own, so . . . I took care of it."

Evan did a double take and stared at Antonio. "What problem?"

"More like 'who' than 'what.' Her problem was

a wannabe thug named Marques," Antonio continued quietly. He didn't look at Evan as he spoke. Instead, he smiled benevolently at his wife and
newborn son. "The one she cheated on me with.
He was blackmailing her, too. She gave me his
name and I Googled his address that very night. It
was easier than I thought. That jackass's name was
plastered all over the Internet for his training services. I showed up at his apartment building and
waited until someone was going inside and I
stepped through the door. I knocked on his apartment door and pretended to be a delivery guy.
When he opened it, I asked him if he knew Paulette.
If he knew about me," Antonio now whispered
through gritted teeth. "He said he did. Honestly,
Ev, I don't know if I would have been more merci-
ful if he would have apologized . . . if he would
have at least pretended that he was sorry for what
he had done. But he didn't. I confronted him
about everything . . . about the affair, about the
blackmail. He talked a lot of shit that night, but by
the time I was done with him, he wasn't talking
shit anymore. He wasn't saying *anything*. The deed
was done. I had it all cleaned up in an hour and I
was back at my mom's to get a good night's sleep."
Antonio turned to Evan. He was still smiling.
"Problem solved."

Jesus Christ, Evan thought, taking a step back.
The deed was done. What *deed*?

Had Antonio just confessed to killing a man?

"Oh, Ev, he is so adorable!" Leila gushed, making Evan jump in surprise. "I forgot what it's like to
hold someone so little. I can't wait to have our
baby." She turned to Antonio, threw her arms

his neck, and hugged him. "Your son is *so* beautiful, Tony! You should be so proud."

"Thanks . . . and I am," Antonio said, hugging her back and giving Evan a meaningful look over her shoulder.

As their eyes met, Evan's throat went dry.

Chapter 28
Dante

Dante slammed his desk drawer shut and impatiently tapped his fingers on the rubber mat near his keyboard as he waited for the computer to shut down.

"Come on. Come on," he muttered, wanting to throttle the swivel post of computer screen like it was a human neck, to squeeze it until it made gagging sounds and choked to death. He angrily shoved back from his desk. "Fuck it!" he muttered before rising to his feet, even as the blue shutdown screen went black and the CPU's green On button flickered to Off.

His rollaway chair sailed across the room and bumped into a nearby bookshelf filled with binders and law books. He grabbed his briefcase off his desk, opened his office door, and walked into the corridor, slamming the door closed behind him. A janitor was bent over a vacuum cleaner in the center of the hall, dancing to whatever tune played in his oversized headphones as he cleaned the law office's carpets. As Dante strode toward him, the janitor looked over the top of his glasses and tugged one of the headphones off his ear. Dante reached into his jacket pocket to pull out a stick of gum.

"Have a good night, sir," the janitor called out as Dante passed.

Dante didn't answer him. Instead, he balled up the metallic wrapping from his peppermint gum and tossed it onto the floor in front of the janitor, making the other man pause mid-cha-cha.

Dante stalked toward the elevator, unabated fury propelling him forward like the engine of a freight train. And he had plenty to be furious about.

"That old bitch," he muttered as he chewed his gum and pressed the Down button. "That old bitch" had called off the lawsuit against Terrence Murdoch because she got an attack of guilt. And now, once again his chance to exact revenge on the Murdochs had eluded him.

"That fucking bitch," he said again as the elevator doors opened and silently slid shut behind him after he stepped into the compartment. He pressed the L button, which would take him to the first-floor level.

Every time he thought about Mavis, about how she had defiantly glared at him when she told him that she had betrayed him and went behind his back to talk to Terrence, he felt fresh rage all over again. He wished he was choking *her* neck right now, watching her gag and scratch at his hands as he squeezed the life out of her.

He closed his eyes, envisioning her features twisted in agony while he strangled her. He opened his eyes again.

They were going to get away with it, he realized as the elevator descended and he listened to the soft beeps marking each passing floor. The Murdochs were going to sail off into the sunset and continue to enjoy their fast cars and big houses and big parties where everyone stood around kissing their asses, telling them how wonderful they were. And once again, he would be left to stew silently and watch them from afar.

"I'll be goddamned," he murmured as the elevator doors opened, revealing a lobby with pale wood paneling lit by custom hand-blown chandeliers. He walked toward the office building's glass revolving doors leading to the adjacent four-story parking garage. "I'll be goddamned if I let that happen."

The sky was already dark. A heavy wind blasted him as he stepped onto a brick courtyard, sending his tie flying like a boat sail. Dante walked across the courtyard and under a concrete overhang that led to the parking garage. He then climbed a flight of metal steps leading to the second floor of the garage. His footfalls sounded like sledgehammers, like ricocheting gunshots in the night.

His siblings might think that his most recent setback would make him back off but they were sorely mistaken. He would find a way to finally get to them. Even though he hated his father—despised the man to the point that his hate was almost palpable—he had inherited one very important trait from George Murdoch: tenacity. Dante wouldn't give up until he was victorious, until he finally made Evan, Terrence, and Paulette suffer. At this point, he didn't know how he would do it or when he would do it, but the opportunity would eventually come again.

Maybe Murdoch Conglomerated had some shady dealings that could be leaked to the press. Maybe he'd finally tell Paulette's husband about the affair she had been carrying on right under his nose. Maybe some dark skeletons lurked in Terrence's closet. Who knows! But Dante did know one thing: He would be careful who he partnered with the next time around. No more weak fools like Mavis and Renee or unstable prima donnas like Charisse. He would choose wisely and make sure whoever helped him was totally on board and would follow orders from beginning to end.

Dante walked across the parking lot asphalt toward his silver Jag. He shifted his leather briefcase to his other hand and dug into his pants pocket, eventually finding his car keys. He opened the car doors with his remote, watching as the headlights flashed and the engine turned on with a soft rumble.

His plans for the future, however tenuous, quelled his anger a little. His face even broke into a smile as he reached for the car door handle, but he paused when he caught the reflection in the tinted window of a dark figure standing behind him.

Dante frowned. He whipped around and stared in surprise at the familiar face. "What the hell are you doing . . ."

His words tapered off when he saw the glint of the handgun. He suddenly brought up his briefcase as a shield and instinctively shut his eyes when he heard the gun fire. He winced at the harsh, echoing sound.

Dante opened his eyes in just enough time to see the person run off.

"What the hell?" he mumbled.

Had they intended to shoot him? Did they miss? Or maybe they had pointed the gun into the air during the split second that he'd closed his eyes. He slowly lowered his briefcase and glared at their retreating back in outrage.

"What the fuck were you thinking?" he shouted after them, angered all over again that someone had scared him that badly. "Are you . . ."

Dante paused and looked down when he felt something wet on his side. He saw a red spot bloom on his dress shirt, then spread across his torso. He touched the spot and marveled at the bright red blood on his fingertips.

So he had been shot after all.

Pinpricks of light dotted his sight. He was going to faint. He slumped against his car's passenger door and slowly fell to the parking lot pavement. That was when he finally felt the pain, which was indescribable. He started shaking. His bladder loosened and another bright spot bloomed on the crotch of his slacks.

"You . . . you shot me," he whispered in shock.

Dante closed his eyes just as his head thumped against the garage floor.

Connect with Us

Visit us online at
KensingtonBooks.com
to read more from your favorite authors, see books
by series, view reading group guides, and more.

for sneak peeks, chances to win books and prize packs,
and to share your thoughts with other readers.

facebook.com/kensingtonpublishing
twitter.com/kensingtonbooks

Tell us what you think!

To share your thoughts, submit a review,
or sign up for our eNewsletters, please visit:
KensingtonBooks.com/TellUs.